MW00678566

Sherlock Holmes And Young Winston

The Deadwood Stage

By

Mike Hogan

First edition published in 2012
© Copyright 2012
Mike Hogan

The right of Mike Hogan to be identified as the author of this work has been asserted by him in accordance with the Copyright, Designs and Patents Act 1998.

All rights reserved. No reproduction, copy or transmission of this publication may be made without express prior written permission. No paragraph of this publication may be reproduced, copied or transmitted except with express prior written permission or in accordance with the provisions of the Copyright Act 1956 (as amended). Any person who commits any unauthorised act in relation to this publication may be liable to criminal prosecution and civil claims for damage.

Although every effort has been made to ensure the accuracy of the information contained in this book, as of the date of publication, nothing herein should be construed as giving advice. The opinions expressed herein are those of the author and not of MX Publishing.

Paperback ISBN 9781780923222
ePub ISBN 9781780923239
PDF ISBN 9781780923246

Published in the UK by MX Publishing
335 Princess Park Manor, Royal Drive,
London, N11 3GX
www.mxpublishing.co.uk

Cover image by www.huntingtown.co.uk
Cover design by www.staunch.com

To Mary

Contents

FORWARD

A very considerable section of the population of Great Britain, the United States, and perhaps of the World, knows that Sherlock Holmes; the first, and still the foremost consulting detective, lived and worked at 221B Baker Street in London.

However, it been recently reported in the Press that some persons believe that Winston Spencer-Churchill, the son of Lord Randolph and Lady Spencer-Churchill, is not a historical figure: that he is a figment of an author's imagination, like Robin Hood or Pinocchio.

Doctor Watson's case notes from 1887 refute this monstrous imputation, and allow the author to set the record straight. Here, in Doctor Watson's own words, is the hitherto untold story of the first meeting of Sherlock Holmes, Watson and young Winston Churchill, their subsequent association, and the adventures they shared.

1. The Marlborough Nephew

An Incident in the Park

On a blustery morning in the Queen's Jubilee summer of 1887, I was examining the breakfast coffee pot in the hope of obtaining a last half-cupful, when my friend, Sherlock Holmes made what was for him a startling suggestion.

"It has the makings of a charming, breezy day, Watson," he said as he gazed out of our open sitting-room window at the busy street below. "It is a perfect day for a stroll in the Park."

I was pleased to accommodate my friend, not only because the weather, after a succession of harsh, baking days, was agreeably fresh, but because I was worried about his health. Holmes's recent exertions in the immensely convoluted Baron Maupertuis fraud had left his exceptionally supple mental faculties dulled and brittle. A nervous prostration had brought on the blackest of depressions. A saunter through Hyde Park with summer flowers in full bloom, the breeze stirring the leaves, and the waterfowl squabbling on the lake was just what this doctor would have ordered.

Our stroll was not the relaxing experience I expected. Holmes set a brisk pace as he threaded through the pre-luncheon crowd circling the Serpentine. He tipped his hat or waved his cane to acquaintances in his easy, informal manner while his angular figure parted the throng of strollers like the cutwater of a twenty-knot armoured cruiser. As we reached the bridge, I was stung into remonstrance.

"Holmes, you suggested a walk in the Park, not a footrace."

"Eh?"

He stopped and turned back with a rueful smile. "Oh, my dear fellow, forgive me. You are puffing like a grampus. Come, we can take a rest here on this convenient bench while you catch your breath. We can smoke a quiet pipe out of the crowd."

He sat on the wrought-iron bench, and I settled gratefully beside him. A cool, refreshing wind blew across Hyde Park as we fumbled for our pipes. I filled my pipe and lit it with a match. Holmes gave me a sly look.

I sighed. "Holmes, you are going to guess what I'm thinking again. It is poor conversation and irksome in the extreme."

He pouted, and blinked at me with a disappointed expression.

"Oh, very well then," I said. "Do your worst. What am I thinking?"

"No, no, I am no stage mesmerist," he said offhandedly. "I do not guess. But I agree with you that the Elizabeth Caspar case —"

"Holmes! That is precisely what I was thinking about. You have deduced my thoughts exactly! How the devil did you read my mind?"

He shrugged in his Continental manner.

"It is a simple enough chain of reasoning. When I explain it, you will sniff and make some remark about how elementary the matter was."

I remained silent, as I knew he could not be. Holmes leaned back and took a pull on his pipe.

"As we sat, an attractive young woman passed our bench. She wore a dark-blue shawl over a green, paisley-patterned dress. She was unchaperoned. Your eyes followed her as you reached into your pocket for your tobacco pouch —"

"I say, Holmes." I reddened.

"You took on a considering expression as you recalled the facts, widely reported in the sensationalist Press, of the latest *cause célèbre*, the arrest of Miss Elizabeth Caspar for soliciting."

"Holmes, there are ladies within earshot!"

"For soliciting for the purpose of prostitution on Regent Street, or perhaps Oxford Street. I understand from Inspector Lestrade that witnesses attest to various locations for the arrest."

He wagged his pipe stem at me. "Untrained observers, Watson: untrained observers. Even the police constables involved gave conflicting testimony. It is a matter of judicial concern that we rely so heavily on witness statements, when it is an oft-proven fact that only a trained observer, such as myself, can offer accurate and reliable evidence."

"Miss Caspar is a respectable woman, Holmes. She is a frock-maker with an established firm."

"Yes," Holmes said. "I saw that thought cross your mind as you lit your pipe. Then your eyes narrowed, and you frowned as you wondered what a respectable young woman was doing out in Regent (or Oxford) Street at nine in the evening."

"The constable was adamant," I said, "He testified that he had seen her twice or thrice before, talking freely with men. She denies it. What motive would he have for lying?"

I heard a splash from the direction of the lake, followed by a cry, a high-pitched screech and a shout of "Stop, thief!"

"A pertinent question," said Holmes, "and one on which the case may — what's the hullabaloo?"

A burly man in a flat cap raced along the path towards us. A park attendant and several strollers took up the view holloa and pointed at him. Holmes and I leapt to our feet.

Holmes adopted a peculiar stance in the centre of the footpath. He set one foot forward, knee bent, and placed the other foot twisted sideways behind him. He waved his arms like a magician casting a spell.

"Stand aside, Watson," he murmured. "I have the fellow."

He stiffened his posture and emitted a strange keening sound interrupted by a succession of high-pitched yelps. The man thundered towards us and crashed full pelt into Holmes, knocking him off his feet and over the park bench. The man stumbled past me, and I brought him down with a rugby tackle.

"I say, Holmes, are you all right, old chap?" I asked.

"Yes, yes," he said groggily. "Is he down?"

"He is out cold. He knocked his head on a 'Kindly Keep off the Grass' sign. I have staunched the bleeding, but he is still out for the count. He was holding this."

I held up a gold pocket watch on a heavy gold chain.

"Splendid." Holmes stood unsteadily. I brushed off the detritus of leaves, grass cuttings, and soil from his coat and replaced his battered bowler hat on his head. He stood over the unconscious felon and smiled triumphantly.

"You will have recognised, of course, the *Shinden Fudo Ryu* technique of *Ninjutsu,* the ancient martial art of Japan. It uses one's opponent's own vital energy against him. You saw how effective it was?"

"Oh, yes," I said with a smile. I did not mention how useful my training with the Blackheath Rugby Club had been.

"The beast!"

A young, fair-haired boy pushed through the ring of spectators that had gathered around the body on the grass. He wore a cutaway Eton jacket and black trousers that were soaked from the knees down.

"He pulled my watch from my pocket, and he pushed me into the lake." The boy shook his fist at the body on the grass. "Beast."

The thief began to stir, and I helped him to his feet. He stood, swaying slightly, looking down with a puzzled frown at the pugnacious boy glaring up at him.

"You are a mean fellow to play such a trick," the boy said as he poked his finger at the thief's chest. "You should give up this shameful activity and take up gainful employment. My father says that they are crying out for men in the building trades."

"Why, you are Bonner," Holmes said to the thief, "Bruiser Bonner. What are you doing up West, Bonner? Your pitch is Bethnal Green, is it not?"

He turned to me. "Bruiser is one of the foremost bare-knuckle boxers in London. I saw him down Sketty George in three hours and forty-one minutes in the backyard of the Horn of Plenty public house at Spitalfields. He is a consummate sportsman."

"He attacked me from behind, sir," the boy said fiercely. "I was feeding the under-duck. That was hardly sporting."

"I never meant any harm to the young gentleman," said Bonner. "I tea-leafed his watch."

"My dear fellow, look at your hands," said Holmes. Bonner held out two bruised and mangled hands with knuckles awry and evidence of several badly mended fingers.

"Are these the hands of a pocket-picker?"

Bonner hung his head. "I don't know, sir, I'm sure."

"I see that a constable is approaching," said Holmes. He turned to the boy. "Do you wish to press charges against this man?"

I handed the boy his watch. He examined it carefully, opening the cover and checking the mechanism.

He looked up. "Not if he will pledge to end his evil ways and search for honest employment."

"Bonner?"

"I will pledge, sir. And sorry for the inconvenience, like."

"Very well," said Holmes. "Be off with you."

Bonner picked up his cap, saluted, and turned away. Holmes took him by the shoulder and slipped a coin into his hand.

"I hope I didn't hurt you, Bruiser. I used the *Ninjutsu*."

"Kind of you I am sure, Mr Holmes," said Bonner with a puzzled look. "And thank you for the shilling."

"You should get home as soon as possible, young man," I told the boy. "There is an unseasonably chill wind in the air today."

The boy checked the time and slipped his watch into a pocket of his jacket. "I am late for an appointment with my mother," he said. "Thank you, gentlemen, for your help. The watch is dear to me."

He solemnly shook our hands.

"Here," said Holmes, holding out a half-crown. "You might like to take a cab, under the circumstances."

"Thank you, sir. I have sufficient funds."

He turned away.

"One question," said Holmes. "You mentioned that you were feeding the under duck when you were attacked. The duck — singular?"

The boy turned. "A mallard chick is backward and does not get its share of the bread. I am training it to stand up for itself and claim its rights. I call it the under-duck."

"I see," said Holmes. "Thank you."

He took my arm and we sauntered down the path.

"What an odd child," he said. "I would have thought that the most discriminating youth could find use for a half-crown. With income tax at eight pence in the pound, it is no mean sum."

"Well, Watson? Come along, out with it," said Holmes as we left Hyde Park at the Piccadilly end.

"I think you know my views on the Law, Holmes," I said stiffly. "We should have given your man Bonner in charge of the constable."

"Come, come, Bruiser is not a bad chap. He succumbed to overwhelming temptation. I expect that the boy fairly swung the watch in his face. Bruiser is a virile fellow. I would bet a sovereign to a halfpenny that he has several wives and dozens of children to support."

I laughed. "Very well."

"Let us take a stroll along Piccadilly. The work at the Shaftesbury Avenue side of the Circus is complete. The boy was correct about the builders; they are turning London into a gigantic construction site."

We braved the heavy traffic at the Circus and, slipping between the cabs, vans, and omnibuses, we gained the north side of the street.

Piccadilly, our nearest approach in London to the Parisian boulevard, was thronged with carriages of every description. There were the fine barouches of rank, the broughams of beauty, the mail-phaetons of the ensign of cavalry, the shabby four-wheel growlers and hansom cabs of the gentleman, and the omnibuses of the humble. I nudged Holmes and nodded at a fine young lady in a glittering mulberry and green equipage with a sleek pair of matched greys. She glared at me and twirled her parasol in a pretty way.

"I say, Holmes," I exclaimed, smoothing my moustache.

Holmes sniffed. "She with the umbrella?"

He lifted his hat in greeting, and I hastily raised mine. The lady nodded distantly.

"You know her, Holmes?"

"She is an infamous poisonatrix, now on her second marquess."

"Oh." I glanced back at the girl just as she turned again, lifted her parasol, and looked over her shoulder. She gave me a brilliant smile.

I was utterly taken aback.

What message had the pretty girl intended to convey? Hers was an arch look, a smile with the slightest hint of a pout; she had fluttered at least one set of eyelashes at me, if not both.

No matter, I thought, tipping my bowler to a jaunty angle. An angelic face, a playful look, and a dazzling smile had uplifted the heart of an ignoble and unattached doctor of medicine.

Holmes smiled and nodded at me, as if to confirm my conclusion. He took my arm, and we walked together in companionable silence.

The Matter of the Watch

We strolled past the entrance to the Criterion Bar and Grill.

"What of the boy, Watson?" asked Holmes. He turned his penetrating gaze to me. "What is your opinion of him?"

I considered. "There is little to go on. He was well spoken and well dressed. His watch was valuable. He had a slight lisp. That is all I can think of."

Holmes smiled. "I might be able to flesh out the picture. Twelve or thirteen, I would suppose: a typical specimen of upper-class English boyhood in the throes of awkward adolescence. Distant parents: you will have remarked the appointment with his mother. They will take luncheon at an hotel. Father will not attend, as he is busy in politics or the City.

"The son idolises his father from afar and has absorbed, or partly digested, his radical conservative political views. In our short ornithological conversation the boy espoused the cause of democratic conservatism. He admonished this ugly duckling (and by analogy, the poor) to pull itself up by its bootstraps. You will have marked the Primrose League pin in his lapel."

"The Primrose League? A Conservative association," I said. "They are pledged to uphold God, Queen, Country, and the Conservative Party."

"In what order of priority?" Holmes asked with a smile.

"The boy seemed self-possessed," I suggested. "He spurned your half-crown with aristocratic disdain."

"Confident to a degree," Holmes answered after a moment of thought. "But he is something of a lonely boy, left to himself or under the feeble discipline of a younger sibling's nurse."

Holmes tipped his hat to an acquaintance.

"He is lightly built, but not altogether sedentary. He has the shoulders of an ardent swimmer, and the good posture of a frequent rider. The creases on his boots, and his threadbare knees and elbows, show that he is an inexpert roller-skater; he bears the marks of frequent spills. Judging from the vile carelessness with which he has knotted his tie, despite his maternal appointment and her inevitable annoyance, he is an untidy and thoughtless boy."

"One shoelace was undone," I offered, thinking hard.

"Oh, yes, he is a procrastinator. His left shoelace is frayed to the point that it will no longer tie; it has not been replaced. He will be scolded, as he has been scolded recently by his father in the matter of the watch."

"The watch, Holmes? What of it?"

"A gold hunter as you saw, rather fine, with a ducal coat of arms engraved on the inside cover. You saw how keenly he examined it when I returned it to him."

"Actually, Holmes, it was I —"

"He values the watch: he took it out twice more after our little *fracas* to see that it was undamaged. When he put it away on leaving us, he was careful, despite his lateness, to ensure that there were no coins in his pocket that might scratch it. Yet, it bears numerous scratches on the case. This extravagant care is of recent foundation and is probably the result of a paternal scolding. The coat of arms suggests a present from his uncle, not his father. I cannot imagine the adolescent scion of a ducal house under such slack supervision."

"It is as if you know the boy."

"I think we have enough data to identify him. The coat of arms was that of the House of Marlborough. The younger brother of the present Duke is the chairman of the Primrose League, and the father of a teenage son. I think we may confidently assert that our young hero is the son of Lord Randolph Churchill, who so recently and dramatically resigned from the Government."

The resignation of Lord Randolph from the post of Chancellor of the Exchequer was still, some months after the event, a matter of intense political speculation. I understood that he had expected his resignation to result in his restoration to office on his terms. In fact, the Prime Minister, Lord Salisbury, had reconstructed the cabinet with a new Chancellor, leaving Lord Randolph out of the government.

"I fear that the boy has inherited his august father's lack of mathematical prowess," said Holmes, picking up the conversation.

"You are referring to Lord Randolph's remark about decimals, when he was in office as Chancellor?" I asked with a smile.

"Yes," said Holmes. "He said that he could make neither head nor tail of those 'damned dots'. His son today carried a mathematical primer in his jacket pocket, but one more suitable for an eight-year-old than a boy of his age."

"No doubt he is cramming for the entrance examination to a great public school," I said. "The Marlboroughs attend Eton."

"He will not pass the mathematical examination into Eton by counting on his fingers."

I laughed. At times, Holmes applied his wry humour with an almost Socialist abandon. "He may inherit other talents. Lord Randolph has a formidable reputation as a parliamentary wit."

Holmes smiled. "At gatherings of the indolent classes, a very little wit goes a very long way. A sharp-witted man may be admired or feared, but he will not be loved."

We passed Wren's lovely St James's Church, much disfigured by a pair of faux-ancient wrought-iron gates. I smiled as I thought of "Old Q", the sporting fourth Duke of Queensberry, whose grave was in the church.

"You know, Holmes," I said. "There is a story —"

"Cricketers. The bet was to convey a letter fifty miles in an hour, a feat that in the middle of the last century, before the advent of steam, was deemed impossible. Queensberry engaged twenty expert cricketers and staked them in a circle a certain distance apart. They tossed a cricket ball, in which the letter was enclosed, from one to another for an hour. They achieved the distance, and Old Q won the bet."

"I was going to say that, Holmes," I said. There were times when Holmes's encyclopaedic knowledge could be wearing on a sensitive spirit.

"Quite so."

He stopped and consulted his watch. "Come Watson, what do you say to a chop and half-bottle of Beaune? We can cut through to Regent Street and the Cafe Royal. I think we deserve a little celebration after our adventure in the Park, and I owe you an apology."

"What, for catching the thief? That Japanese nonsense?"

Holmes gave me a stern look.

"No, not at all. I took the last cup of breakfast coffee."

The Displeasure of Lady Randolph

After a pleasant luncheon, we took a cab back to our digs in Baker Street.

"It is your turn to pay," said Holmes.

He paused at the door of our lodging house. "You know Watson, when you are required to pay nine shillings and sixpence, as we were today, for a bottle of Claret but three years old, then something must be wrong with the world."

We entered the hall, and found it bustling with activity. Mrs Hudson, the maid Bessie, and young Billy, our pageboy, plied brooms and feather dusters in the hall and waiting room.

"Whatever are you doing, Mrs Hudson?" cried Holmes. "We endured spring-cleaning in its usual month. This hygienic obsession is wearing on your paying guests. Dust undisturbed poses no threat to health, as Doctor Watson will agree, while the same quantity wantonly beaten into the air, from a carpet or curtains, may cause severe respiratory effects."

Holmes tossed his hat to Billy and started up the stairs two at a time.

"Coffee!" he called back.

"I am changing the curtains in the front parlour before Her Ladyship returns," Mrs Hudson said, taking me by the arm. "These old ones hadn't been touched since ever so."

She displayed a roll of soft, shiny green cloth. "I got some handsome, bright-green curtains down from the attic."

Holmes stopped at the landing at the top the stairs and turned back.

"Her Ladyship? We had a caller while we were out. There, Watson," he said fiercely. "That is what comes of your walks in the Park."

He darted out of sight.

I sighed and hung my hat on the stand. "Her Ladyship, Mrs Hudson?"

Billy handed me a gold-embossed visiting card.

"Lady Randolph Churchill," I read.

"With her son," said Mrs Hudson. "A most polite young gentleman."

"Beautiful carriage with the coat of arms on the door," added Billy. "Two footmen and the driver on top, all nice and proper."

"Did Her Ladyship leave any message?" I asked.

"Yes, Doctor," said Mrs Hudson. "She will allow herself the pleasure of calling again in an hour. That was forty minutes ago."

"Thank you, Mrs Hudson. Some coffee, if you please — when you have a moment, of course."

I followed Holmes upstairs and found him leafing through a stack of correspondence.

"I expect she wants to thank us for saving the watch, Holmes," I offered as I sat in my usual seat by the empty fireplace.

He waved my speculation away and continued to read his letters. I settled in my armchair with the latest copy of *The Lancet*. I had recently written a note to the editor stating that, while I accepted the claims of Doctor Lister and the germ-theorists, I believed that the role of the body's own mechanisms for resisting and repelling these newly-discovered microscopic menaces had been underestimated. I saw that my letter had not been published. I threw the magazine onto a chair and mixed a whisky and soda.

A carriage drew up in the street below. Our doorbell rang, and I heard a murmur of voices and the measured tread of footsteps on the stairs. Holmes swung open the door to our sitting room with a flourish. He bowed.

"Good afternoon, Lady Randolph," he said. He looked up. "Eh? It is you, Mrs Hudson. You are not Lady Randolph Churchill. Where is Lady Randolph Churchill?"

"In the waiting room."

"Well, show her up."

"She is waiting for you to come down."

"Good Lord, woman. The King of the Netherlands and the Chief Rabbi of all England did not scruple to attend me in my rooms."

"Holmes, keep your voice down," I whispered. I held the door open.

He swept out, and I followed him downstairs.

Lady Randolph stood by the newly curtained windows of our ground floor waiting room looking out into the street. She wore a grey coat over a lemon-yellow silk dress, and a matching feathered hat set slantwise across her head in the antique Duchess-of-Devonshire manner. The boy from our fracas in the Park stood by the fireplace looking nervous. He now wore a blue and white sailor suit that made him look very young.

"Good afternoon, Lady Randolph. I am Sherlock Holmes, and this is my friend and colleague Doctor John Watson. Do sit down. Would you care for tea?"

"Good afternoon, Mr Holmes," Lady Randolph said with a slight American accent. "I am afraid that this is not a social call."

She indicated the boy.

"My son, Winston, has informed me that an attempt was made this morning to rob him. A ruffian assaulted him, threw him into the Serpentine and snatched his watch. A constable was called, and the thief was apprehended. My son says that you have a connection with the thief and, on your orders, sir, he was let go. Are these the facts?"

"Mama," said the boy. "Let me explain."

Lady Randolph gave her son a dark look that silenced him instantly.

"Those are indeed the raw facts," said Holmes, "but not in their correct sequence and not glossed for relevance or importance. It was early afternoon, and your son —"

"I hardly think the time of day is of consequence," Lady Randolph interrupted.

A cold silence followed that observation.

"Perhaps," I said, "as a simple bystander, I could give an unbiased account of the incident."

Lady Randolph nodded.

I described the cry for help, our capture of the thief, his identity, and the decision to release him. Her ladyship considered.

"Are you the Doctor Watson who consulted with our family physician, Doctor Roose on — on a certain case last year?"

I bowed. "I had that honour."

"Very well."

She took off her gloves.

"Winston and I would be delighted to take tea with you, Doctor."

She handed her parasol and gloves to Holmes and sat on the sofa.

"What a charming lady," I exclaimed, as Holmes and I returned to our rooms a half-hour later. "Though daunting at first."

"Indeed."

"Ha, yes." I cackled. "She had you by the collar, Holmes. She was going to drag you off to Bow Street Police Court for aiding and abetting. We should have seen you in broad stripes on the treadmill at the penitentiary."

I continued to chuckle as Billy entered with a letter.

"Note from Her Ladyship," he announced.

"Give it here," said Holmes.

"It's addressed to the Doctor."

Holmes sniffed and turned away.

I took the sealed envelope and opened it.

Holmes went to the window. "Lady Randolph's carriage is still at the kerb," he observed.

"Good Lord, Holmes," I said. "Oh, thank you, Billy."

Billy left, closing the door. I joined Holmes at the window.

"This is extraordinary. Her ladyship wants me to consult on her son. She says Lord Randolph has doubts about the boy's mental capacity. Their family physician, Doctor Roose, has examined him with inconclusive results. She says she would value my opinion. Holmes, what shall I do?"

Holmes considered. "He seemed sharp enough in the Park. Not overly bright, of course, nor particularly gifted: note the mathematics primer. Given his aristocratic heritage, he will not be called upon to shine intellectually. I expect he will govern Barbados, or minister to his flock as suffragan Bishop of Saskatchewan."

I read the note again more carefully.

"I have to accept; I owe it to Doctor Roose. He was very kind to me when I started in practice."

I hesitated. "And there are some, well, other circumstances."

Holmes gave me a penetrating look. He nodded. "I think I understand. You mean the sins of the father may have been visited on the son."

I penned a short note and sent it down with Billy.

A few moments later, there was a soft knock on the door and young Winston Spencer-Churchill stood before us again. I was about to offer him a seat when I heard a shriek downstairs and a pattering of naked feet on the stairs. A troupe of ragged street boys surged into the room, shoved Spencer-Churchill aside, and lined up as if for inspection.

"Ah," said Holmes. "The Baker Street Irregulars. What are you doing here, Wiggins? I did not send for you."

The tallest boy, a redhead of fourteen or fifteen, stepped forward and saluted smartly. "No, Mr Holmes. We come of our own accord, like, on particular business."

Holmes draped himself over an armchair and lit a cigar.

"Pick two lieutenants to stay with you. The others must wait down in the street."

"Len and Monty step forward," said Wiggins. "The rest bugger off."

Two boys stayed, and the others started for the door.

"Stop!" said Holmes. "You in the black cap — yes, you, sir — give Master Spencer-Churchill back his watch and handkerchief."

The boy returned the articles with a cheerful grin. Spencer-Churchill backed warily to the window clutching his possessions. I checked my watch and pocketbook. The last visit of the Baker Street Irregulars had cost me a silver pencil holder and an autographed score of Sir Arthur Sullivan's 'The Lost Chord'.

"Continue, Wiggins."

"It's a case of missing persons, Mr Holmes — and maybe worse."

"Go on."

"We was down the Belvedere, sir, having a jar and a smoke when two coves turn up —"

"That's the Belvedere Road, behind Waterloo Station," Holmes said. "When? Precision, Wiggins. You know my methods: I must have data."

"Six months ago, sir. Bleeding cold, it was, and snowing something awful. We had a fire going under an archway; a proper fire, sir, in a watchman's brazier that we found in the road, as was not wanted by its owner. It was about eight at night."

Holmes nodded for him to continue.

"Describe the coves."

"One was a tall, black fellah, a Negro, nineteen, as we found out. He was in a footman's rig, but with a swell overcoat — moleskin lapels — and a bundle under his arm. The boy with him was a white boy, younger, maybe thirteen, and yellow-haired. He wore a bowler and a posh suit and coat. He had a fat cloth bag with him."

"You decided to relieve these travellers of their burdens," said Holmes.

"Infamous," I said.

"Well, sir," said Wiggins, turning to me. "Some terrible rough fellahs was up the road drinking at the George and Dragon. We thought it would be a kindliness to help the young gents before they got into bad trouble. They'd have been knocked on the head, robbed, and stuffed down the sewer else, sure as toast."

"What a good Samaritan you are, Wiggins," said Holmes with a pleasant smile.

I frowned. Holmes was perfectly aware that the street children that he employed as his 'Baker Street Irregulars' derived whatever income they had from various forms of crime. Their recruiting ground in a vile section of Lambeth was a notorious nest of thieves, fraudsters and coiners. They were expert pickpockets, as I had learned to my cost. Yet Holmes, despite his considerable influence over the boys, had made no effort to improve them.

Their leader, Wiggins, was an exceptionally intelligent boy. He squandered this aptitude in developing ingenious schemes to rob his betters. I sensed in him a potential for reform. I had given him a copy of a remarkable book on self-help by Mr Samuel Smiles. I felt sure that the many anecdotes it contained of people who had raised themselves from poverty by self-education and healthy bodily exercise would excite the boy's curiosity. The book described how young men from the lowest stratum of society acquired wealth, or reached positions of social eminence, lauded with honours, by following the precepts advocated by the admirable Mr Smiles. Their successes were a noble example for any young fellow.

Naturally, I also wanted Wiggins to realise that money and position were not the only goals in life: knowledge itself was one of the highest enjoyments. The ignorant man passed through life dead to all the higher pleasures: art, music, comradely intercourse on the great matters of the day —

"Are you with us, Doctor?" Holmes asked. "Do try to keep up."

I blinked at him.

"Go on, Wiggins," he said.

"Well, the tall, brown geezer looked nervy when I asked him what's in the bundle. He saw we was mob-handed, so he was ready to do a runner. The boy, he put the bag down, stood there with his hands on his hips, and asked us what business it was of ours. I explained as how we was cold and hungry, and that the Jew stall in the Lower Marsh would give three bob for a hanky and a lot more for a moleskin lapel coat. We could get hot tongue and tattie stew all round for three bob at the back of the George, if we trod careful, like.

"The boy thought it over, then he opened his cloth bag, rummaged around, and pulled out a handful of silver spoons. He held them up and said, 'What would you get for these, then?', bold as brass. He had a funny accent."

"What sort of accent?" I asked.

Holmes waved my question away. "In good time, Doctor. Let the story unfold in its natural rhythm."

I turned away in some irritation and helped myself to a whisky from the tantalus. It did not seem so irrelevant a question. At times, Holmes could be quite curt. When I turned back, I saw that Wiggins and his lieutenants stared hard at me.

"Refreshment for Wiggins and his men, Watson," said Holmes.

"Really, Holmes, I hardly think — and there are only three glasses."

"Wiggins's companions can share."

I poured two small whiskies and added a great deal of soda water.

"Master Spencer-Churchill?" Holmes asked, pointing to the whisky decanter.

"Thank you, no," he answered softly, slipping into a chair at our dining table.

"The silver spoons was the real thing," Wiggins continued. "I grabbed them and sent Lenny here down to the pawn shop, and he got three quid. Meanwhile, the blond boy — he says his name is Bobby and his mate's Aaron — pulled a half-sovereign out of his coat pocket and bought drinks and beefsteak pies all round."

He smiled. "We thought about duffing them up and nicking the lot, but it wouldn't have been right, like. What with him being already such a open-handed young gent."

Holmes nodded.

"They joined up with us," said Wiggins. "He put us on to some good lays: the parcel dodge, the dead faint, the dizzy German —"

"The parcel dodge I know," said Holmes. "You follow a messenger from the parcel office on his round, or maybe the delivery boy for a hatter. He delivers the package. When the messenger is out of sight, you run up to the door of the house and tell the servants that the delivery from so-and-so shop was an error, and that their goods are on the way. You take custody of the delivered package and wish them good day. Is that it, Wiggins?"

"Exact, sir. Bobby could do it just right. He had the looks, see, and all his teeth."

"Scoundrel," I muttered. I could not imagine where this catalogue of nefarious tricks would lead us.

"The dizzy German?" asked Holmes, smiling at me.

"We changed it, like, to the dizzy Yankee-Doodle on account of Bobby doing a posh Yankee to a 'T', and the Buffalo Bill posters all over town. Bobby gets dolled up in his gent's finery, with his gloves and such, and he goes up West with his manservant, Aaron. He picks out a walking stick, or a silk cravat or whatever, and asks the price. They say two or three quid, and Bobby offers a couple of fivers. He says he never could understand this English money. Aaron gives the assistant a wink over his master's shoulder. Bobby walks out with the loot. Aaron gets a tip from the assistant and everyone's happy."

"I don't understand," I said with a puzzled frown. "The boy paid ten pounds for goods worth two or three."

I got five pitying looks.

"Master Spencer-Churchill? Can you solve Doctor Watson's conundrum?" Holmes asked.

"Fake money, sir," he said shyly.

"Very well. Bobby and Aaron became valuable members of your gang. Come to the meat of the matter."

"A week ago, he and Aaron buggered off. Or at least that's what we —"

The sitting-room door crashed open. Our pageboy staggered into the room looking pale and clutching his throat.

"Watch your valuables, gents," said Wiggins, jumping up. "It's the Dead Faint."

"Doctor," said Billy as I helped him to a chair. "Mrs Hudson — she's dead."

He slipped into unconsciousness.

2. Element of Danger

The Science of Diagnostics

I left Holmes with Billy and ran downstairs. Mrs Hudson was on the floor in the hall in her street clothes.

"She just dropped, sir, right there," said Bessie. "She was going for a fine turbot to be seethed for the gentlemen's tea, kept special at the fish shop. She reached to open the front door, and she dropped like a stone. And now she's — oh, Doctor."

I knelt and checked Mrs Hudson's pulse; it was racing.

"Help me put her on the couch in the waiting room."

"Is she dead, sir?"

"She is not."

We stretched Mrs Hudson out on the sofa so recently vacated by Lady Randolph. I sent Bessie to my room for my medical bag. Holmes appeared at the door.

"She is alive," I said in reply to his questioning look. "Her breathing is irregular, and her pulse is abnormally fast and reedy. She may have had a seizure of some sort. How is Billy?"

"Revived."

Bessie returned with my medical bag.

"I have some *sal volatile*."

"Never mind, Watson," said Holmes. "Cognac sufficed. Billy snorted, woke, drank, and asked for a refill. I have planted him on the window seat in the alcove."

I pulled my stethoscope from my bag and checked the patient's vital signs. I was amazed that the hale Mrs Hudson of less than an hour previously was now febrile, pale, and in a coma-like condition.

"Whatever malady this is, Holmes, it has acted with astonishing swiftness. I can see no signs of typhus, cholera or the ague. The best we can do is to make her comfortable and observe how the disease, if disease it is, manifests itself. I shall also examine Billy."

"You think that his fainting spell was not a reaction to Mrs Hudson's sudden attack. That his condition and Mrs Hudson's have the same cause."

"I do not know, Holmes. That is why I must examine the boy."

I turned to Bessie. "Did Mrs Hudson complain of any ailment today, or in recent days?"

"Oh, no sir, she was right bonnie, but for the heat. It was an awful freezing winter, and now it's been terrible hot the last few days."

I immediately checked the patient's skin for dryness and reached for my thermometer case.

"Might it be heat-stroke?" asked Holmes.

"It is possible; the last few days have been sweltering, and then there was a chill breeze this afternoon." I turned up the cuffs of my jacket and rolled up my sleeves. "Bessie will loosen Mrs Hudson's clothes, and I will check her temperature."

"I shall withdraw," said Holmes.

I returned to the sitting room upstairs an hour or so later to find that Holmes and Spencer-Churchill were alone.

The boy sat at our dining table with a dozen reference and commonplace books piled before him. He wrote furiously in one of Holmes's notebooks.

"I hope that your Irregulars did not take advantage of our disarray to take souvenirs again," I said in an acid tone.

"No, no, Watson," said Holmes from his usual chair by the fireplace. "Wiggins gave his word they'd touched nothing. Spencer-Churchill watched them like a kite hawk as he noted the details of the case. How is your patient?"

"She is awake, and I venture to say that she is more comfortable. It may well have been a heat syncope. However, she has exhibited other symptoms, a furred tongue, for example, that led me to suspect another cause. Mrs Hudson is a robust woman, and the effect of the disease has been strangely speedy."

"Should she be transferred to a hospital?" asked Holmes.

"I cannot think what a hospital would offer over skilled home-nursing. I have sent for a lady-nurse who has proven herself entirely reliable. I will ask for Doctor Roose and Mr Philpot to attend. Have you a couple of telegram forms?"

I wrote out my messages.

"I'll call for Billy — oh."

"He's lying down in the alcove. I can go to the telegraph office," Spencer-Churchill said eagerly.

"Thank you. It is a matter of the gravest urgency. Billy will tell you where the nearest office is."

"Why, it's on the corner, Doctor. It's beside the silver and glass emporium."

I gave him the forms and money, and he slipped out the door.

"That was good observation by the boy," said Holmes as the door closed behind him. "Pass me the notebook."

He read for a moment. "A childlike, round hand, but legible. He has noted all the salient facts, though he does include more 'l's in moleskin than is usual."

He tossed the notebook back onto the table. "Have you formed an opinion on the nature of the malady that has laid Mrs Hudson low?"

"I have several causations in mind," I answered. "I need to examine Billy."

I drew back the curtains of the alcove where Billy reclined on the window seat.

"Billy, how do you feel?"

"All right, sir; as well as can be expected."

I took his temperature; it was normal. "But you felt poorly earlier, before you fainted."

He avoided my eyes and reddened. "Wasn't a faint, sir. I stumbled on the carpet."

"Were you well before that?"

"Top-hole, sir, mostly. I had a wart come up on my big toe day before yesterday, but Mrs H burnt it off with a red-hot poker."

I sighed. "Did you eat luncheon with Mrs Hudson and Bessie today, as you usually do?"

He looked blankly up at me.

"The doctor means dinner," Holmes called from his chair by the fireplace. "Did you eat dinner at twelve or so, as usual?"

"I did," answered Billy.

"Describe the meal," I said.

"Nice bit of rabbit stew, with dumplings done in the juice. Very tasty."

"And you all ate the same?"

"Well, I had a bit more than the ladies. Mrs H says I need building up."

"Ha! I'd say you need a new pageboy uniform, young man. You are popping out of the sleeves and cuffs of that one. All right, get along with you downstairs. I'll have an errand for you soon."

I lit a cigar and settled in my usual armchair as Spencer-Churchill returned and handed me the telegraph receipts and change.

"You suspect food poisoning, Watson?" Holmes asked as he stubbed out his cigar. "Or perhaps one of these new-fangled germs?"

"Food poisoning is possible, but I would expect symptoms that have not yet presented themselves: gastric pain, for example, or vomiting and other evacuations. The body, as we physicians have recently come to realise, puts up its own fight against disease. It attempts to expel toxins: *vis medicatrix naturae*."

"Nature's own power of healing," said Holmes, smiling at Spencer-Churchill.

He steepled his hands and gave me a considering look.

"Watson, I have been remiss. You have frequently referred to the science of detection, of which I am the foremost practitioner, and we have discussed its intellectual foundation and methods. I have never asked you about the philosophy of your profession. I am afraid that I have taken it for granted. It is clear to me that medicine must offer opportunities for exercising the same faculties of logical inference as the science of detection. I track down the fell murderer by his motive and methods. You pursue the deadly disease agent by its signs and symptoms."

I helped myself to a whisky and splashed in soda water from the gasogene while I considered Holmes's remark.

"Philosophy, Holmes? Yes, we may say that there is a philosophy of medicine. I am no mere empiric. However, I must confess to you that much of my business is trial and error; many of my remedies are mere placebos. I would throw out half the *Materia Medica* if I could keep only two medicines of whose effectiveness I am convinced: opium and —"

The bell rang downstairs. I jumped up. "That will be Mrs Levine."

I caught a look between Holmes and Spencer-Churchill.

"She is a Jewess. She is the District Nurse in one of the vilest sets of streets off the Waterloo Road in Lambeth. She can walk unmolested through the darkest, filthiest courts inhabited by the toughest and most despicable Irish drunkards. She is universally respected and admired; indeed, they treat her with the respect they would accord to a bishop of their own faith. She is a most remarkable woman."

I briefed Mrs Levine and together we examined our patient again. I returned to the sitting room and reported to Holmes.

"Mrs Hudson is awake and wracked with head- and stomach-aches; she is evacuating copiously. Now we have data, Holmes. The problem is that these symptoms are associated with several illnesses. But, nausea, vomiting, diarrhoea, abdominal cramps, and fever, together with the sudden onset of the malady, do suggest at least one likely cause."

I called down the stairs for Billy.

"As you intimated, Holmes," I said, as I returned to my usual chair, "medical symptomatology may be said to parallel your science of detection. It is a matter of acute observation, weighing the evidence for or against a diagnosis, and finding a cause that fits the evidence. When we peel away the impossible, what is left, however unlikely, must be the true cause."

Holmes regarded me with a look of scepticism. He seemed prepared to accept the connection between the science of deduction and the science of symptomatology, except when the latter was practised by his co-lodger.

"Tainted rabbit or tainted dumplings," he said with an impertinent smirk as Billy brought up a tray of coffee.

"Possibly," I answered stiffly. "I have prepared samples of both to send off for analysis. Ah, Billy, go to the public commissionaire's station; get Peterson for choice. Tell him to take this package to Herr Voelcker at 11, Salisbury Square. This will cover cab fare, hourly payment for the commissionaire, and thruppence tip."

He left with the package and money. I turned back to Holmes. "I have included samples of her evacuations —"

"Did you use a stomach pump?" asked Spencer-Churchill.

"Nature provided an efficient alternative. I should describe Mrs Hudson's evacuations as —"

Holmes held up a restraining hand.

"Suffice it to say, then, that no intervention was necessary."

Twenty minutes later, there was another knock on the door and Billy returned. "Package sent, Doctor, and a Mr Philpot is waiting at the back door."

"The back door, Watson?" said Holmes. "This Mr Philpot is a strangely retiring sort of medical specialist."

I smiled. "Mr Philpot is not a physician, Holmes. He is a plumber."

The Miasmatic Plumber

I left Holmes and Spencer-Churchill to mull on that as I went into the backyard with Billy.

A stooped elderly man in a leather jerkin waited there, attended by two boys carrying toolboxes and lengths of pipe. After mutual salutations, I outlined the medical situation.

Mr Philpot scratched his chin. "Could be, Doctor, might well be. I'll need to investigate, like."

"Get on, then, Mr Philpot. Billy will be your guide to the house."

There was a knock at the front door, and Bessie opened it for Doctor Roose. I left the plumber and hurried along the corridor to greet him.

We shook hands. "Thank you so much for coming at such short notice, Doctor."

"Not at all, Doctor," he said, removing his gloves.

I took Doctor Roose's top hat, noting the stethoscope coiled inside the crown that, with the faint smell of ether, was the mark of the general practitioner.

I showed my colleague into the waiting room where Mrs Hudson lay in a bed made up on the sofa. We examined the patient again, extremely thoroughly. The doctor's calm and methodical bedside manner impressed me deeply. He led Mrs Hudson through the days and hours before the onset of the disease, if disease it was, and elicited information on her diet, her health, and her doings with the calm assurance that he doubtless extended to his far more august patients. Mrs Hudson answered in a weak voice, sometimes stumbling over words and misplacing thoughts.

I felt a profound unease as I looked down at her. She was restless, groaning occasionally, and clearly in pain, despite the opium draught that I had administered earlier. I took her damp and trembling hand in mine and squeezed it in a reassuring gesture. Mrs Hudson looked up at me, smiled, and then grimaced as a spasm of pain wracked her body. I coughed to disguise a half-sob. It was impossible for me to maintain a professional distance with someone who had shared so many of our adventures. I ordered Nurse Levine to administer an increased dose of opium, squeezed Mrs Hudson's hand again, and assured her that all would be well. I was touched, and embarrassed to a degree, that my assurances seemed to calm her.

Doctor Roose and I left the patient in the waiting room and crossed the hall to Mrs Hudson's private sitting room.

"She was perfectly well this morning," Doctor Roose summarised. "She had a fainting spell, or seizure, at lunchtime, and now she is confused, febrile, and nauseous. There was a copious evacuation."

"There was indeed."

He took out a cigar case and offered me one.

"I concur with your suspicions of food poisoning, Doctor Watson, although it is a puzzle that the boy was hardly affected, and the maid not at all."

I explained that Billy was rendered dizzy and faint, although he denied it out of masculine bravado, and that he and Bessie had strong constitutions.

"I should have said the same for Mrs Hudson, Doctor," I said. "If I had not just left her in such a pitiful condition."

"Fluids," said Doctor Roose. "We must replace those lost fluids."

He buttoned up his gloves.

"That is the key," he said with the professional gravitas that had won him so many aristocratic clients.

Billy showed in Mr Philpot.

I introduced Doctor Roose and desired the plumber to give his report.

"It might be best, Doctors," said Philpot, puffing up like a pigeon, "was I to show you the evidence."

We followed him out of the room and along the corridor to the room opposite the kitchen.

"That, gentlemen," said Philpot gravely, "is the lady's bedroom; it is where, you have to understand, she habitually sleeps."

He led us out into the backyard.

"Now, next to that plane tree is your cess-pit. The boys sounded it, and it's in good nick, but full, or nearly so. If I was you, Doctor, I'd get the night-soil men to pump it out. I know a reliable firm, sir. I shall send you their card."

He indicated a pipe that ran up the wall of the house and disappeared into the eaves.

"That's your four-inch soil pipe, all right, tight and proper, with a neat water trap and ventilating chamber; everything hunky-dory and Bristol fashion."

He shook his head.

"I was fair foxed for a while, I will admit, gents." He chuckled wryly. "But as the Lord says, 'There is nothing covered, that shall not be revealed; and hid, that shall not be known'."

Doctor Roose gave him an irritated look.

Philpot squatted and pointed at a section of the pipe near the window of Mrs Hudson's bedroom.

"There's a good deal on plumbing in the Good Book, sirs: 'They have ears, but they hear not: noses have they, but they smell not'. I followed my nose and all was revealed. See that?"

He pointed to the back of the pipe, next to the wall.

"A crack six inches long, and half an inch of pipe gone off."

He straightened and nodded sagely.

"Windows opened for the first time in the warm weather after the chill of last winter; sewer gas building up and escaping through this here hole. What you have, Doctors, is a miasma, sure and certain, or you can call me Ishmael, son of Abraham and Hagar."

I left the plumber and his assistants mending the cracked pipe and saw Doctor Roose to the door.

"Sewer gas poisoning," said Doctor Roose as he took his hat and stick. He smiled. "You will have an article for *The Lancet*. You can champion us experienced practitioners against Lister and his germ fanatics."

Doctor Roose retrieved his hat from the stand in the hall. "I spoke with Lady Randolph. I understand that she has requested that you examine Winston."

"Instructed, not requested," I replied.

He chuckled. "Yes, she has a way about her. It is all nonsense, of course, or at least I hope it is. When Winston was born, the father's terrible disease had not fully manifested itself; I do not believe that the child was affected in the least. However, you have seen a great deal more of the disease in your Army service, Doctor. If the boy is not up to snuff—"

"He seems to be a normal boy."

"That he is not," said Doctor Roose firmly. "Winston requires a firm hand. He stayed with me twice last year: in March, he nearly died of pneumonia, and then there was an outbreak of cholera in the servants' hall. He is a wilful and lazy boy, precocious, but not given to study or application of any description. He would far rather play with his toy soldiers than read his Scripture."

He put on his top hat and considered.

"However, he is a loyal and truthful young fellow, and he will have a devil of a time with his father if this period of remission gives way to the full horror of the disease we suspect. As we know, Doctor, it is ineluctable: it is no respecter of rank. It will kill Lord Randolph as it would a costermonger of the lowest order."

He stopped at the door.

"You need not concern yourself about the younger brother, Jack. His conception took place in Ireland, while Lord Randolph was about his occasions elsewhere in the Kingdom. Lord Randolph was not involved in any phase of the boy's formation."

I bade Doctor Roose farewell, then returned to the waiting room and prescribed a further course of opiate painkillers and cool barley water for my patient. It was a balmy evening, and I ordered the nurse to draw the curtains and open the windows wide to allow the soft breeze to remove any trace of miasma that might have penetrated the room.

I stomped upstairs. Holmes was alone, pasting articles cut out from the newspapers into one of his scrapbooks. He looked up inquiringly as I entered.

"She is much the same, I am afraid. She drifts in and out of consciousness. I have administered opiates."

I sat in my usual chair in front of the empty fireplace.

"There is a possibility of miasmatic poisoning," I said. "I suspected poisoning because of the rapid onset of symptoms and their intensity. That is why I engaged Mr Philpot. He examined the drains at the new St Thomas Hospital last year after an outbreak of unexplained fevers, and he made some intelligent suggestions. He found a broken escape pipe below Mrs Hudson's bedroom window. Numerous cases are reported in the medical journals of unwholesome fumes from the sewers causing reactions similar to those we have seen today. If you took a map and marked the districts that are the constant seat of fevers, fits, and infant deaths, you would be able to trace with mathematical exactitude the line of the sewers of London."

I leaned forward in my seat.

"It is not just a question of sewer gas explosions levelling a house here and there. We have under our streets a dark and fecund jungle as dangerous to civilized man as the leech-infested jungles of the Congo basin. Incidences of cholera precisely follow the pestilential tunnels of the Metropolitan Line Underground Railway. Rats the size of cats infest the workings and think nothing of taking down a man."

"How would the miasmatic theory account for Billy's indisposition?" said Holmes, looking pale.

"Perhaps you were right; perhaps he was in shock at Mrs Hudson's sudden illness."

"I propose," said Holmes, shaking his head, "notwithstanding my earlier remarks, that our Billy has not previously shown the slightest signs of sensitivity on any matter whatsoever."

I laughed. "Spencer-Churchill has gone home?"

Holmes nodded and opened the afternoon newspaper.

"I did not have much chance to observe the boy," I said. "He seemed normal enough, though rather shy. I expect he leads a rather sheltered life at Blenheim Palace."

Holmes flipped down a corner of his paper. "On the contrary, he strikes me as a feisty little fellow. He spends very little time at Blenheim Palace, or at Connaught Place, his family's London abode. He told me that he stayed with Doctor Roose for much of last year, recovering from illness, and he often remains at his prep school, or stays with school friends, during the holidays."

"Connaught Place. That's in Bayswater; not so far."

"Not far enough, I think we will find," Holmes replied with a smile. "I strongly suspect that young Spencer-Churchill will find it convenient to visit us again. You saw the gleam of excitement in the boy's eye as Wiggins described his meeting with the American and his companion. I do not think that the Spencer-Churchills are a close, or doting family; you will remember the luncheon appointment with his mother. I am quite certain that you will have more than ample opportunity to examine the boy."

We sat for a while in companionable silence. I went through the day in my mind and tried to think of any steps that I had omitted to take. It was a strange and unnerving experience ministering to someone who was so much a part — the centre in fact — of our little household. It reminded me of my time on the line in Afghanistan, when I operated on and nursed officers that I had messed with; so many had been lost.

I looked up to see that Holmes regarded me steadily over his pipe stem.

"Pass me the evening paper, Watson. I saw a poster in Regent Street advertising Madame Neruda at St James's Hall."

He scanned the notices.

"Yes, we have just missed the Philharmonic Society with Sir Arthur Sullivan conducting. Today is Monday, the usual day for the 'Pops' concerts, and unfortunately for the vile blackface Christy Minstrels nearby."

"I do not think that I should —"

"Old friend," Holmes said. "You will forgive me for saying that while I smoke a pipe or two over a problem and search for a solution, you smoke your cigars and worry on consequences. You must clear your mind and approach the problem from a fresh perspective. Neruda's exquisite violin playing will refresh your diagnostic faculties. There is also a fine dining room at the Hall and, my dear fellow, we are unlikely to be provided for at home this evening unless our pageboy and maid have undiscovered culinary skills."

He was undoubtedly right.

"Oh, very well," I said. "Let me change, and I'm your man."

"No need," said Holmes. "One does not dress for the 'Pops'."

A Footrace in the Fog

As we rode towards Piccadilly in a hansom, I asked Holmes about the case brought to him by Wiggins and the Irregulars.

"The matter is devoid of interest, Watson. The gist is that the American boy, Bobby, and his older Negro companion, have disappeared from their rookery in one of the darkest and most infamous courts of the New Cut, Lambeth. He has moved on to another nest of vipers elsewhere. There is no case."

"The fact that he is an American boy adds a touch of topical interest to the tale."

Holmes looked blankly at me.

I laughed. "I meant the Buffalo Bill exhibition at Olympia. You must have seen the posters and advertisements. They are all over the city."

My laugh sounded hollow, even to me. My mind was still fully taken up with my patient in Baker Street. I had little interest to spare for the affairs of Lambeth roughs and missing American boys.

Our cab dropped us outside the Piccadilly entrance to St James's Hall, the principal concert hall of London. I had not been there before, so I viewed the huge building with interest. It was a massive gothic construction with restaurants and bars on the ground floor, and concert halls on the upper floors. According to a placard at the door, the building could seat more than two thousand people.

We dined, and then went upstairs to one of the balconies of the Grand Hall. The long chamber was decorated, according to our elaborately printed concert programmes, in the Florentine style. We took our seats on one of many rows of threadbare, green benches.

The audience was indeed democratic. I saw people who were, from their dress and deportment, from the lower-middle class. Soberly dressed clerks filled the front rows in what looked like club or office groups; people at the back of the Hall might have come from the more respectable upper reaches of the working class. The atmosphere was, nonetheless, respectful and subdued.

"Just a bob for the cheap seats," Holmes said, following my gaze. "The same price as a back-row music-hall seat. There is a universality about music that almost transcends class."

He saw my expression and laughed. "I said almost."

He tapped his elaborately printed programme. "Look, we have the Joachim Quartet with Bach and Beethoven, then Neruda with a Haydn violin sonata."

I flicked through my programme as the house lights dimmed and the gas flared brightly around the stage. The Joachim Quartet, consisting of Mrs Neruda and three foreign-looking gentlemen, was warmly greeted by the audience.

The music, an early Beethoven quartet, began. I saw my companion lean forward as if to better absorb the sound; he surrendered to the power of the music and was transported.

I could not put out of my mind the most melancholy thoughts. I was unable to shake off a sense of inadequacy. I had boasted to Holmes that modern medicine was a matter of deductive reasoning, but I had not fully acknowledged the trial-and-error nature of much of the modern physician's work, or the limited number of proven remedies that he could safely employ for even the most common maladies.

Holmes's remark on the differences in our approach to problems had vexed me. It was true: I did worry on consequences. Was it a violation of professional dispassion to be concerned for Mrs Hudson? I thought of her with affection and respect: I thought of her as a friend. I could not retreat from emotion and, like Holmes, envelop my mind and heart in a hard carapace of cold detachment.

I turned to my companion. He was in profile: his hawk-like nose and determined chin were in silhouette against the gaslights.

He had often claimed to be immune to sentimental attachments. His profound immersion in the music while Mrs Hudson lay so gravely ill was an apt and convincing demonstration of the truth of his statements.

I almost allowed myself a mawkish attempt to characterise my own relations with Holmes in terms of real and abiding friendship, or mere companionship and domestic convenience. I instantly suppressed such unmanly and uncomradely thoughts.

I loosened my collar slightly. The evening was warm, and the heat emanating from the close-packed audience and the bright gas jets made me uncomfortable. I found myself nervously twisting the green silk tassel that adorned the concert programme. My fingers were damp, and I wiped them with my handkerchief. As I stuffed it back into my sleeve, a tiny green sparkle caught my eye. I held the cloth up to the bright light from the flaring gas jets on the stage and saw a cluster of minute green glitters where I had wiped my sweaty fingers.

I shot bolt upright. Holmes gave me a surprised look that turned to one of concern.

"Watson, are you —"

"We must go, Holmes — instantly. There is not a moment to be lost."

I stumbled and pushed my way along the row of seats, stepping on toes and eliciting annoyed 'tuts' and several more direct expressions of disapprobation. I reached the aisle, pushed past an attendant and dashed for the exit. I took the stairs two at a time to the Piccadilly side entrance and rushed to the porter's kiosk in which an elderly man in uniform sat on a stool drinking tea.

"A cab, I must have a cab."

Holmes appeared beside me.

"What about our hats and gloves, shall I —"

I gave him a look that silenced him. I pushed through the heavy glass doors and stepped into the street. I stared. It was not yet eight-thirty in the evening, but the street was dark and deserted; greasy coils of musty, foul, yellow vapour hung in the air and obscured the sky.

Holmes came out and stood next to me.

"Fog," he said. "It has the makings of an absolute pea-souper."

"We must get back home to Baker Street, Holmes," I said. "I believe that it is a matter of life and death."

"Very well." He cupped his hands around his mouth and called 'Cab!' across, down, and up Piccadilly. There was no answering cry or echo. He disappeared back inside the foyer and returned with a police rattle and an anxious porter.

"You mustn't spring the rattle, sir, except on police business. And not never during a performance."

I looked up to the lighted windows of the concert hall above us. The fog was already dimming them and dampening the sound of Mrs Neruda's violin.

Holmes looked quizzically at me.

I nodded.

He held the rattle high above his head and swung it furiously. The noise was tremendous. The porter shrank back inside.

Holmes paused and we listened: nothing. I nodded again and he gave the rattle another long, long swing.

He paused: all was still.

"I am afraid that we have silenced the great Neruda," said Holmes.

I heard the faint sound of a whistle, followed by another, and another.

Holmes swung the rattle wildly.

A light flickered through the thickening fog, and a heavily built police sergeant appeared holding a bull's eye lantern.

He shone his light on Holmes, then on me. Two young police constables ran up, also carrying lanterns.

"Well, sir," the sergeant addressed Holmes. "What's going on?"

Holmes turned to me. "Doctor?"

"I must get back to our lodgings at 221B Baker Street, by the station. It is literally a matter of life and death."

The porter and several attendants came from the foyer of St James's Hall.

"Madame Neruda requests that you refrain from noise-making," said the porter.

Holmes handed him the rattle.

"You are a medical man?" asked the sergeant.

"I am," I replied. "We must hurry. The fog is getting worse."

The sergeant bent forward and took a deep breath.

"No, Sergeant," said Holmes, "We are not in drink. I see that you are from C division. You will know Inspector Lestrade, now with the detective force at Scotland Yard. He may have spoken of me: I am Sherlock Holmes, the consulting detective. We need a cab."

The sergeant considered.

"No, sir, if you'll pardon the liberty, you do not. A cabby would have to lead his horse through this muck. You'll be faster on foot."

He turned to his men.

"Baker Street lads, on the jog. You two lead the way. Ten paces ahead with your lanterns on the street. I will follow with the gents on either side. Keep to the centre of the roadway. The omnibuses and carriages will have parked against the kerb."

We set off in formation, Holmes on one side of the sergeant, me on the other, and the constables ranging ahead.

The fog thickened as we passed Piccadilly Circus. Twice the constables crashed into stationary cabs and carriages, and with a few shouted insults, we passed on. We were the only creatures, as far as I could tell, moving through the choking, soot- and sulphur-tasting, yellow-brown murk.

Our way was clearer at Oxford Circus as the gaslights were lit. We paused for breath.

"Straight up Portland Place, Sergeant?" asked Holmes.

"Clearest way, sir," he answered, his eyes gleaming in the lantern light. "Then left along the Marylebone Road to the station."

One of the policemen disappeared for a moment and returned with a half dozen ragged boys. They carried bundles of twigs topped with tarred cloth.

"Link boys, sir: always a mob of them at the corner there for the drunks spilling out of the pubs."

"Baker Street," I said, bending over my knees and gasping for breath. "Two-bob a nob."

The sergeant lit the boys' torches with a match and reorganised our convoy. The boys fanned ten paces ahead, the constables took station in front of the sergeant, and Holmes and I were positioned once again on his left and right.

We started off again at a steady jog, faster now that we had a screen of lights. The boys excited yelps and whoops, like those of a pack of Mr Buffalo Bill's Red Indians, echoed strangely, sometimes near, sometimes far away in the fog. The flaming torches lost formation and veered left. We followed.

"Marylebone Road," the sergeant called back to us.

Left again. I stumbled against the kerb and felt a searing pain in my leg. I fell on one knee, panting and coughing. Arms gripped me on either side, and I was lifted almost off my feet.

"Nearly home, Watson," said Holmes. "Is it the Jezail bullet?"

"Damn my leg, Holmes," I cried. "And damn me for a fool. We may be too late."

"The boys are almost at the station, sir," said the sergeant patting me on the shoulder. "Never say die."

I was half dragged to the junction with Baker Street. I hobbled to where the street Arabs congregated outside the entrance to the railway station. I glimpsed lighted windows on the other side of the street through dense banks of fog. A racking cough from one side was answered by another farther along.

Holmes thrust out his arm and pointed. "Our lodgings are there, Watson, at precisely twenty-three degrees —"

I heard a shout of 'Ahoy', and saw a moving point of light as one of the policemen waved his lantern from across the street. There was another shout and flash of light as his colleague joined him and hammered on a door. It opened and a vague figure appeared, silhouetted against the diffused glow of gaslights.

Holmes arm swung to the lights. "Exactly one hundred and fifty-five degrees left."

"Pay the boys, Holmes."

I staggered across the street on the sergeant's arm, up the steps, past Bessie and into the lobby of 221B.

"All of you," I ordered. "Cover your mouths and noses." I rested against the stair balustrade and took out my handkerchief. I was folding it into a kerchief or mask when I spotted the bright green sparkles again. I threw it down. Holmes came into the lobby and covered his nose and mouth with a handkerchief tied behind his head. His bright eyes regarded me with reassuring confidence.

"In there, Holmes," I said, pointing to the waiting room. "Bring out Mrs Hudson and the nurse. Stay well clear of the windows."

"Miasma, is it, sir?" the sergeant asked with a grim look. "Is it mortal, like?" He gravely tied his handkerchief over his face, and the other policemen, wide-eyed with dread, covered theirs.

"There is little danger if you are quick, but you must not stir the atmosphere; move speedily but temperately."

Holmes opened the waiting room door and stalked inside followed by the sergeant and the two trembling police constables.

They reappeared a moment later carrying two inert bodies.

"In here." I opened the door of Mrs Hudson's sitting room and watched as they lay Mrs Hudson on the sofa and Nurse Levine in a chair.

"Hot water, sponges, brushes, and my medical bag, Bessie," I ordered. "Gentlemen, throw your handkerchiefs to the floor, throw them down instantly. Close the door of the waiting room. No one is to enter there or here. You are safe outside. Leave the front door open."

As I hobbled into the sitting room, I heard Holmes murmur to the policemen.

"Do any of you know how to make coffee from the raw bean?"

The Power to Cure and to Kill

"Ah, there you are, Holmes. Good morning."

"Good morning, Watson. I see by your smiling countenance that you have some positive news."

"Indeed. It is a beautiful clear day outside, and Mrs Hudson is much improved. She imbibed a half-pint of beef tea early this morning and roundly criticised it as too salty."

"I am heartily glad. What of the district nurse?"

"She is resting, but already planning her afternoon safari into the rank jungles of Lambeth."

Holmes joined me at our breakfast table and lifted the lid of the chafing dish in the centre.

"What is this?"

"That is a curried chop, Holmes, braised with onions."

"Where is my customary six-minute boiled egg?" he asked stiffly.

"My dear fellow, Mrs Hudson is still unwell. We must make do."

"Who prepared this repast?"

"I did."

He gave me a sceptical look.

"I campaigned through Afghanistan, Holmes," I said warmly. "My soldier servant Murray, though as brave as a lion, ate his meat raw. I have mastered the art of camp cooking, and with the aid of Mrs Beeton's compendious book, I expect to hold the culinary fort until Mrs Hudson relieves me."

Holmes contented himself with tea and toast.

Billy let in Master Spencer-Churchill. He wore the same Eton jacket he had worn in the park.

"Ah, good morning," I said. "Have you breakfasted?"

"Somewhat, sir."

"Could you manage a curried chop?"

"With delight, Doctor."

The boy helped himself; not without, as I was pleased to see, commendable relish.

"How is your leg, sir?" he asked.

"Better, thank you."

"I understand that Mrs Hudson and the lady nurse are recovering," he said. "And that it was not the miasma after all."

"It was not," I answered. "They were poisoned."

"Was it the Mormons, Doctor?"

"Eh?" exclaimed Holmes from across the room. "Oh, you have been reading the manuscript of Doctor Watson's account of the Mormon case."

"Yes, sir," said Spencer-Churchill. "I'm almost at the end of 'A Study in Scarlet'. It is very exciting."

Holmes turned up his nose and sniffed.

"No," I said with some satisfaction. "It was not the Mormons: it was the curtains. They have been coloured with a solution of Scheele's dye: they are furiously arsenical. The fashion twenty or thirty years ago for all things green led to a deplorable competition among manufacturers for the most brilliant hue. Arsenic compounds provide a deep, lustrous green, but at a terrible cost. Mrs Hudson breathed in a quantity of Scheele's —"

"Schweinfurt Green, rather than Scheele's," Holmes interrupted. "At the remarkable density of sixty-eight grains of arsenic per square yard, and so loosely incorporated into the fabric that the poison can be dusted out with ease. Two or three grains will kill if ingested, as I am sure you are aware, Doctor."

He smiled at my look of astonishment.

"I took a sample of the drapery while you were busy reviving your patients, Doctor. I subjected it to the standard Marsh test, with the Gutzeit additions: the test that exonerated Smethurst, the bigamist. I added zinc to sulphuric acid to create hydrogen, with which any arsenic present will combine to form arsine gas. I ignited the gas, and metallic arsenic precipitated as a black mirror on a sheet of glass.

"I would caution you, Spencer-Churchill, not to try that experiment at home. It requires more than ordinary laboratory experience to perform safely. A leak in his apparatus poisoned the great Adolph Gehlen. He died in agony."

Spencer-Churchill gave Holmes a wide-eyed look that bordered on veneration. He promised to avoid all chemical experiments other than those specifically recommended by Holmes.

"I had hoped —" I said stiffly. "I had expected to conduct that experiment myself. I thought of preparing an article for *The Lancet*."

"Indeed?" said Holmes with an impenitent grin. "Then I have saved you some trouble. The tassel on our concert programmes yielded only four grains of arsenic; much has no doubt already rubbed off on the gloves and hands of music aficionados. I have written to the proprietors of St James's Hall."

He stood.

"May I visit the patient, Doctor?"

"Yes, of course, but she is not to be tired."

Holmes smiled and left the room.

I did not know whether to be pleased that I did not have to test the curtain material myself, or provoked at Holmes's gratuitous intervention in my case. I had to admit, at least inwardly, that I was not in the first class of experimental chemists; I had forgotten, if I had ever known, that the great Adolph Gehlen died while performing the arsenic test. I should therefore have felt grateful to my friend for performing the risky experiment himself.

However, my notes on the case, written up, would have provided a strong *per contra* to the Lister fanatics who insisted than all ailments were the result of germ infestation. There might have been a minor or — who knew? — an important shift in opinion away from the germ theorists and towards those medical professionals who had their feet more on the firm, empirical, ground of experience.

What would my medical colleagues remember of a paper written by me, based on experiments conducted by the famous Sherlock Holmes? Ha!

If Holmes undertook the experiment because of his poor opinion of my laboratory skills, then I had a right to the peevish sense of resentment that I could detect in a dark ignoble corner of my inner spirit. If, on the other hand, he had risked himself for a friend, the matter took on a different complexion —

"I say, Doctor," said Spencer-Churchill. "This chop is first rate."

"Thank you," I said. "The gravy is a mixture of Mrs Beeton's and my own recipe. Carrots have no business in gravy, as I am sure you are aware."

I regarded the boy with some benevolence. "My dear fellow, we cannot keep calling you Master Spencer-Churchill."

"The chaps at my school in Brighton call me Winston, but that will not do for Harrow. I am thinking of styling myself Winston S. Churchill to be higher in the class list: a 'C' and not an 'S'."

"You are at Harrow, not Eton? Your father was at Eton."

The boy coloured and looked down at his plate. "My father thinks that my constitution is too frail for Eton; Harrow is on a hill, and enjoys healthy breezes. After Harrow, I will aim for Sandhurst and the Cavalry."

"The Cavalry: that's a fine ambition. I will call you Churchill, if that is not too familiar?"

The door opened, and Holmes returned.

"Well done, Doctor. We will have our old Mrs Hudson back in no time."

"I hope that you did not harass her."

"I did not. I merely tallied our expenses: the linkboys, twelve shillings; the constables, five-bob a bobby; the estimable Sergeant Baynes, a half-sovereign. Then two-shillings a head to the navvies I hired to take away the arsenical curtains. They assure me that they will chop them up, sugar the fibres, and sell them as fly bait. I merely acquainted Mrs Hudson of the costs incurred during her illness so far. I am sure that will be a capital bucker-upper."

"Holmes, how could you?"

"What? I did not mention my breakfast egg and toast soldiers, or lack of same." He snatched the morning papers and slumped into his armchair.

"Mrs Hudson is recovering remarkably quickly," Churchill said.

"Yes, it is often the case when the source of the poisoning is removed, or, as in this case, the victim is removed from the source. As I recently explained to Holmes, there are only two remedies in my medical arsenal on which I feel I can absolutely rely: opium and arsenic. Both have the power to cure and to kill."

"Why was Billy hardly affected, Doctor? And Bessie not affected at all?"

"I would not like it generally known, no doctor would, but I have no idea. Billy is young and fit, of course, and he was less exposed to the curtains."

"He said that poisoning is a woman's business, sir. He says that hot, spiced gin, taken regular with —"

"Regularly," I corrected.

"Taken regularly with cayenne pepper, fortifies the constitution."

"He may be right, at least in his case. Bessie is temperance, or perhaps teetotal. I understand that there are peasants in the Styrian area in Austria who ingest massive amounts of arsenic to improve their health and stamina. They are sleek and rosy-cheeked. Perhaps Bessie has some Styrian blood in her ancestry."

Billy appeared at the door with a tray.

"Telegram, Doctor."

I took the form and opened it.

"It's from the analyst, Herr Voelcker," I said. "He says that he can find nothing amiss with the rabbit or dumplings, but that the other samples heave with arsenic. Well, I suppose that a second, or in this case third, opinion is always useful, however late."

Holmes grunted something unintelligible from behind his newspaper.

I helped myself to another cup of coffee.

"I will not, however, completely discount Mr Philpot's miasmatic — eh?"

Billy caught Churchill's eye and they both collapsed in giggles.

Holmes flicked down a corner of his newspaper. "What?"

Billy looked down at his feet.

"It's a remark of Doctor Watson's," said Churchill. "When we got back from Lambeth last night."

"Why, the boys are blushing furiously, Watson. You must have been vehement to embarrass Billy."

It came back to me in a rush.

"Oh, it was nothing, Holmes. I may have been intemperate. I was tired. I may have said 'Bother, miasmas,' or something very like."

The two boys convulsed in laughter.

"What is this about Lambeth?" said Holmes dropping his paper into his lap.

Billy and Churchill exchanged nervous looks.

"We went down Lambeth way to have a look-see," Billy said. "We thought we might find out more about —"

Holmes jumped up and stood in front of the fireplace, arms folded. "You took Spencer-Churchill on a tour of Lambeth?"

"Just Churchill, Holmes," I corrected. "He has decided to drop the Spencer."

Holmes ignored me. "Do you realise that the Doctor is *in loco parentis*? Imagine his position if something had happened to the boy."

Billy gave me a strange look.

"Holmes means that I am responsible to Churchill's parents for anything that might happen to him while he is in my care," I said. "You do understand that, I'm sure."

He looked back down at his toes. "I'm sure I didn't mean no harm, sir. We were with Harry and his mob. We didn't go near the George and Dragon. We met in the Duke of Sussex, like we'd agreed."

"Harry? Do you mean Harry Wiggins of the Irregulars?" said Holmes. "Good Lord, it gets worse and worse."

"Calm, Holmes," I said. "They are back safe."

They were indeed not only safe and sound, but eager to talk about their adventures. I could not find it in me to scold them too harshly. I turned back to Billy.

"Sit there at the table with Churchill and explain yourself."

He exchanged another nervous glance with Churchill and perched on the edge of a chair.

"Well, sir, we could see that you and Mr Holmes was taken up with Mrs Hudson's ailment, and you'd not have time for the missing American boy case for a while, so I thought that we might help by —"

"That is not so," Churchill interrupted. "It was entirely my idea. I made my plan with Harry Wiggins and persuaded Billy to accompany me."

"I see," I said. "You went to North Lambeth in a sailor suit. That was brave. You heard what Wiggins said about the rough crowd that frequent the Waterloo area. You might have been knocked on the head and popped down a drain."

Holmes chuckled, and Churchill reddened.

"I borrowed suitable clothes from Billy," he said. "They belonged to your previous pageboy; he was about my size. We met Harry and his men outside the Duke of Sussex, and they showed us where Bobby and his dark friend lived."

He stood and took up a pugilistic stance.

"I can defend myself, if necessary. Raines, one of the under-gardeners at Blenheim, is teaching me the Noble Art. He says I have a formidable left hook."

He demonstrated the punch, and sat down again. "And Mr Holmes needed his data on the case checked by someone on the spot. You know his methods, Doctor."

"Churchill," I said shaking my head. "People of that character, thieves, vagabonds, and so on, do not stay in one place for long. Things get too hot, the authorities close in, and they move on. I am sure that is what this American boy has done."

"But what about Mutton-chops?"

"Eh?"

"Doctor Watson missed most of the testimony of the Irregulars when he left to tend Mrs Hudson," Holmes said as he picked up a notebook from the table and tossed it to Churchill.

The boy found his page, and read. "Wiggins said that Bobby and Aaron went missing about a fortnight ago; a few days later, a cove turned up at pubs and lodging houses along the Waterloo Road asking after a young American boy with blond hair, aged thirteen, and an older Negro footman. He had a photograph of Bobby when he was a bit younger, maybe eleven or so. He said the boy was Robert W Taylor, and the servant, Aaron Long. The man accused Long of stealing clothes and silver. He offered a reward of ten pounds."

"Move on to the description," said Holmes.

"A tall cove with big, red, mutton-chop whiskers. He was in a sandy-coloured coat and a soft hat. He had a funny accent like the pot man at the Horse and Groom in the Westminster Bridge Road."

"This mutton-chop fellow must be the footman's previous employer," I said. "It is likely that they stole the silver spoons and clothes from him. The mutton-chop-whiskered man is searching for his lost possessions. What is singular about that?"

"You will remember, Doctor," said Churchill, "that the boy, Bobby, wore expensive clothes that fitted him. He also had a high-class American accent."

"If such a thing there be," said Holmes.

"All very well," I said. "And what else did your nocturnal perambulations in Lambeth turn up?"

"Not very nocturnal, Doctor," said Churchill. "We got back before the fog. We discovered that the pot man is from Cape Town. He has a strong Germanic accent. And we got this."

He handed me a pen and ink drawing of a young boy. "It's Bobby."

The drawing was exquisitely crafted. The artist had caught the boy's pensive expression wonderfully. He leaned against a wall with his hands in his pockets and dared anyone to challenge his right to do so. His grey-green eyes displayed confrontation and defiance: he faced the world with a mixture of bravado and alarm.

"Who drew this? Who was the artist? It is very fine."

Churchill and Billy chuckled.

"It was drawn by Wiggins's uncle Josiah," said Holmes. "He specialises in drawings of Britannia."

"Eh?"

"Five-pound notes: he is a forger."

There was a long, loud ring at the doorbell.

"Damnation," I said, hobbling to the window. "That will disturb Mrs Hudson's rest. Quick Billy, go down and answer — oh."

Holmes joined me at the window.

"It is a police officer," he said. He turned to Churchill. "If there is anything we should know about your adventure last night, young man, now is the time to confess it."

3. The Police Constable and the Milliner

The Stalking of PC DR42

Billy led a tall police constable with a fine, black walrus moustache into our sitting room.

"Good morning, Constable," I said. "You can put your helmet on the table." I ushered him to the sofa where he sat stiffly, looking ill at ease. He turned to Holmes.

"Am I correct in assuming, sir, that I am addressing Mr Sherlock Holmes?"

"You are," said Holmes. "May I ask how you knew?"

"My sergeant gave me a description of you, sir, and of Doctor Watson."

I bowed.

"Your informant is Sergeant Baynes?" I asked.

"Indeed, sir. He was most insistent that I put my position fairly before you, and ask for your help. I am in the most awkward bind any police officer has ever been in. It is the women, sirs: they dog me night and day."

"Well," said Holmes reaching for his pipe. "Constable DR42 Endaby, why don't you tell us your side of this unfortunate Caspar affair."

The policeman sprang up, bewildered.

"How did you know, Mr Holmes?"

Holmes shook his head and blew a smoke ring across the room.

"Your number is on your collar, Endaby," I said. "Come to the window."

PC Endaby and I looked down at Baker Street. A half-dozen respectably dressed young women congregated on the pavement below talking animatedly. Two held banners on poles: the first said 'Women's Rights', the second simply, 'Fiend'.

"They've dogged me from Tottenham Court Road," said Endaby shaking his head.

One of the women looked up and spotted us. She pointed and let out a shrill cry that the others instantly took up.

"Dogged," said Holmes, "is hardly the *mot juste*."

Holmes settled in his accustomed chair before the fireplace, bent forward with his elbows on his knees and his hands steepled before his face.

"Endaby, you will understand that I, like the rest of London town, have read the newspaper version of events in the Elizabeth Caspar affair. Pray you sit down and begin your tale."

I took my pocket notebook from my jacket pocket and hunted on the desk for a pencil.

"Spencer-Churchill," said Holmes, "take notes."

I replaced my notebook as the boy sat at the table, opened a large notebook and regarded PC Endaby with the eagerness of a hunting dog on point. I noted with some annoyance that the pencil he held was mine.

"It's like this, sirs," said Endaby. "On the day in question, I was on fixed-point duty in Regent Street —"

"Where exactly?" asked Holmes. "Be as exact as you can. I need precise data."

"The west side, sir, at the corner of Conduit Street. A constable is on duty there day and night. I came off my shift at eight in the evening, and I thought I would take a turn along Regent Street towards Oxford Circus."

"Why?" asked Holmes.

"It was a fine evening, sir. And I hoped to meet one of my colleagues stationed there to arrange a quiet drink or two after work."

"You trace this route habitually?"

"Mostly of a Friday. I walked up Regent Street at a steady pace and reached Oxford Circus. My pal wasn't in sight, so I crossed Oxford Street —"

Holmes held up his hand.

"Your simplest way back to Tottenham Court Road and your station would be to turn right into Oxford Street, would it not?"

"Yes, sir, but I thought I might catch my pal on the corner of Great Castle Street."

Holmes nodded.

"The crowd thinned after I left the Circus behind. I noticed a well-dressed young woman walking in a certain manner, sir. She was swinging her bag and her parasol, and stepping, almost dancing along the pavement in a way that attracted attention. I saw a gentleman, and then another, move up to her and say a word or two. She talked to them quite freely and with a smile, so I was immediately suspicious that she might be inebriated or a —" He stopped.

"What is it?" Holmes asked.

Endaby nodded at young Churchill.

"Eh? Oh, I see. Master Spencer-Churchill," said Holmes. "Why don't you trot downstairs for a while? You can play in the backyard."

Churchill gave Holmes a furious look and stalked out the door. It closed with a loud crash.

I raised my eyebrows.

"What?" said Holmes looking back at me with a puzzled frown.

I took out my notebook and retrieved my pencil from the table where Churchill had flung it down.

Holmes turned to the policeman. "Continue."

"I watched as this spectacle continued, sirs, with several men talking with the lady."

"She was accosted by the men," I said. "She did not start the conversation."

Endaby laughed. "No, no, these street ladies are much too fly for that, sir. They flaunt themselves and the customers cluster around them. That area near Peter Robinson's is a well-known pickup point. I saw the same lady there on at least three other occasions, although she denies it."

"You arrested Miss Caspar and took her to Tottenham Court Road Police Station," said Holmes. "Did she protest her innocence?"

Endaby shrugged in an ill-bred fashion. "Most vehemently."

"I understand that Miss Caspar was found innocent," I said.

"She appeared the next morning at Great Marlborough Street Police Court before Chief Magistrate Newton," said Endaby. "I gave evidence of the arrest and testified that I had seen her three times before in Regent Street, late at night, soliciting for prostitution. Miss Caspar's employer, Mrs Barker, testified in her defence that she had been in London only a few months and that she could not have been in central London on the dates I gave in evidence; she further said that Miss Caspar had never been out late at night before the day she was arrested. She said that Miss Caspar was a respectable woman of perfect character in a good job. Mrs Barker was unshakeable in her evidence. Faced with this, the magistrate had no option but to find Miss Caspar not guilty. However, the judge gave her a warning."

Endaby pulled his police notebook out of his breast pocket and read from it.

"Just take my advice: if you are a respectable girl, as you say you are, don't walk in Regent Street at night, for if you do, you will either be fined or sent to prison after the caution I have given you".

Endaby closed his notebook with a snap.

"So," said Holmes, "it seems, from this statement, that the magistrate believed Miss Caspar was guilty and that she had persuaded Mrs Barker to perjure herself to secure her acquittal."

"That seemed obvious at the time, sir."

I recalled from the *Pall Mall Gazette* that the case was taken up by Llewellyn Atherley-Jones, MP, barrister and a rising star on the radical wing of the Liberal Party. The Home Secretary was forced to order the Commissioner of Police, Sir Charles Warren, to undertake an inquiry into the case. The Metropolitan Police held six days of hearings and sent a report to the Home Secretary. The contents were not released.

"Did you testify at the hearing?" I asked Endaby.

"Yes, sir. I was suspended, and I gave my evidence. And now I am sued for perjury in a private prosecution by Mrs Barker and Miss Caspar. However, I have been assured by certain personages —"

Holmes stood.

"Thirsty work, Watson. Let us have a whisky and soda. I suppose I cannot tempt you constable, as you are in uniform."

"I am under suspension, Mr Holmes. And those shrieking harpies would drive any man to drink. I wore my uniform as protection against them. They are camped outside my house."

"A large Scotch for the constable, Watson."

Hyenas at the Door

I watched from the window of our study as a cab stopped at the kerb below.

Our pageboy leapt out before the cab halted. PC Endaby left the house at the run and jumped in to take his place. The cabby, warned by Billy, took off at a great rate. He flicked his horsewhip at the women protesters on the pavement as he passed them.

"I say, Holmes, that is too much. The cab driver took his crop to those women downstairs. I hope that Endaby noted his number."

"One does not reason with hyenas, Watson. One flogs them away."

The protesters, jibbed of their quarry, continued to shout up at our windows.

"Well," I conceded. "They do sound like hyenas. Do you not feel, Holmes, that women in groups, fired up to a frenzy, are unfeminine to a gross degree?"

I sat and took a cigar from the scuttle. "Was Endaby telling the truth?"

"Ignoring, for the moment, the fool of a magistrate," Holmes answered. "Why do we keep these old dodderers on the bench until they are half in the land of gaga — ignoring him, I say, leaves us with three possibilities."

He counted them on his fingers.

"One: Endaby saw Miss Caspar apparently soliciting and arrested her in good faith. Two: ditto, but after the arrest and before they arrived at the station, she convinced him by her vehement denials and behaviour that she was innocent. To avoid an action for false arrest, he made up the circumstantial evidence of the three earlier sightings in Regent Street. Three: he is the lying hound that those harpies below think him to be."

I considered. "He seemed a truthful person. He must have a good moral character, or he would not have been accepted into the Metropolitan Police."

"He meets the height specification, and he has the requisite facial hair," said Holmes. "Nothing more is necessary. There are no intellectual or ethical requirements."

He took a pipe from the mantel and filled it with tobacco from the Persian slipper.

Holmes's flippant gibe against the police had, I thought, some basis in truth. The police officers that we encountered did not give a very professional impression as they stumbled in Holmes's wake, tripping over clues and thumping into dead-end walls. However, I believed that the canny distrust, doggedness in pursuit, and evident bravery of Inspector Lestrade and his kin were as much tools of the detective trade as the application of abstruse theory.

I had often shared Holmes's intellectual and moral satisfaction when a complex case was solved through our efforts, but it was an undeniable fact that most crime was as degenerate as it was commonplace. Not every solution to a case turned on the texture of the killer's cigar tobacco; not every murder was committed by a one-legged dwarf who condescended to leave pockmarks in the doormat. Most cases were solved by arresting the nearest person with a blood-stained knife or bludgeon.

I put that thought aside, and concentrated on the case of the unfortunate Miss Caspar. I was much concerned at the circumstances in which she had been taken into charge.

"What strikes me, Holmes, is the randomness of the arrest. It is almost *Continental* in character. We do not expect our police force to arrest people on the streets of London, even young women, and even in the late evening, without firm evidence that they have done wrong. This is not St Petersburg or Berlin."

"I agree," said Holmes. "And the charge levelled against her is almost impossible to disprove. It will scar the lady for life, whether true or not."

"As the charge of lying in court will confound Endaby's hopes of career and promotion."

"Yes," said Holmes. "In his shoes I would not rely on the assurances of his 'certain personages', especially not with the Press aroused. I should be more, rather than less concerned at the involvement of the mighty. The case does not have the international colour or forensic profundity of some of my recent cases, Watson, but it has demonstrably serious repercussions. Lives may be ruined."

"So you will help the constable's defence?"

"I shall work to determine the truth." He jumped up from his chair and rubbed his hands together. "Luncheon: something simple in the circumstances. I will see what Bessie can provide."

He left the door open and bounded down the stairs.

"Oh, dear," I said to myself.

A moment later, there was a shout, a screech, and Holmes came pounding back up the stairs. He strode to the window.

"I am a simple man, Watson," he said grimly. "I have simple tastes. All I require for lunch is a pot of piping hot coffee and two roast-beef sandwiches. You would think I am asking for *Culotte de bœuf Salomon avec pommes Anna* for all the cooperation I received downstairs. Your nurse is out on an errand, and Bessie flatly refuses to leave the Sick Room. She says that she is under your orders."

"Mrs Hudson is still unwell, Holmes. She must be carefully watched."

I stood. "I will check the larder and see what there is."

"There's a fair bit of leftover rabbit stew with dumplings," said Churchill softly from the doorway. "I looked."

I sat. We stared glumly at one another.

"The stew has been tested," I said. "It is completely unarsenical."

Churchill sighed and sat at the dining table.

"Wait," said Holmes. "Watson, you are a member of the Junior United Services Club, are you not?"

"I am."

"Excellent. Come, Spencer-Churchill," said Holmes making for the door. "Watson, my dear friend, you are allowed up to three guests per visit for your seven guineas a year subscription. They do an excellent roast beef luncheon on Tuesdays; the last sitting ends at two. We will just manage it if you tip the driver sufficiently. There is not a moment to be lost."

We followed him downstairs into the hall. He whispered instructions to Billy; the boy slipped out the front door, closing it behind him.

"I thought that those female harpies had marched off," Holmes said softly. "But there are still two hyenas dawdling on the pavement outside, no doubt gathering sufficient courage to come in and face us. They are minions of the Caspar female come to complain that we act for Endaby — ah."

Billy opened the door, and Holmes darted across the pavement to a waiting hansom cab. The older of two well-dressed ladies standing outside our door moved to accost him, but he waved her away with his top hat.

"Urgent business, Madam, that will brook no delay. I act for the Akond of Swat."

He jumped into the cab. I followed him across the pavement leaning on my stick. My wound still troubled me a little.

"Come along, Watson," Holmes shouted. "Spencer-Churchill will perch on your knee."

"Doctor Watson, I presume." A pretty young lady in a sober grey dress and jacket, a white blouse, and a straw hat touched my arm as I passed her.

"Good afternoon." I doffed my hat and endeavoured to slip past her to the cab from which Holmes furiously beckoned me.

"You are Miss Caspar," said Churchill coming up beside me. "I saw your picture in the newspaper."

"I am," said the lady. "And this is my employer, Mrs Barker." She indicated a short older lady dressed in black. "We are here to see Mr Sherlock Holmes."

"I am Winston S Churchill, how do you do?"

"Oh, ah, Doctor John Watson at your service," I said.

The two ladies demurely acknowledged our bows. We all turned to the cab, where Holmes sat immobile.

"Holmes —" I began.

He sprang down and stalked between us.

"Have the cab wait, Watson. We shall not be long."

He disappeared back through the front door of our lodgings held open by our bemused pageboy.

I ushered the ladies into the hall.

We followed Holmes through the open door of the waiting room. The walls, carpet, and furniture had been carefully cleaned, but the curtains had not yet been replaced. Bright sunlight streamed through the light, netted lace that covered the windows.

Miss Caspar and Mrs Barker sat together on the sofa. Miss Caspar looked to be in her early twenties. Her oval face was pale, but her blue eyes sparkled clear in the bright light. Her hair was auburn and pulled back into a bun at the back of her head. Her straw hat with its violet band was tilted at a slight, but modest, angle. She gave me a reserved look and a shy smile.

Mrs Barker glared at me, and I looked away, abashed.

Holmes stood with his back to the window, in shadow. I sat in an armchair by the door. I noticed that Churchill had slipped in and taken his place by the fireplace. I motioned for him to leave, but he ignored me.

"Now, ladies," said Holmes after I made the introductions. "You should know that this morning we received Police Constable Endaby. I understand that you have initiated a private prosecution against him for perjury. He has told us his side of the story, and requested that we act for him in the matter. Although I have not given Endaby a firm acceptance of the case, I feel it would not be correct for me to enter into communication with his accusers. I suggest therefore —"

"His accusers!" cried Mrs Barker. "And what of this cruelly wronged woman?"

"Hush, Mary, my dear," said Miss Caspar softly in a voice with a Northern tone. "As Mr Holmes is not yet engaged in the case, I am sure that he will agree to hear the facts of the arrest from the lips of both principals before he decides on his course of action. That would be fair and prudent, would you not agree, Doctor?"

She turned to me with a sweet smile and a flutter of eyelashes.

"I think," I said. "I am of the opinion. That is to say —"

"Very well, Miss Caspar," said Holmes, much to my relief. "You have a valid point. You must understand, however, that anything you tell me may be made available to the supporters of PC Endaby, should I decide to act for him."

"I understand and agree. I have nothing to hide."

Holmes sat in the armchair by the window with his face in shadow.

"Pray, state the facts."

"Thank you." Miss Caspar folded her hands in her lap and began her story.

"I am Elizabeth Anne Caspar, twenty-four years old, unmarried, born in Grantham in 1863, and residing until recently in Stockton in County Durham. I made my living first as a seamstress, and then I had the good fortune to be noticed by Mrs Barker and offered a position in London as a dress designer. I left Stockton earlier this year, and I now live and work at Mrs Barker's residence and workshop in Southampton Row."

"Number nineteen," said Mrs Barker. "It is a most respectable neighbourhood."

"Thank you, Madam," said Holmes. "I do not doubt it for an instant. Perhaps we could move on to the day of the incident."

"I went out on the evening in question to Jay's Shop in Regent Street. They are a large retailer of silk and millinery. I wanted to buy gloves. The Jubilee decorations were up, and people were out enjoying the warm weather. It took me longer than expected to get to Jay's, as the crowds were so dense. When I arrived I found that the premises were closed."

"What did you do?" asked Holmes leaning forward in his seat.

"I stood for a moment in the doorway of Jay's deciding whether to press on to another shop or go back home," said Miss Caspar. "It was getting late, so I decided to return home. I retraced my steps through the crowds across Oxford Circus, intending to take the omnibus back to Holborn. I was walking along Oxford Street to the 'bus stop, when a policeman grabbed my arm most forcibly and took me in custody on a charge of — of —"

She buried her face in her hands and let out a low sob.

"Spencer-Churchill," said Holmes, glancing at his watch. "Would you pop outside and dismiss the cabman. You may then sit upstairs in the sitting room. Watson, give the boy eight pence for the cab waiting charge."

Churchill left, glowering at Holmes. The door slammed behind him.

"We must take that boy in hand, Watson," said Holmes. "I have a solidly made hairbrush that may be used to persuade the child to exit rooms in a more orderly fashion. Our door hinges are Georgian; they will not stand this abuse."

Holmes snapped his watch closed. "The boy is vexed. We have unfortunately missed the last luncheon sitting at the Junior United Services Club."

He stood. "Were you walking along happily, Miss Caspar?" he asked, smiling. "Were you dancing? Swinging your parasol?"

She looked up, and returned a wan smile. "Not at all, Mr Holmes. I was in something of a bad mood. I wanted a new pair of gloves to wear for the Jubilee celebration and on our company excursion to see the Wild West Show at the Olympia Grounds in July."

"Your demeanour was not cheerful and high-spirited?"

"Quite the opposite, I was hot, bothered by the crowds, and morose at my lack of success with the gloves."

"And you were taken into charge in Regent Street, between Oxford Circus and Great Castle Street. That is the testimony of PC Endaby."

"That is not the case. I am certain I was in Oxford Street. I was looking in the windows of the Crystal Bazaar when Constable Endaby accosted me. I cannot understand his insistence that the arrest took place elsewhere. It seems of little importance where I was at the time."

Holmes considered for a long moment.

"Miss Caspar," he said. "I put it to you that you were tripping gaily along Oxford Street, enjoying the warm weather and the jolly throng of shoppers and sightseers as you have done in perfect innocence on a number of previous occasions. You found yourself accosted by a man, perhaps by several men in succession. Flustered, you took a wrong turn away from your route and from the crowds, north into Regent Street. The man or men accosted you again, and you flew into a panic. You were relieved to see a policeman come up, but horrified when he took you in charge for —"

Miss Caspar jumped to her feet. "No, sir, that is not so!" she cried. "That was my first visit to the centre of the city, and I was not accosted. I am wholly innocent of this disgusting charge!"

"I say, Holmes," I said. I sprang up, proffered my handkerchief, and helped Miss Caspar back to her seat.

"Oh, how remiss of me," said Holmes. "We have not offered you any refreshment. Watson, would you be good enough to instruct Bessie to brew tea?"

Miss Caspar returned my handkerchief with a murmur of thanks.

I opened the door and found Bessie outside with the tea tray. Churchill followed her in with a plate of biscuits.

"You must try some of this new lump sugar," said Holmes. "One piece or two, ladies?"

"You were hard on Miss Caspar, Holmes," I said, as Billy showed the ladies out, and we settled ourselves upstairs in our sitting room.

"Nonsense. The magistrate was far more unpleasant, the old reprobate."

He filled his pipe with tobacco.

"There is more to this than meets the eye, Watson. I am convinced that everything hinges on the place of arrest."

"Could it be, Holmes, that Endaby places the arrest north of the Circus because, as he says, the area in front of Peter Robinson's is notorious for —" I looked across at Churchill seated at the dining table. "For street-walkers?"

"Prostitutes," said Churchill with a sly smile. "Gay ladies, women of the Town, *Femmes* —"

"Or could it be," said Holmes overriding him, "that Miss Caspar was mistaken. She says herself that she is a stranger in London. You have the list of witnesses she gave you?"

"The persons whose evidence are relevant, apart from the principals," I said, "are witnesses Madame Fernand Audet and Major Edgar Massingham, and the two policemen on duty in the area, PC Twyman and PC Dyer."

"We shall get to the witnesses in due course," said Holmes glancing at the clock. "It is three-twenty. If we can hold famine at bay with café and biscotti at the Italian coffee house by Baker Street Station, we can travel to Oxford Circus, view the scenes of arrest and then repair to the Criterion Grill. The table-d'hôte starts at five-thirty, and they offer capital roast beef in a fine room on the Piccadilly side for half-a-crown a head, excluding wine. You are cordially invited, Spencer-Churchill, provided you can manage to learn how to close a door like a Christian. Come, it is your turn to pay, Watson."

The doorbell rang.

"I shall snip the wire," cried Holmes.

Churchill went to the window.

"It is a police detective," he said.

Billy showed in a stooped, narrow-faced man with a sharp nose and a sallow complexion. He wore a brown tweed suit and a bowler hat.

"Inspector Lestrade," said Holmes with a sigh. "How good it is to see you."

"And you too, Mr Holmes, Doctor."

He looked quizzically at Churchill.

"This is Winston Churchill," I said. "He is — ah —"

"A cadet in the Consulting Detective profession," said Holmes. "An apprentice: he is learning the trade."

Churchill beamed.

"Well," said Lestrade, taking his usual seat on our sofa and placing his hat in his lap. "It's this Caspar affair. The Commissioner himself put me on the case. I don't mind telling you, Mr Holmes, it's been an embarrassment to the Force, and, if I may make so bold, to the Government."

"Miss Caspar is bringing a private prosecution against Endaby," I said. "How are the police involved?"

"The Law Officers have offered to take over the case, or to direct it. It'll be official whatever way."

"I see," said Holmes. "I should inform you, Lestrade, that we have been visited by Endaby and by Caspar. Each party has requested that we act in the matter. We have not yet concluded an agreement, but I feel bound to respect the private nature of any information imparted to us today."

"Quite so, Mr Holmes," said Lestrade tapping the side of his nose. "One cannot be too fastidious in these cases. I could tell you tales that would curl your toes, gentlemen. The Press is in a state of high excitement. Have you seen the afternoon editions?"

"We have been much taken up with business," said Holmes. "To the point of missing luncheon: missing luncheon entirely,

Inspector. I would be grateful if you could let me know how I may be of assistance to Scotland Yard."

"Well, sir," said Lestrade. "When I heard that you might have an interest in the case — news travels fast, sir, especially when the gutter newspapers are on the track — I thought that I might pop around to have a quiet word. You've been a good friend to the Force, Mr Holmes, and I would not like you to think that we are ungrateful."

He bent towards Holmes and lowered his voice.

"A particular person, sir, a luminary of the Metropolitan Police, suggested that I should acquaint you with certain facts that we have unearthed. We thought to let you have this information before you take a position as to the innocence or otherwise of the lady."

"You have something on Miss Caspar," said Holmes in a cold tone.

Lestrade nodded. He looked left and right as if searching for eavesdroppers.

"In Stockton, Mr Holmes, oh —" Lestrade glanced across at Churchill and back to Holmes. He raised his eyebrows.

The boy sighed, got up and slouched out of the room. He closed the door with a quiet click.

"The poor fellow is starving," said Holmes, shaking his head. "He has lost his vim. What of Stockton?"

"We are about to acquire evidence, sir, that Miss Caspar had a reputation for drink and disorderly conduct. We understand that the police there cautioned her for soliciting. I have sent a pair of my best officers to Stockton to gather data."

He sat back.

"There, sir," said Lestrade with a sniff. "I have been as open with you as I can be."

Holmes was lost in thought for a while.

"Your luminary at the Yard, Lestrade. He would be content if the case against Endaby were dropped. He would not pursue Miss Caspar, or let out the Stockton allegations."

"He would not. The affair would be forgotten in a fortnight."

Lestrade stood and put on his bowler.

"There is a particular reason for urgency, Mr Holmes. That news reporter, Mr Stead of the *Pall Mall Gazette*, is doing a piece on what he calls 'Police assaults on Women'. He says that we allow foreign women and their bullies to infest the West End, while innocent and respectable English girls are pounced upon. Stead is a convicted felon, as you may know, sir."

"Thank you for your warning, Inspector."

"Time?" asked Holmes as we settled into a cab.

"Five past five," said Churchill. He perched on my knees.

"Excellent. To the Criterion Grill, then. We can visit the crime scenes after our roast. Their apple pie and custard is the best north of the River."

He tapped the cab roof with his cane.

"Drive on!"

"Holmes," I said.

"What?" he snapped.

We drove in silence until we crossed Mortimer Street into Regent Street.

"Cabby!" Holmes tapped again on the cab roof. "Go to nineteen, Southampton Row."

Churchill gave me a puzzled look.

I winked.

Holmes came out of the house at a run. He clapped his top hat on his head and vaulted into the cab.

"The Criterion, Cabby. Two bob tip if you get us there before we die of hunger!"

We took off at the trot.

"Are we still on the case, Holmes?"

"We are not. Miss Caspar all but threw me out. She would hear nothing of Stockton. She vows her innocence and that the prosecution will proceed. She says that the Law Lords will direct the case, and that the *Pall Mall Gazette* has offered to defray costs. She is a determined woman, Watson."

"I thought that," I said with a smile.

"And a poor liar."

"Eh?"

"Oh, yes, she lied about Stockton. This is a dark business; darker than we thought in every particular."

He smiled.

"I must confess that at first I thought it dull fare, but Stockton has added a relish."

"What happened in Stockton?" asked Churchill.

"How did you know, young Spencer-Churchill, that Lestrade is a detective?" asked Holmes in the pause that followed. "You said that there was a detective at the door."

"Well," said Churchill. "He has that furtive hole-in-the-corner manner that sneaks have at school. And his carriage had a dingy government-issue look."

"And?"

"His picture was in the newspapers last month: the vitriol throwing in the Mall. Inspector Lestrade is his name. He looks older than in the newspaper drawings."

"Fling the boy from the cab, Watson. We'll have to pay sixpence extra for him otherwise, and it is your turn to pay."

"Perhaps the driver would accept him as extra baggage for tuppence," I suggested.

Churchill gave me a grin and a sharp dig in the ribs.

4. Arresting Points

Infamous Conduct

Holmes pushed through the heavy swing doors of the Criterion Grill and led us back out into Piccadilly.

"Gentlemen, you will agree with me that there is nothing more satisfying to the inner man than a good English roast. The three emperors were not better served at the Café Anglais in Paris than we three here in the heart of Empire."

He turned to me.

"Shall we take a cab?"

"Not on my account," I answered. "My leg is much improved; a walk will do it good."

I offered Holmes my cigar case. He turned to Churchill as he lit his cigar with a match.

"Do you smoke, Spencer-Churchill?"

Churchill looked up at Holmes and wrinkled his nose. "I do not, sir."

"You might think about taking it up," said Holmes as he led us across the Circus and into Regent Street. "It is a wholesome, gentlemanly practice. A good cigar excites the nervous system and exalts the mind. In conversation, a cigar, or particularly a pipe, affords time for cogitation, for thoughts to be marshalled and ideas organised. Tobacco smoke is, as Watson will agree, a notable invigorator."

"I find cigars rather sick-making," said Churchill.

We strolled along Regent Street at a pace suited to my impairment, through a moderate throng of evening shoppers and theatregoers. Posters for Gilbert and Sullivan's latest piece, *Ruddigore*, were on every wall.

"Did you see *The Mikado* last year, Churchill?" I asked.

"No, Doctor. I missed it due to illness. I was behind in conversation with the other fellows at school until my mother's friend, Prince Kinski, sent me a score and I could learn the songs and patter."

I hummed the first bars of 'A Wand'ring Minstrel, I'. Churchill sang the song in a sweet treble voice. Passers-by smiled indulgently or picked up the tune. Holmes drew ahead of us, hunching his shoulders in irritation.

We reached Oxford Circus after a pleasant walk and darted across the road through a jam of cabs, omnibuses, and heavy carriages.

"Here we are," said Holmes waving his stick at the row of handsome shops between the Circus and Portland Street. "The Crystal Palace Bazaar is before us. There is Peter Robinson's establishment. It is on this stretch of pavement that Miss Caspar insists Officer Endaby apprehended her. Good, let us now —"

"There is a policeman over there," said Churchill. "He is watching Mr Holmes."

I followed his gaze. A policeman in the doorway of the Bazaar peered out. He walked across the pavement to us.

"Is everything all right here, sir?" he asked, addressing me. "This gentleman seems agitated."

"You are PC Dyer," said Holmes.

"If you are newspaper reporters," the policeman said, "I will have you in charge for loitering. Be off with you."

"I am Sherlock Holmes."

"Bless me," said the policeman puffing up. "You used your detective powers to identify me, sir. It is like a magic trick. I shall tell the lads —"

"Dyer, I act in the case of your colleague Endaby and Miss Caspar. Is there anything that you can tell me that might shed light on the affair? You were here on the night in question, I believe."

"Exactly there, sir, where you saw me. I was on fixed-point duty, watching the Circus."

"Did you see the arrest?"

"I saw nothing, sir. There was no arrest here, sir; no *fracas* if I may use the term." He rhymed the word with jackass.

"You did not see PC Endaby or Miss Caspar at all."

"I did not."

"Was it a busy evening, constable?" I asked.

"Very quiet. A warm evening, with folks about on account of the Jubilee decorations, but no incidents. I cautioned a couple of sergeants of dragoons that was in drink, and I put them in a cab to the barracks. I lent omnibus fare home to an old clergyman in reduced circumstances who'd lost his boot heel. He was fuddled by the traffic and the noise."

He shook his head.

"No, no incidents, despite the crowds. It has been that way from the start of the Queen's Jubilee celebrations, sirs. The lads and I put it down to loyal affection for Her Majesty and the wish not to spoil the occasion, like."

"Very well," said Holmes. "Do you know the exact location at which Endaby claims he arrested Miss Caspar?"

"Follow me, sirs, if you will."

PC Dyer led us at a steady constabulary pace back towards Oxford Circus and around the corner into the northern section of Regent Street, a distance of no more than sixty or seventy yards. He pointed across the road.

"See, sirs, they are at their little games."

Two women in bright frocks and bonnets were on the opposite pavement. They smiled coquettishly at passing men, even those with ladies on their arms, and offered tiny bouquets of flowers for sale. Another woman stood under a gas light flapping her gloves in a highly suggestive fashion.

"Infamous," I said, smoothing my moustache.

A policeman came up beside us.

"This is Sherlock Holmes," said Dyer.

"Good evening, Constable Twyman," said Holmes.

Dyer nudged his companion in the ribs. "He's a caution, ain't he? He should be on the boards at the Empire. He asking about 42 Endaby and the pro —"

He looked down at Churchill.

"It's all right, officers," said Holmes. "You may speak freely. He is Spencer, the Ratcliff Highway penny-a-peek midget. He is sixty-eight next Tuesday fortnight."

The policemen examined Churchill with interest. He coloured a bright and pleasant pink in the bright gaslight from a nearby chemist's.

"PC Dyer says that he saw nothing of the arrest in Oxford Street," said Holmes. "So it must have taken place here."

"No, sir, it did not," said PC Twyman firmly. "I was stationed right here, on this very spot. I cautioned half a dozen of the women, sir, mostly regulars, but with one or two new faces. That Caspar woman was not arrested on my beat, Mr Holmes. I've already sworn to that on oath to the Metropolitan Commissioner of the London Constabulary."

"It seems that Miss Caspar and Endaby dreamt up the whole affair," said Holmes as we alighted from our cab in Baker Street.

"Are they in league? Is there a dark undercurrent that has eluded our investigations? Each is adamant that the arrest took place in a separate location patrolled by police constables who flatly deny the fact. Do not haggle over the fare, Watson. A penny a minute is fair to cab and passengers, plus sixpence, no seven pence, for Master Spencer-Churchill. He had three portions of Criterion apple pie, and he must weigh half a stone more than when we left."

Holmes and Churchill went upstairs to our sitting room. I excused myself to check Mrs Hudson. I found my patient sleeping gently under the watchful eye of Nurse Levine. I sent her home with instructions to report in the morning.

Upstairs, Holmes and Churchill were engrossed in a game of chess.

I opened the evening paper. It was full of the Caspar affair. There were drawings of the principals and of the arrest. The tone of the articles was critical of the police conduct of the case and of the police inquiry that had failed to publish its report. The letter columns were active.

"Listen to this, Holmes. A lady styling herself 'Indignation' writes on the 'Police Outrage in Regent Street'. She says that she is respectably married, and that she habitually wears sober blue or black garb. She states that when she frequents the West End shops, she is often accosted, in the middle of the day, by male pests who speak to her or follow her. The police, she says, do nothing when applied to."

"Check," said Holmes.

"A self-confessed male pest replies: 'There are hundreds of girls, who, without being vicious, *will* enter into conversation'. The blackguard continues, 'There is nothing that tens, hundreds or thousands of girls more desire than to be addressed by unknown men in the streets.' Infamous hound; I should take a dog whip to him."

"Checkmate," said Holmes. "I know one invaluable specific that will keep all male pests away from a virtuous woman wherever she may roam."

I flipped down a corner of my paper.

"And what is that, pray tell?"

"She must wear a Salvation Army bonnet. Spencer-Churchill, do not pout; it is a game. You must learn to lose gracefully if you are to thrive at Harrow School. Pass me down the Bradshaw."

"You are going somewhere?" I asked.

"One of us must go North, Watson, and at the moment you are discommoded by your injury. I am convinced that the answer to everything lies in Stockton, County Durham."

"Is that necessary, Holmes?" I asked. "Lestrade was certain that he had proof of Miss Caspar's insalubrious life in her hometown, or that he soon would have. Why not wait to see his proofs?"

Holmes flicked through the pages of the railway guide.

"Because his detectives will ask all the wrong people the right questions, and vice versa. They will be tight as clams by the time I get there, you know Northern folk, but an effort must be made."

He gave us a sly smile.

"Aren't you going to ask me how I knew who the police constables were?"

I returned to my newspaper. "You tell him, Churchill."

"By their collar numbers," said Churchill. "Their names and numbers were in the morning paper a week or more ago."

The door slammed. I closed my newspaper and found Holmes gone and Churchill grinning at me from the dining table.

"Chess, Doctor?"

The Distraught Sweet Lady

I entered the sitting room the next morning and found thc breakfast table laid for one. Bessie entered with a steaming coffee pot and a covered dish on a tray.

"Mr Holmes?"

"Gone, sir. Left in a cab to catch an early train. There's a note for you on the mantel."

"Thank you, Bessie."

She placed the dish on the table and took the cover off.

"Bacon and eggs!"

She poured me a cup of coffee; the aroma was delicious.

"Bessie, my dear girl, you have surpassed yourself. How did you learn the coffee-making art? I hope that Mrs Hudson had no hand in this. She needs her rest."

"No, Doctor. Master Churchill got it out of a book."

Churchill came in smiling shyly.

"Well done, sir," I cried. "But what about your own breakfast?"

He sat.

"I found it a simple plan to eat the first batch while the second fried, sir. It's what we do in our dormitory at my school in Brighton."

"They allow you to cook?"

"No, Doctor. But it is one of those traditional activities to which a blind eye is turned."

"And a blind nose," I said.

"The technique of roasting and grinding the coffee beans is explained in that great thick book in the kitchen. It took two goes to get it pat. It smells right, sir, how is the taste?"

"Superb. What a pity Holmes is not here. Pass me down that note on the mantel."

I skimmed through the note and handed it to Churchill.

"We have some work to do this morning," I said. "That is, if you are available. You might want to spend some time with your family at home. Are you sure that your mother suffered no ill-effects from her exposure to the arsenical curtains?"

Churchill looked up and smiled.

"She is very well, Doctor. My parents are busy preparing for the receptions, dinners and balls to celebrate the Queen's jubilee. And my father is fully occupied denouncing Mr Gladstone and Home Rule for Ireland. I believe that they are satisfied not having me under their feet for a few days."

"Good," I said draining my third cup of excellent coffee. "Get us a cab, my boy. Arrange a hire by the hour: five bob for two hours is the rate in Town. Show the cabman the two addresses in Mr Holmes's note so there is no confusion. I will look in on my patient and join you outside in five minutes."

Our first call was to a small confectionary shop at Margaret Court, not far from Oxford Circus.

The name above the shop was that of our first witness, Madame F Audet.

I led the way inside. I took off my hat, an action that instantly enraged a thickset teenage boy behind the counter. He pulled a heavy leather cosh from under the counter and smacked it into his hand.

"Out! Or you'll feel the weight of this life preserver across your skull."

Churchill slipped past me into the shop.

"A quarter of jelly snakes, please."

The boy stood, blinking at us.

"And," said Churchill, "a penn'orth of sherbet."

The boy replaced the club under the counter.

"Lemon or orange?"

"Lemon, please."

He weighed out the sweets.

"I'm sorry, gents, it's just we've been plagued with newspaper reporters this last week or more on account of Madame being a witness in a public case. She's all over nerves. What with you not being from around here, and the gentleman taking off his hat like he was planning to stay the night, my suspicions was aroused. I'll not let anyone near her, that I won't. I said the same to the two jacks from Scotland Yard yesterday. You'll forgive me, I hope. That'll be tuppence farthing."

I passed him a thruppenny bit and took my change.

"He's not a reporter or a detective," said Churchill nodding to the open door behind the counter. "He's a doctor."

"Oh," said the boy lifting a section of the counter-top. "Go on through. Madame is in the bedroom on the left. She's in a right state."

Churchill gave me a strong push. "I'll wait for you here, Doctor, sir."

I came back into the shop some twenty minutes later. Churchill and the shop boy were in deep conversation at the counter. I gathered that the subject was the Wild West Show at the new Olympia ground.

"Do you have Turkish delight?" I asked the boy.

"We do, Doctor."

"Put me up a pound, no, two separate pounds, would you?"

We stepped back into our cab and set off for South Kensington.

"Jelly snake, Doctor?" Churchill offered.

"Thank you. You know, I could be struck off the medical register for what I just did. I prescribed an opiate. Her regular practitioner will be livid."

"We gave no names, Doctor. They'll think that you were an enterprising gutter newspaperman posing as a doctor. My father says that there are no depths to which the breed will not stoop."

I wondered whether young Churchill was learning fly ways from us, or we from him.

"And I wasted my time. She is a perfectly unreliable witness, sobbing, crying out to the saints and getting names, dates, and streets hopelessly mixed up. She seems to support Constable Endaby's location, but I would hesitate, if I were his barrister, to put her before a jury. A competent prosecutor will goad her into hysterics. I say, this jelly snake is delicious."

The Oriental Major

Our second destination was a small but pleasant Georgian townhouse in the shadow of St. Luke's church, just off the Fulham Road.

I mounted the three whitewashed steps and grasped the brass, dolphin-shaped doorknocker; the door opened silently before I had a chance to knock.

A slim, brown-skinned, black-haired girl dressed in an Oriental robe and flowery headdress held the door open and stood aside to invite us in. I took off my hat (not without some small trepidation) and entered, followed by Churchill. The partitions had been removed and we found ourselves not in a hall, but in a large sitting room that stretched to the back of the house. It was well lit by casement windows at the front and two sets of French windows that gave out on to a garden. A steep curved staircase stood in the far-left corner.

The room was curiously furnished. A red-and-gold Oriental carpet covered the floor, and upon it were thrown, apparently at random, bright-hued rugs and druggets. A noble tiger skin lay before the fireplace.

Plump sofas or backless divans, upholstered in gold silk and covered in cushions, faced each other in two groups, one in front of the fireplace, and the other facing the garden view.

Silver-filigreed oil lamps hung from the ceiling and from wall brackets. The wall on our left was covered with weapons: curved swords and scimitars, jewelled daggers, and long muskets with stocks carved into fantastic shapes.

The only homely, English feature of the room was a large gold-framed painting above the crackling log fire in the fireplace. It showed a group of naked, white-skinned boys bathing from a skiff in what looked to be the estuary of a wide river.

The girl showed us to the divans at the fireplace, and wordlessly indicated that we should sit. Churchill patted some cushions into a pile and squatted on his sofa, quite at ease. I found mine too low for comfort. My leg had started to play up again.

Churchill twisted around at a sound, and I followed his gaze. A short, grey-haired man with a thin moustache descended the staircase. He wore a crimson smoking jacket, baggy yellow pantaloons, a tasselled gold fez, and white silk slippers. He reminded me instantly of the bath attendants at the Turkish hammam in Jermyn Street. I could sense Churchill trying to catch my eye, but I kept my gaze away from him lest I should lose my composure.

The man padded silently to where we sat, and held out his hand. I struggled off my sofa and shook it.

"Major Edgar Massingham. You, I presume, are Mr Sherlock Holmes."

"I do not have that honour, sir. I am Doctor John Watson, and this is Winston Churchill. We are associates of Mr Holmes, and we are here at his bidding."

"I see," said Major Massingham in a disappointed tone. He waved us back to our seats and sat primly on the divan next to Churchill. "When I read in the afternoon edition of the newspaper that Mr Holmes had condescended to act in the Caspar affair, I expected that he would wire or visit. I am, of course, the only disinterested and reliable witness to the arrest."

"You forget Madame Audet," I said. "I have just come from interviewing her."

He laughed an unpleasant, high-pitched laugh.

"Then you will know that she is a foreigner and devoid of even the tiny amount of common sense one would expect from a female of her type. Ah, tea."

The girl appeared again with a large tray on legs. She stood it on the tiger skin rug before Major Massingham.

"There is Darjeeling," he said. "But perhaps you would like to try a blend made up for me by a plantation at Kandy, in Ceylon. It goes well with these little rice-cakes that Ahmad makes."

The girl passed me a china cup of dark, aromatic tea. She was a beauty, I thought, although very young; she was not yet out of her teens. Her eyes were wide, almond shaped, and outlined in kohl, like the ladies I had glimpsed in Afghanistan during my war service there.

The girl smiled — her face lit up — and winked.

"Do you care for sugar, Doctor?" the Major asked. "I have the new lump sugar. It is so convenient."

I dropped a tiny lump of sugar into my tea and stirred it furiously. Had the girl winked at me in that astonishingly lewd fashion, or had I imagined it? The room felt warm, and I ran a finger inside my shirt collar.

"That is a fine painting," I said looking for a neutral topic. I indicated the large canvas of boys bathing.

"Yes," said the Major. "I picked it up in Cornwall in the spring. The artist is a gentleman who specialises in maritime and Uranian themes."

I stood, partly from the necessity of stretching my legs, and examined the painting more closely.

"He has caught the wind on the water. And the light on the boys' skin."

Churchill coughed and gave me a look that brought me back to the subject at hand.

"Major," I said, sitting down. "I am here at the request of Mr Holmes to ask you to describe what happened on the evening of Miss Caspar's apprehension. We understand that you witnessed the arrest and that you accompanied Constable Endaby and Miss Caspar back to the police station. On arrival there you made a statement."

"That is correct." Major Massingham astonished me by slipping off his silk shoes and tucking his stockinged feet under him like an Indian fakir. I again avoided Churchill's eyes or we would have broken into peals of unforgivably impolite mirth.

"You should know that I was for many, many years in the Indian Service. My billet was in Colombo in Ceylon. As you see, I developed a taste for the Oriental, and I live, as far as one can in this frigid and foggy city, in that style. On the evening in question, I visited Messrs Fortnum and Mason in Piccadilly to restock my supply of various small items. I then made my way in a cab to the Crystal Bazaar, where I recently saw some fine peacock feathers that I knew would do well in that Chinese vase in the corner."

He pointed to the only corner of the room that was not weighted with Oriental bric-a-brac.

"It was a short journey, but I do not choose to walk unless I am obliged to; I detest crowds. I alighted farther along than I had intended owing to a distracted and possibly deaf cabman with a wilful horse, and so I was obliged to make my way back along Oxford Street through a mob of pedestrians. I noticed a young lady ahead of me walking at about my pace, slowly and steadily. I noticed her in particular because she wore a straw hat with a silken band of precisely the shade of pale lavender that I am contemplating for the curtains in my study upstairs."

"Was the lady not tripping along, twirling her parasol?" Churchill asked.

"Quite the contrary, young man. As I have described, she was moving in a sober fashion at my pace. I saw no parasol. I followed her — I mean that without any connotation of a connection between us, we merely followed a similar path — for at least thirty yards until we both veered towards the brightly lit windows of the Crystal Bazaar. It was coming on for dusk. In the shadow of the tall buildings that line Oxford Street and outside the pools of light from the streetlamps and the light spilling from the shop windows, it was dark already."

"Did the lady talk with anyone — any man — while she was in your view?" I asked. "Did any gentleman accost her?"

"No, not one," said Major Massingham.

"And you saw the arrest?"

"A burly police constable pushed past me in an intemperate fashion and came up behind the lady, Miss Caspar as I now know. He took her arm most violently. Shc attempted to defend herself. She then saw that her assailant was a police constable, and she remonstrated with him."

"Did you hear what they said?"

"He said something like, 'Got you, My Lovely'. She protested and demanded to know what offence she had committed. On hearing that the policeman alleged, ah, that infamous charge, she fainted; I, and the Audet person, assisted her. I offered the strongest representations to the officer that the lady had behaved in a respectable manner while she was under my observation. He replied that 'I did not know the half of it', so I took his number and followed them to the police station."

"And you are sure, Major, that the arrest took place in Oxford Street outside the Bazaar?"

"Yes, on the pavement near Peter Robinson's."

I caught a puzzled look from Churchill.

"Well," I said, struggling from the divan. "We will take up no more of your time, Major. You have been of inestimable help."

"Oh, are you going?" he said. "As you admired the painting, I had thought to show you and your young companion some of the artist's photographs. Mr Tuke was kind enough to lend me several of his albums."

Churchill instantly doubled over in a coughing fit that was relieved by a half-cup of tepid tea. I made our excuses and we left. The pretty, brown-complexioned girl showed us to the door and, as she returned my hat and cane, I received a look that I can only describe as arch. I smiled a thank-you. I saw that Churchill noticed the exchange.

I ignored his indecorous smirk as I tripped down the steps, adjusted my tiepin and set my bowler to a jaunty angle. It does a gentleman, especially one just out of the first bloom of youth, no harm to see that he can still strike a pretty girl's fancy; even if, as in this case, she was a mere child.

I looked at my watch as we climbed back into the hansom.

"I say, driver," I called. "We are almost at our time, and I know the traffic is building up, but I should like to drive back to Baker Street via Peter Robinson's in the West End."

"The one in Oxford Street, sir, or the one in Regent Street?"

"Ha!" I said. "You have saved us the journey and earned yourself a half-crown."

We returned directly to Baker Street where I quizzed the cabby on the exact location of the two shops in question. He pointed them out in a large-scale map of London in our sitting room and thumped downstairs whistling and jingling his tip.

With Churchill's help, Mrs Beeton's guidance, and using groceries obtained by Bessie during the morning, I was able to provide the household with a luncheon of curried beef and rice followed by stewed apples and a thick custard.

After lunch, I took out the map of London again and puzzled over the discrepancies in the testimony of the two policemen and the two witnesses. I found it hard to concentrate, as my thoughts were still with poor Miss Caspar. I could see no good coming from her libel case against PC Endaby. It would be widely reported in the penny newspapers; her servants and neighbours would read the details. Even if she won the case, her reputation would be smudged, if not irretrievably tarnished.

I determined to visit Miss Caspar to suggest that she drop the case, and perhaps return to the bosom of her family in Stockton until the fuss died down.

A telegram from Holmes arrived. He said that he would be home before lunch on the following day. I instructed Billy to ask the telegraph boy to wait while I wrote a short telegram to Miss Caspar asking whether I might visit in the early evening. I looked forward to a pleasant afternoon preparing my notes on the arsenical curtains for publication, and then a drive across Town to Mrs Barker's residence in Southampton Row for tea with Miss Caspar. I had saved one packet of Turkish delight as an offering.

I heard a rumble of footsteps outside. The door was flung open and Wiggins, the leader of the Irregulars appeared. Churchill was behind him looking grave.

"Go away, Wiggins," I said. "I am busy. Churchill, give this to the telegraph boy."

"It's Aaron," said Churchill. "Bobby's Negro friend."

"What of him?" I asked.

"His head is cracked in," said Wiggins. "He's dead as mutton."

5. The Corpse in the River

The Dipper's Narrative

"Sit, Wiggins, and give us the circumstances of the boy's death," I said.

"Be as precise as possible, Harry," said Churchill opening a notebook. "You know our methods."

Wiggins took a seat at the table. Luncheon had not yet been cleared, and he devoured two bread rolls before he began his tale.

"It's like this. We was doing the Faint outside Charing Cross station. I'm on the ground, see, spitting and foaming, and the boys are working the crowd."

He shrugged.

"A railway copper on the top of a bus spots the lay, and grabs Monty for dipping a wipe —"

"Stealing a pocket handkerchief," Churchill explained.

"The copper takes him to the police station and sits him on a bench with the derbies on, I mean handcuffs, Doctor. While he's sat there, he hears the desk coppers talking about a Negro lad they'd fished from the River the night before. His head was proper bashed in, they say; it is awful to behold. They say they found nothing in his pockets save for a small photograph of a white boy in a Yankee hat. There's nothing else to show who this body is, despite he'd not been in the water more than a minute or two judging by the evidence."

"What evidence?" I asked.

"Don't know, Doctor. The coppers played a close hand on that. Anyway, Monty tells them that he might claim an acquaintance with this black fellah. They bring him down to the ice store at the coroner's and show him the body. Monty says he did the Dead Faint for real when he saw Aaron's brains all over the shop. He knew Bobby too, when they showed him the photograph. No doubt at all, sir."

I turned the matter over in my mind. Bobby and his friend Aaron had left Wiggins's gang without a word and decamped to an unknown destination. A man in mutton-chop whiskers subsequently haunted the Waterloo Road offering a substantial reward for news of the two boys. A week or more later, Aaron was dead: foully murdered. Bobby was either dead too, or in grave danger.

"We must find Bobby," I concluded.

I saw Churchill and Wiggins exchange satisfied looks.

"How, Doctor?" asked Churchill.

I grabbed a sheaf of telegram forms. I wrote out the two messages, willing myself to write slowly and clearly. I passed the forms and a half-sovereign to Wiggins.

"Pop down and give these to the telegraph boy. Ask him to have them sent, and pay for answers."

Wiggins tried to read the addresses, slowly sounding out the letters one by one. Churchill read them over his shoulder.

"Scotland Yard," said Churchill. "And the coroner."

I nodded. "The telegraph clerk will have to look up the address of the coroner's office. Hurry, now."

Wiggins ran out.

"Let me look again at that likeness of the missing boy."

Churchill slipped the picture from his notebook and unfolded it.

"It is very fine. You say that the artist is a forger of banknotes. I thought to commission a portrait of Holmes for his Christmas present, but I suppose it would not do to employ a felon."

I handed him back the picture. "Tell to me more about your excursion to Lambeth."

Churchill described his evening's entertainment with some humour. He and Billy first visited the Royal Victoria Hall, popularly known as the Old Vic', a music hall, theatre, and coffee public house run by its lady owner on strict temperance lines. They then met Wiggins and his crew at the back of the Horse and Groom pub, run by its proprietor on strictly alcoholic lines, and ate a supper of boiled beef, potatoes, and carrots alfresco in the yard. Churchill took the testimony of four boys from various localities in the district that Mr Mutton-chop Whiskers had accosted. The man had offered a reward of ten pounds for information on a young American boy and a thieving footman. The missing boy was Robert W Taylor, and the servant Aaron Long. He had shown around a photograph of Bobby looking a year or so younger than he was when he met Wiggins and his crew. There was no doubt that the boy was Bobby, and the thief was his companion, Aaron.

"How were the informers to receive the reward?" I asked.

"They would take Mutton-chops to Bobby's lodgings and get a tenner then and there," said Churchill. He said that Wiggins was of the opinion that Mutton-chops couldn't be very fly if he advertised that he carried ten pounds in his pocketbook.

"Perhaps he was knocked on the head and robbed," I suggested.

"Wiggins says that he would have heard of it. He thinks that the cove gave up and tried elsewhere."

Churchill's account impressed me. He acquitted himself well in circumstances well out of his normal way of life. He conversed easily and unpretentiously with boys far below his caste. I could find no reason for his father's apprehensions concerning the boy's intellectual capacity. I resolved to acquaint his mother with my conclusions and return him to his family. I realised, as I watched him draw a sketch of the Horse and Groom pub in his notebook, the tip of his tongue peeping out of his mouth as he drew, that I would miss him.

Wiggins returned with the telegram receipts and change.

"Now, gentlemen," I said. "Let us examine the evidence. Mutton-chops is searching for a boy by name and description. He has a photograph of Bobby that shows him to be younger than he is now. That surely argues for some long acquaintance. Bobby wore respectable clothes that fitted well, and he spoke with an American accent. Mr Mutton-chops had a different accent."

"Like the pot man at the Horse and Groom," said Churchill. "He's from the Cape Colony in Southern Africa."

"He and Aaron," I continued, "had a considerable amount of money and loot on them, probably stolen from the house of Mr Mutton-chops. Agreed?"

The boys nodded their heads.

"This again argues for a strong relationship between Mutton-chops and Bobby. Even though he has suffered a serious loss, it does not seem that the man went to the police, or they would have soon picked the boys up. What?"

Wiggins was quietly chuckling.

"I would say that Harry does not share your belief in the efficiency of the police, Doctor," Churchill said with a smile. He turned to Wiggins. "Did they lock Monty for the dip?"

"Gawd bless you, no. He slipped the derbies like a good 'un. He hopped it as they opened the door of the police van back at the station."

Churchill turned to me and shrugged.

"Well, there is no evidence that Mutton-chops went to the police," I said. "Or that he advertised in the papers. I saw nothing. He made his own enquiries; not very effectively. He was something of a flat, was he not?"

Wiggins looked at me with astonishment.

"I read the *Police Gazette*," I said not without some inner triumph. "I am not unconversant with the jargon of the criminal classes. Mutton-chops was unfamiliar with the street, easily gammoned or fooled, a flat fellow, not fly in his ways."

Wiggins nodded. "I will tell you, Doctor, that we did him for a fiver by describing Bobby exact and saying he was in a dead lurk."

He gave me an expectant look.

"Empty building," said Churchill after a long pause.

"I see. You stung Mutton-chops for five pounds pretending that you knew Bobby's whereabouts. That's good. It supports my theory that he is not of the criminal fraternity. Yes, so now we have a chance."

I took a page of letter paper from the drawer of Holmes's desk and wrote a paragraph.

"I want this in the agony columns of the evening newspapers."

"Which ones, Doctor?" asked Churchill.

"All of them."

Billy came in with a telegram on a tray. It was the answer to my previous enquiry.

"Ha," I said as I read the telegram. "The Middlesex Coroner has a sense of humour. I wired for directions to the Coroner's Court and he writes, 'Quickest way is to step in front of racing omnibus. Otherwise take cab to 9, St Laurence, Pountney Hill, EC'."

"Billy, get us a four-wheeler. Come, we will to the City. The game's afoot!"

"May I come, sir?" asked Billy.

"No."

"Oh, go on, Doctor," said Churchill. "He'll be jolly useful, I bet."

"Oh, very well. If Mrs Hudson agrees."

The boys thundered down the stairs.

The Phrenological Coroner

We spilled from the cab at the Middlesex Coroner's office.

Inspector Lestrade waited at the kerb, furiously blowing his nose. He stuffed his handkerchief back into his pocket and offered me his hand. I shook it reluctantly.

"Fine day, Doctor. Where is Mr Holmes?"

"He was called away on an urgent matter."

"I see." He waved a telegram in my face. "This telegram asked me to meet him here."

"The telegram was from me, Inspector."

Lestrade sniffed. "Signed by you; yes, that is technically correct."

He turned to Billy and gave him a long, suspicious look.

"I know you."

"Pageboy to Mr Holmes and the Doctor, sir."

Lestrade peered at Churchill.

"I am Winston Churchill." He held out his hand. "We met at Doctor Watson's digs."

Lestrade ignored him and focused his narrow gaze on Wiggins.

"I know you too."

"I'm his brother, Inspector." Wiggins gestured vaguely at Churchill and Billy.

"Shall we go in?" I said. "We may be able to shed some light on a ghastly murder that took place last night."

Lestrade nodded curtly and led the way up a short flight of stairs and into the coroner's offices. A clerk guided us to the back of the building and into a large room lined with bookshelves. A black, solid-looking desk stood between two sets of windows with a swivel chair behind it. On the desk were a carved mahogany penholder and a large, shiny ivory-coloured human head marked with coloured lines and strange symbols. The boys were examining this with interest when a short, bald man in a dark suit bustled in from behind us.

"Welcome," he said in a faint Welsh accent. "Deputy-Coroner Ivor Purchase at your service." He shook hands with me, with Lestrade and with each of the boys, chuckling to himself and bidding us to make ourselves comfortable. He dropped into his seat behind the desk, put on a pair of gold-rimmed spectacles, and regarded us benignly.

"You must be Doctor Watson."

I bowed.

"I can always tell a fellow practitioner, my dear Doctor, even when they arrive feet first."

He turned to Lestrade.

"And you are Inspector Lestrade of Scotland Yard, the scourge of the criminal classes."

The inspector beamed.

"And the boys are, the boys."

He turned back to me with a bright smile.

"The young gentlemen were looking at the head on my desk, Doctor. I wonder what they make of it."

"Is it to do with phrenology, sir?" asked Churchill.

"Well done, young man, very well done. It is indeed. These marks and squiggles show the various sections of the brain and their special functions. Protuberances of the skull — lumps if you like — indicate features of the brain beneath, and therefore certain character traits. The region just above the eye is associated with concentration and introspection. You can see that this area is prominent on the inspector's head."

We all turned to stare at Lestrade. He blinked back at us in astonishment.

"And in my own case, these two areas are visible."

He pointed to the top of his own skull.

"Self-esteem and love of approbation, ha-ha! All nonsense, of course."

He bent forward and peered at us over his steepled hands. "You came to see me about the young Negro man washed up at Limehouse. Is that correct?"

"It is, Doctor," I said. "We believe that we can confirm his identity and furnish some clues to his likely murderer."

"Murder, Doctor Watson," said Lestrade in his irritating nasal bray. "Aren't we getting a little ahead of ourselves?"

The coroner opened a drawer in his desk and took out a slim folder. He slid it across to me with a smile. I opened it and found a two-page document. I read the heading on the first page and the summary on the last.

"It is your report, Mr Purchase," I said. "It details the autopsy and your findings. You have ruled that the boy was killed by a series of savage blows to the head with a blunt instrument, by a person or persons unknown."

Lestrade pursed his lips, pulled out his handkerchief and blew his nose loudly.

Doctor Purchase bounded out from behind his desk.

"Come, then, sirs, and you may view the remains. We can then speak of my conclusions."

"The boys may stay here," I said.

"But, Doctor," said Wiggins. "I'm the one what knows Aaron!"

"Do you then?" Lestrade gave him a narrow-eyed look. "Come along the lot of you. I don't want you out of my sight."

We followed the coroner along several corridors, down a flight of steps and through a pair of double doors marked 'Mortuary' in green letters. The temperature dropped as we entered a large white-tiled room. Wall-mounted and hanging gas jets lit the room as brightly as a butcher's shop. Along one wall was a framework of polished wood in which rows of metal doors were set. A handwritten notice hung on one: 'Bodies Feet First If You Please'.

A row of five dissecting tables occupied the centre of the room, each with a nude body laid out on it. At the farthest bench, two young men in white coats were at work on the corpse of an old man. Aaron's body was on the first bench, the only Negro. He lay face down; even from a distance, I could see that the back of his head had been laid open by what must have been a tremendous blow or blows. I took out my handkerchief and held it over my nose in a vain effort to mask the penetrating odour of decay.

"It is quite five or six degrees cooler in here than outside," I said.

"Yes," said the coroner. "We have a patent system of steam-driven fans that blow air over blocks of American ice. The Indian railways used the system first, without the fans. They stored the ice in louvred boxes and air passed over it with the motion of the train. I am afraid that the record temperatures these last few days have overwhelmed us, and we are not coping as well as we might. Help me turn him over. Just hold his head."

I rolled up my sleeves and held the young man's head as Doctor Purchase turned the body onto its back with practised ease.

He beckoned the boys forward.

"Which of you can confirm this young man's identity?"

Wiggins stepped forward reluctantly and stared down at the face for a long minute.

"Can I see his hands, sir? Just the left one."

The coroner held up the left arm and Wiggins peered closely at it.

"Well, boy?" said Lestrade.

Wiggins shook his head. "That's not Aaron, Doctor Watson," he said. "I'd stake my life on it."

Impulsive and Violent Behaviour

We assembled back in the coroner's office.

Lestrade poked a bony finger at Wiggins. "Another boy, a pickpocketing young rascal, identified the body as Aaron no-middle-or-family-name, last seen in Lambeth. Now you say nay. What's your game, then, eh?"

Wiggins turned to me.

"He's like him, Doctor, but that's not him. Aaron had a cut across his left hand. A long scar from when he played with a knife and got cut, accidental, like."

Lestrade snorted. "What about this, eh?"

He waved a crumpled photograph about the size of a playing card in front of Wiggins face.

"This was in the victim's pocket. Again, a positive identification from the dipper for an American boy named Bobby no-family-name, last seen in Lambeth in the company of the Negro Aaron. What have you got to say to that?"

"Never saw him before in my life, Inspector," Wiggins said.

"Well, Doctor," said Lestrade, turning his sharp nose to me. "You've got me out here on a wild-goose chase and wasted this gentleman's valuable time. I shall bid you good day."

He jammed the photograph back into his pocket and made for the door. He stopped and pointed at the three boys deliberately one-by-one.

"I've got my eye on you lot," he growled. "So you just watch it."

He tipped his hat to the coroner and left.

"I am very much persuaded," said Doctor Purchase as the inspector's footsteps echoed down the corridor. "I am almost certain that this area of the brain is the organ for impulsive and violent behaviour."

He tapped a blank area on the forehead of the head on his desk.

"It was prominent on the inspector's skull, as you will have instantly noticed."

He laughed. It was a most infectious laugh, and I, and the boys, chuckled with him.

He gave the head an affectionate pat. "All nonsense, of course. Now, what's all this about?"

Wiggins looked down at his toes.

"*Quid pro quo*, young man," said Doctor Purchase. "I will tell you what I know, and you may tell me your thoughts, or not, as you please."

Wiggins nodded agreement.

"According to witness statements that I have obtained from the files of the local police," Doctor Purchase continued, "the young man was killed last night at about a quarter past midnight. Four dock labourers, just off their shift, had each picked up a pint of ale at the bar of the Grapes public house, on the River in Narrow Street, Limehouse. They decided to sup their beer on the terrace overlooking the tideway. They had hardly taken their first gulp when they heard a cry and a splash from a short way upstream. Looking down, they saw a man in the water at the edge by the steps. Thinking he had fallen in drunk, they had a laugh at his expense, took another sup, then they ran down and hauled him out. He was wet, but not thoroughly soaked, so he had been in the water just a few moments. That accords with the cry and the splash. When they saw his terrible wound on his head they knew that they had a corpse on their hands. They called the potboy, who called the landlord, who sprang his police rattle and summoned a constable. Tea?"

Doctor Purchase opened the door of his office a crack and called out for tea. An answering cry came from within the building.

"Now," he said. "You, young man, Wiggins, is it? Would you stand here in the centre of the room? You are about five-one or two, I would guess."

Wiggins shrugged.

"You'll do for the dead man. And you, Doctor, stand a pace behind, thank you. Swing your stick, Doctor, against the boy's head so that the blow lies from above and behind the right ear down to just below the left ear. No? It is awkward, is it not? Try your left hand. You see? Thank you both. Here is tea already; it must have been brewing."

A young clerk brought in a tray of tea and biscuits. Doctor Purchase teased him about his fancy tiepin, and the man replied in kind. That was not the atmosphere I had expected in a mortuary.

"The police searched the houses on the riverbank adjacent to the Grapes and found nothing," said Doctor Purchase reading from his notes. "The house next door was empty; the tenant moved out a week earlier. Next along was a failed hurdy-gurdy manufactory, and then a sisal warehouse; all three premises were securely locked, and showed no sign of forced entry."

He opened a cupboard and brought out a whisky bottle.

"Would anyone care for a little fortification?"

Wiggins offered his cup; I stared Churchill and Billy into submission.

"The attacker was left-handed," I said. "And my height or so."

"Mutton-chops was left-handed," said Wiggins. "He gave me the fiver in his left hand."

Doctor Purchase looked up at me and smiled.

I described the facts of the case, the nature of the involvement of Holmes and myself as private investigators, and our suspicions.

Doctor Purchase mulled this over while we drank our tea.

"And our man is not your Aaron," he said. "You are certain, Master Wiggins?"

"Certain sure, sir. I knew when I set eyes on him. He is like Aaron though, very like; maybe a relation. It is not him, the dead man's an older-looking lad. The boy in the photograph was Bobby; I didn't want the inspector to tag me in the case, so I lied."

He lowered in head in patently false contrition.

"I see," said Doctor Purchase. "Why did you also lie about the knife scar?"

Wiggins jumped up. "I never."

Doctor Purchase chuckled. "You saw immediately that the body was not your friend, yet you asked to look at the left hand. You stared not at the palm, where you claim there is a scar, but at the finger ends, at the nails. You noticed a yellow discoloration there, under the nails. It was much more pronounced before we washed the body. We found yellow marks on his arms, and spots in his hair too. I have not yet analysed the substance, but I am sure it is water-based paint. Was he a painter?"

Wiggins looked across at Billy.

"He was a canary painter," said Billy.

Doctor Purchase beamed at me.

"You must find this detective business enthralling, Doctor," he said with a chuckle. "I guessed that he might be a house painter, although the yellow is a startling one and I could not imagine it on my walls. The true answer is much more exotic."

"I do not understand," I admitted. "Do you, Churchill?"

Churchill shook his head.

"When you buy a canary," said Billy, "you look for two things: colour and chirpy singing. Some folks like red birds, but yellow is the fashion now; bright yellow is all people want. The yellow birds are hard to get wholesale, and expensive, so the trade makes them up."

"The canaries are painted!" I said in astonishment.

"The factory is down my way in Whitechapel," said Billy. "That's where that bloke worked, I bet."

I looked at my watch.

"Coroner," I said. "We must leave you. We have another appointment. I cannot thank you enough for your help. That is not our friend on your slab, but I have not the slightest doubt that his death is related to the case. The photograph of the young American boy found in his pocket is conclusive."

Doctor Purchase stood and shook our hands. He tapped the folder on his desk.

"I will make a note of what we have discussed today. If you have any information as to the identity of the young man, I would be grateful if you could communicate it to me. As coroner, I am legally obliged to pass on anything I learn to the police. Inspector Lestrade seems reluctant to proceed in the case, so I will continue to work with my local people; they are very manageable."

"Thank you, Doctor."

We took our leave and the coroner was kind enough to show us to the front door.

"*À bientôt!*" called Doctor Purchase as we tumbled into a cab.

Wiggins gave me a puzzled look.

"It means 'See you soon', in French," Churchill explained with a chuckle.

"Gawd," said Wiggins looking back. "I bleeding hope not."

I smiled at him. "I have a job for you."

6. The Cape Colonial Visitor

A Mexican Standoff

We dropped Wiggins off at a ferry pier on the River and made our way back to Baker Street.

I sent Billy to the back kitchen to help with chicken plucking, potato peeling, and vegetable scraping. I intended to cook a pair of roast chickens with all the trimmings for our dinner, followed by bergamot pears and hothouse apricots in red wine. I knocked on the door of Mrs Hudson's sitting room. Churchill followed me in.

I found her sitting on her sofa, pale, but bright-eyed, reading *Tit-Bits* and eating Turkish delight. Bessie poured tea. I was glad to find that my patient continued to make an excellent recovery from the poison that almost killed her.

"Oh, sir," said Bessie. "You must speak to Mrs Hudson. She insists on getting up to make the supper."

"I am perfectly fine," said Mrs Hudson firmly. "Oh dear, young sir," she said catching sight of Churchill. "I do hope that your lady mother wasn't troubled by those old green curtains. I'm sure I didn't mean any harm."

She dabbed at her eyes with a handkerchief.

"No, Mrs Hudson," said Churchill with a smile. "Mama is very well."

Mrs Hudson looked up at me over her handkerchief and narrowed her eyes.

"I don't know, then, Doctor," she said. "Maybe Mr Philpot wasn't so wrong. Maybe I was the victim of a miasma, and a good pair of flock curtains bought by my mother at a respectable establishment in the London Road for eight pence farthing a yard was sacrificed in error. Yes, in error, Doctor, and at a cost of a pound or more, not counting nearly two pounds in expenses to the police and the street riffraff. What do you say to that, sir?"

"I'll leave you to rest, Mrs Hudson. Drink your beef tea and your barley water."

I nodded to Churchill. "Come, let us go upstairs. We have some preparations to make for our visitor."

The clock in our sitting room struck seven as we finished our dinner. Bessie brought coffee and cleared the table.

"How was dinner, Bessie?" I asked as I lit a cigar. "I hope that Mrs Hudson, you and Billy enjoyed the roast chicken as much as Churchill and I did."

"It was nice, sir, very tasty."

"And what had Mrs Hudson to say?"

"She said that you forgot to butter the carrots, Doctor."

Churchill chuckled, which set Bessie off giggling. I strode to the window and looked down on the grey street below and across to the grey houses opposite. I could not readily share their simple mirth. I wondered what chance we had of finding Bobby and his friend in a city teeming with four million or more people, each intent on his or her own occasions and without thought for their neighbours.

I had taken the Metropolitan Line underground railway from Baker Street a few weeks earlier, and I was surprised at the way Londoners had adapted to the dreadful conditions of heat and smoke that prevailed in its tunnels. We endured and ignored each other. On an omnibus, one nodded to one's neighbour. On the Metropolitan Line one tried to read one's paper in the flickering lamplight, gasped for breath in the fug of engine and cigar smoke, and emerged into the light covered in sooty smuts.

"I wonder how Holmes is getting on with his case," I said softly. "He missed dinner."

"And how Wiggins is getting on in Limehouse," said Churchill.

I nodded. "We will soon know. Bezique, Churchill? We have an hour, if the Fates allow, before our appointment."

At a quarter to the hour of eight, I made my final preparations.

I wondered again whether I should have wired to fetch Inspector Lestrade to Baker Street. I reminded myself that he had complained when I brought him to the coroner's office on what he called a wild-goose chase. I did not feel justified in calling him out again when I was not certain that my plan would succeed in beating our bird from cover.

"If I had a guinea, Doctor," said Churchill in an imitation of Holmes's parlour trick. "I'd bet that he would come."

"If so," I said severely, "you will immediately hide yourself in Holmes's bedroom and make not a squeak of noise. Is that understood, young man? Or I shall pack you off back to your parents in Connaught Place this instant."

Churchill nodded reluctantly.

"But I may come out when he is in the derbies, mayn't, I?"

I heard a squeal of carriage wheels against the kerb outside. I flicked aside the curtains and looked down. A heavyset man in a sandy-coloured coat and flaming red mutton-chop whiskers alighted from a cab. The doorbell rang.

I was pleased to see that Churchill had retreated to his hiding place. I checked the action of my service revolver and slipped it back into my waistband. I drew the lapels of my frock coat together to hide it.

Billy showed in my visitor. The man surveyed the room calmly as he gave his bowler, heavy stick and gloves to the boy with his left hand. He was taller than I, well over six feet, and powerfully built. He was perhaps in his late fifties. His red mutton-chop whiskers framed a square head and a much-seamed and wrinkled face with a ruddy, brown complexion.

He crossed the room and held out his hand.

"Maxwell P Taylor, at your service, sir," he said in a strong Cape Colony accent.

"Doctor John Watson. Please take a seat."

I indicated our sofa, but he sat instead in Holmes's usual armchair. I sat opposite him, and as I did, my coat fell open.

"That's a piece of artillery you have there, Doctor. It outranks mine by a wide margin." He pulled open the right lapel of his coat to reveal a small shoulder holster. He took out a two-barrel palm pistol and laid it on the table. "That's what we in the United States call a 'Derringer' after the inventor."

"You are from the United States, Mr Taylor?" I asked.

"No, I am English, by birth if not inclination. I was born in London. As you can likely hear from my accent, I grew up among the Boers in Natal. I have lived the last several years in America, in business, and I came back to the old country some months ago to put my son to school and to spend my declining years in comfort at my place of birth. I am not a Boer, you understand, but I have little experience in the ways of Englishmen."

He sat back.

"And you, Doctor, placed an advertisement in the evening papers concerning the whereabouts of Robert W Taylor and the servant, Aaron Long. Anyone who wanted news of them was to come here at eight. I see that I am your only customer, sir. Unless another party has been in touch with you."

He leant forward in his seat.

"Has anyone else contacted you?"

"No."

"I see. Then, may I ask what information you have? You should know that I am willing to pay handsomely for any information that helps me find the boy. May I?"

He drew out a cigar case and indicated a large cigar. He lit it with a match.

"Before we go on," I said. "I must ask you what your relationship is with Robert W Taylor and with Long."

"I am Maxwell Taylor, and Robert is my son," he said matter-of-factly. "I brought him up in Natal, where my wife died.

We moved to America when he was six. I came here with him a little under a year ago because I wanted him to go to a great English school and learn the ways of a gentleman. You may believe me when I say, Doctor, that Milwaukee is no place to learn fine manners."

"And Long?"

He shrugged. "A thieving servant. I care about him only in the particular that he is with Bobby. My concern is to find Bobby. Long may go to the devil."

His eyes met mine with a determined expression and firm brow. I stiffened as he picked up his pistol, but he slipped it back into its holster.

"Someone is in that room behind you," he said softly. "Is it Bobby?"

"Come out, Churchill," I called.

Churchill appeared at once. He slipped across the room and took his usual seat at the dining table.

I introduced him to Taylor, who nodded a wary greeting and gave me a questioning look.

"I should tell you at once, Mr Taylor, that the police are investigating a murder in connection with the disappearance of your son."

Taylor leapt from his seat. My hand went instinctively for the butt of my revolver.

"Bobby?" he cried.

"No, sir. It is a Negro."

"Is Bobby hurt?"

"Not that we know."

Taylor sat heavily and sighed. "Was it Long? He was a thieving scoundrel, and he persuaded my son to run with him, but I am sorry that he is dead. He was with me in America for more than six years. I brought him to England as a companion for Bobby. Now Bobby is alone. You say in your advertisement that you have news of the boy."

"News, yes," I said. "But I do not know where he is."

Taylor slumped back in the chair.

"I would give every cent I have to get my son back, Doctor. I would give every cent I possess."

"I believe you, sir," I said. "Let us acquaint you with what we do know."

I described our first visit from Wiggins and his engagement of Sherlock Holmes to find Bobby. Taylor had no knowledge of Holmes or the profession of consulting detective.

"I would have employed him myself otherwise," he said. "I hired a thief-taker here in London on the recommendation of the Pinkerton Agency in America. He pointed me in many, mostly wrong, directions. I got closest when some boys in Lambeth tracked my son and Long to a house there, but the house was empty."

The doorbell rang downstairs.

Taylor looked quizzically at me.

"One of our agents, perhaps" I said. "He may have news."

The door opened, and Billy peeked in and looked a question at me. I nodded. Wiggins pushed past him and into the room. He caught sight of our visitor.

"Mutton-chops!" he yelled raising his walking cane.

"Damn you for a fraud." Taylor jumped up and reached for his pistol.

I pulled out my revolver and covered him.

Taylor looked from Wiggins to me and chuckled.

"In Milwaukee," he said. "They call this the 'Mexican standoff'."

Wiggins Reports

"Let us all regain our composures," I said softly. "Wiggins, give your hat and cane to Billy and sit you down with Churchill. Mr Taylor and I will put away our weaponry and sit quietly while Wiggins brings us up-to-date."

I put my pistol back in my waistband as Taylor holstered his.

"Tea, Billy. Or do you prefer coffee, Mr Taylor?"

He smiled. "I can't tell the difference here in England, at least the way it is prepared at my hotel."

"I think you will find that we know our business here, sir. Wiggins, report."

Wiggins explained that I had requested him to visit the scene of the crime and see what he could discover. He said that he had spoken to two of the dockworkers — nine pence to be refunded for three pints of half-and-half and two meat pasties — and had verified the facts. The body had fallen into the water a few yards from the pub and the dockworkers had fished it out less than a minute later. The landlord called the police. They searched the nearest houses on the upstream side of the Grapes. All had river access by steps or stairways, and all had overhanging terraces. They had found nothing.

The landlord of the pub had offered a reward of a guinea for information on the crime; he said that it was a diabolical liberty to dump bodies outside the Grapes and have blood and brains dripping through the bar when, as everyone knew, the proper dumping place for bodies was downstream, in the marshes.

Wiggins had entered the premises next to the pub: a simple lock. It was unoccupied. All the furniture was draped with sheets, and the floors showed signs of having been swept clean recently. He saw no bloodstains and no signs of a quarrel. The two shops next along were also closed and locked. Again, he had made entry and discovered disused storehouses with dusty hurdy-gurdy parts in one and coils of old rope in the other. He could make nothing out despite the abundant dust, as the police had tramped all over the floor in their big boots.

He went back to the pub where the owners of the three properties were huddled at the bar with a group of locals discussing the incident over hot, peppered gins. They were annoyed that they'd been dragged out by the police in the early morning to open their premises for the search. Mrs Plum, owner of the house next door to the pub, had explained to the police that her tenant had moved out a week previously, so there was nobody in the house and the doors were locked. They had still made her open up.

"Could the body have been dumped from a boat?" Taylor asked.

"No, sir," said Wiggins. "The dockers would have seen a boat. It was a cloudless, moonlit night. They heard a loud splash, as if the body had dropped into the water from a way up."

"Was there any news of Bobby? Was he with Long?" Taylor asked.

Wiggins looked at me.

I shook my head.

"I told my piece," said Wiggins. "Nothing of Bobby."

"You should know," I said to Taylor after a long pause, "that the murdered Negro was not the lad with Bobby. Wiggins says that they looked alike, but it was not he. However, the police found a small photograph of Bobby in the coat pocket of the corpse."

Taylor looked at me in confusion.

"Not Long? Then who was it?"

"I hoped that you would tell us that," I answered.

"I have no idea."

My eyes flicked to Wiggins, then to Churchill. Both wore noncommittal expressions.

"Could I ask you then, Mr Taylor," I said, "What induced your son to run away?"

"I don't see what bearing that has on the problem. My son is missing, and I mean to find him. I am his father."

"The boy's motive for absconding can hardly be irrelevant to the case. It is the central fact."

"May I?" Mr Taylor indicated the match box on the table.

"Of course."

He relit his cigar with a match.

"You must understand, Doctor, that Bobby is a wilful boy. In that, I guess he takes after his father. I had to put him to school by compulsion, and he would frequently play hooky and mix with the street boys in downtown Milwaukee. He was often in mischief. He is not a bad child, you understand, but he bored easy and he did not settle to schoolwork. I believe, and his schoolmasters agree, that his intelligence and resourcefulness are far above his years.

"I used every means at my disposal to bring him to his books and to shield him from the influence of the bad elements he had become associated with."

"He was beaten?" I asked.

Taylor shrugged. "Not often, and never without reason."

"You decided to come to England."

"Yes," said Taylor. "I thought that I could remove him from the temptations of the street in Milwaukee and that a change of environment, different customs, and above all, the intellectual and physical challenges he would meet at one of the public schools here would direct his talents to a more positive end."

I nodded. "A sensible procedure, sir." Nothing, I thought, could be more calculated to bring out the best in a boy than exposure at an early age to the moral and virile atmosphere of a great school. I was surprised to see that Wiggins's expression was one of open scorn, and that Churchill looked unimpressed.

"Did you visit any schools, sir?" asked Churchill.

"Five. Let me see: Eton, Winchester, Harrow, uh, and two others. They were the ones recommended to me by the American authorities. There were unexpected delays in securing interviews.

References from my bankers in America were not considered sufficient —"

"The fees are substantial at some schools," I said. "I believe fees and living expenses for boarders at Eton can reach a hundred and fifty guineas or more. Winchester and Harrow would no doubt be cheaper — oh."

I avoided Churchill's eyes.

The door opened and Billy appeared with a tray.

"Here is our coffee." I busied myself with the cups and plates.

"This is good coffee, Doctor," said Mr Taylor. "Coming back to the schools, the cost was not a factor. I was in the diamond-mining business at the Cape until I sold out to Cecil Rhodes. I have an ample sufficiency. The problem was not money; it was a lack of social connections here in England. Even so, I believe that an accommodation could have been reached, but for the behaviour of my son at the interviews. He was disrespectful and insolent. The headmaster at Eton offered to thrash him for me at no charge, then and there."

He chuckled, and Wiggins and I smiled. Churchill looked distressed.

"But it was no laughing matter. Bobby grew more and more scornful of me. He demanded that we return to America. When I refused, he disappeared. He was abetted by the servant Long. He stole some items of plate and clothing from the house."

I nodded to Wiggins.

"We met Bobby down Lambeth way, sir," he said. "He sort of joined up with us."

"He was with Long?"

"He was with a Negro gent that said he'd been a footman and that his name was Aaron. He had some stuff they pawned to meet their expenses. After they hopped it, you turned up asking questions. So we put the case before Mr Holmes and the Doctor."

"Well, that was a Christian thing to do, Mr Wiggins. You must let me pay whatever fees are necessary in the case."

"Just a bob, sir," said Wiggins. "We can take it out of the fiver you paid us."

Taylor laughed.

"I put that down to experience." He turned to me. "I will, if I may, take over as the principal in this case. I will stump up whatever it takes to find Bobby."

"You are now staying at an hotel?" I asked.

"The Langham, Suite 55. I gave up the lease on the house; it was too painful to retain. My sole aim now is to find Bobby and return to the States with him. We will make a new start and try our luck out West in Nevada or Wyoming."

"Very well, Mr Taylor. We will contact you when we have more information. I can assure you that we will use all our resources to find the boy."

"What are our conclusions?" I asked, as Billy closed the door behind Mr Taylor.

"Do we believe our Mr Taylor? Or did he kill the young man on the slab at the coroner's?"

"I don't think he did, Doctor," said Wiggins. "He was shocked when he heard that the man was not Aaron. He spoke true when he talked of his love for his son. It was in his eyes, like."

"He lied, though," said Churchill. "When Cresswell Minor at my school in Brighton lies, his eyes are right on you, you wouldn't guess a thing: he is an accomplished fibber. Mr Taylor's eyes were all over the room when he talked about Bobby's reason for running away. He looked in the ceiling; he looked at his feet. Mr Taylor lied in an amateur fashion. I agree with Harry that he's not the killer."

"I admit that Mr Taylor made a good impression," I said. "But we cannot be guided by impressions."

I was reminded of the handsome young lady in the elegant carriage in Piccadilly. I wondered whether Holmes was indulging in one of his occasional embellishments when he said that he knew her to be guilty of murders by poisoning. Notwithstanding his awareness of her misdeeds, Holmes had doffed his hat, and she had acknowledged him with a smile and a bow in return. Could it be —

"Ahem," said Churchill. Both boys were looking oddly at me.

"Could it be," I said, "that Taylor did the foul deed thinking the young man was his servant, Aaron Long? I have to say that Negroes, like Orientals, look alike if you are not used to them. There was no love lost between him and Aaron. He accused the young man of inveigling his son to run off."

"I don't think Taylor would mistake a servant if he knew him well," said Churchill after a long pause. "He said that Aaron had come with him from Milwaukee, and had been in his employ there for six years, then for several months here in London. We have two footmen at Blenheim who are brothers from Balham. They have been with the Duke for just two years, but despite the uniforms and powdered wigs, we can all tell them apart — except for Grandmamma, the Duchess of Marlborough, who calls all servants, 'You there'."

Wiggins and I digested that slice of aristocratic life *chez* Marlborough.

"The dead man looked enough like Aaron to be his brother," said Wiggins.

"Mr Taylor is old to be the father of a thirteen-year-old," I said. "Although he perhaps looks older than he is."

"Why did Bobby disown him?" asked Wiggins.

"Perhaps Taylor was cruel to him," I said. "He admitted beating the boy, but that is not unusual. He had rough-and-ready manners, but I do not think he is a cruel person. He had ambitions for his son to be a gentleman."

"My headmaster at Ascot carried himself like a gentleman," said Churchill stiffly. "And he was a fiend."

Wiggins and I looked blankly at Churchill.

"We should go to Limehouse," he said.

"Why?" said Wiggins. "I've already —"

The doorbell rang downstairs.

"Perhaps another enquirer about Bobby," I said.

Churchill sprang to the window.

"Oh lawks," he cried. He turned back to us looking pale.

"What is it Churchill? Is it Taylor again?"

"No, Doctor," said Churchill with an appalled look. "It is my nurse."

A short, red-faced woman in a voluminous black dress and shawl bustled into the sitting room. Churchill introduced her in a quavering voice as Mrs Everest.

"Well, Doctor Watson," she said, "you can see why I had to come, despite the hour; it's as plain as a pikestaff. Look at the state of that boy's shirt. I ask you, sir, I really do, is it not a public disgrace?"

She twisted Churchill's head towards the gas light.

"Look you here, sir, behind his ears; Lord love us, you could grow potatoes. He missed his bath last Monday. And has he had his daily cold-water douche and colic syrup that Doctor Roose insists upon? No offence to yourself, Doctor, but Doctor Roose is physician to the family, as is well known. The doctor prescribed a cold douche after Winston's bout of you-know-what last year. Has he had his douche every day, regular like, as he should? If so, I am the Emperor of Japan."

I tried to assemble a remark that would avoid a particular position on Churchill's ablutions — although I had to admit he was becoming somewhat rank — while assuring the lady that she bore no resemblance, as far my little knowledge went, to the Mikado.

"Pneumonia," explained Churchill, blushing pink and looking down at his toes. "I had pneumonia last year. Doctor Roose says that I must bathe in cold water every morning to toughen my system."

"Ah," I said, grateful for a topic on which I could offer a safe opinion. "I have a cousin who bathes in seawater every morning, winter or summer, rain or shine. Of course, he lives in Eastbourne, where the weather —"

"I had to bring a new suit of clothes," Mrs Everest said, overriding me. "That filthy suit could catch a cab home, pay a grateful tip to the cabby, and smoke a long cigar at the fireside in the sitting room without so much as a nod or a wink. What her Ladyship would say if she saw the state of him, I do not know. Sneaking in and out; he's not been seen for three days or more, not even for his rice pudding with brown sugar that the cook makes special on Tuesdays. I don't know, I'm sure."

She took off her black wrap-around bonnet and took me by the arm.

I stiffened and backed to the wall.

"I asked the lady downstairs, Doctor, for the use of a tin bath and enough buckets of hot water to fill it," she confided quietly. "Very polite I was mind, as is my nature, unless put upon. I have to say, sir, that neither she, nor the slavey, was co-operative. I wonder if you might be good enough to intervene, Doctor? You can see that I had to call, sir. I could not wait another moment. Winston needs a good scrub up, down and sideways. I brought my own carbolic soap and nit powder."

She unpacked soap and scrubbing brushes from a large basket.

"He's twisted Her Ladyship around his little finger with his talk of investigating this and detecting that; and she and His Lordship busy with the Jubilee and their official engagements with Her Majesty and the lords of the realm."

She wagged her finger at Churchill.

"He won't come home, the wilful mite."

"But, Woomany," Churchill squeaked as he backed to the window. "I'm on a case with Mr Holmes and Doctor Watson."

"I should inform you, my good woman," I said, "that I have written to Lady Randolph to advise her that, in my professional opinion, her son is perfectly —"

Mrs Everest rolled up her sleeves. "What state his under linen must be in, I cannot conceive."

I retreated towards the door; Wiggins followed, grinning.

"We'll be in the waiting room downstairs, Master Churchill," I said. "Do join us when you are — when you have been — ah. Billy, bring the remains of the coffee."

The door of the waiting room opened slowly and the sound of shrill female contention outside in the hall was instantly magnified.

Churchill tiptoed into the room and softly closed the door. He wore the blue and white sailor suit that I had seen on earlier occasions, and he shone with scrubbed wholesomeness.

"She gave Billy a shilling to bring hot water and soap," he said with a slight, engaging lisp. "I shall never thpeak to him again."

"Mrs Everest is a persuasive personage, Churchill," I said. "I should go halves with Billy on the tip, if I were you, and forgive him."

"Why should we go back to Limehouse?" asked Wiggins. "I got all the information as was going."

Churchill smiled and touched his finger to the side of his nose in an unseemly manner. "I borrowed Mr Holmes's magnifying glass, Doctor. He said I could."

"Be careful with it."

I made to open the door, then paused and listened. I consulted my watch. "As time is not pressing, we might wait until the hubbub has died down before we venture forth."

7. The Grapes, Limehouse

Thoughts on Empire

Our four-wheeler made good time through quiet, darkening backstreets.

The cabby avoided the main thoroughfares that still thronged with late-diners and theatregoers. Wiggins fell asleep as soon as we boarded the cab. Churchill sat opposite me with his sailor suit decently covered by a coat borrowed from Billy and his eyes shining with excitement.

"This Cresswell Minor of yours at school, the accomplished liar," I asked, "Is he any relation to Baron Cresswell, the Old Bailey judge?"

"His grandson," said Churchill.

"Dear me," I said.

We made good progress until we turned in to Narrow Street in Limehouse. The roadway was lined with sail warehouses and ships' tackle manufacturers. Provision agents showed cases of meat and biscuit in their dusty windows. Slop shops had hammocks, pilot coats, shiny black dreadnought jackets, and well-oiled nor'wester hats hanging across the frontage of their dingy open-faced premises. Low lodging houses for sailors and dockworkers filled the courts and alleys on either side of the street.

The cabby grew more nervous as we pushed through groups of raggedly dressed, chattering men coming out of long warehouses that smelt strongly of malt, hemp, tobacco, or tar. Their shift had just ended, and they were in a boisterous mood. Hurdy-gurdy players plinked out the latest music hall tunes and the men, and a surprising number of women considering the hour, sang the ditties with less tunefulness than vigour.

Our cabman refused to wait outside the Grapes. He said that there was a stable up the road in the mews in Shoulder of Mutton Alley and that we could send a boy to fetch him when we were done. I had to agree with this strange procedure, as we would otherwise have had little chance of getting another cab in the district.

The Grapes was a tall, thin, Elizabethan building of three or four floors. The upper stories overhung the lower, giving the house a drooping appearance like the public house in a similar situation by the River that I recalled from one of Charles Dickens's novels. We pushed through the door and into a long narrow room, no more than fifteen feet across, with a small bar on the left side. Men in working clothes occupied the rough mismatched chairs and tables grouped on both sides of the room. Hand-tinted prints of riverside scenes lined the left wall, and the flotsam and jetsam of maritime life: hooks, blocks, coils of intricately knotted ropes, brass lamps, and braided masters' caps festooned the other. A long harpoon hung over the bar. There was a steady hum of conversation, interrupted by loud laughter and shouted drink orders. The air was pungent with tobacco and rum fumes.

I followed Wiggins as he slipped between the benches to the back of the room to a more open space, about the size of our parlour in Baker Street, furnished with a half-dozen sets of tables and chairs. All were occupied except for a table by the window that he ignored. He led us up a couple of steps and through a door onto a narrow terrace open to the River. The over-hanging upper story of the pub formed the roof. There was room for one table and three or four chairs. Churchill and I sat as Wiggins disappeared back inside to fetch drinks.

"It's like the captain's balcony at the back of a sailing man o' war," said Churchill with a wide grin. "We could be on a ship-of-the-line with Nelson."

I nodded. The analogy was perfect. I looked over the rickety balustrade straight down to the River Thames. A set of wooden steps led down perhaps ten or twelve feet to the water.

I looked to my right, upstream, at the house next door. The structure was taller and wider than the Grapes. It also had a set of steps down to the water and a terrace at our level. There was a much larger balcony jutting over the River from the upper floor. Above that, twenty feet or more above us, a balustrade ran around the roof of the building. The building was a huge Spanish first-rate towering over our simple English ship-of-the-line.

A rowing boat was tied up at the bottom of the steps.

The door behind me opened, and Wiggins appeared with a tray of pint glasses and a small, wizened old man in a dark suit and cap.

"Half and halves all round, Gents. This is Mr Mould, what was one of them good Samaritans that pulled the young Negro gentleman's body from the waters of the Thames." He passed out the beers, sat Mr Mould in his chair and propped himself against the balustrade behind him.

A strong, acrid smell at once pervaded the atmosphere. I frowned and looked about as I tried to find its source.

Wiggins grinned at me from behind the old man. He pointed to his nose and then to Mr Mould.

"He works down the Spice Wharf, don't you, Mr Mould?"

"I do," he said grinning and showing a single black tooth. "I've been on the Spice these forty-two years. Before that I was in Sugar."

"Sugar and spice and all things nice, eh?" I quipped.

"You what, sir?"

Wiggins jumped in and led the man through the events of the previous night. He described the cry, the splash and the discovery of the body.

"Right there it was, sir," said Mr Mould in a quavering voice. "Just where that boat is now."

He pointed to the rowing boat moored at the next-door house. "We pulled the poor gent out at the steps below you. All the back of his head was gone, sirs; you could see his intellectuals, plain as porridge. He was a Negro gentleman and brown all over."

We thanked him, and Wiggins steered him back inside.

"Well," said Wiggins on his return. "What's next?"

I looked blankly at Churchill.

"I'd like to speak with the lady who owns the house next door," he said.

Wiggins turned to me. "Money for the beers, Doctor, and we'll need a hot gin for madam. She's a tough old bird, so I'd go easy."

I gave him a half-crown, and he disappeared inside.

"Never," I remarked, "was a man more aptly named than Mr Mould."

I sipped my beer and gazed upstream along the curve of the Thames towards Wapping and the Lower Pool. The view of the river was stupendous. Vessels of all kinds created a forest of masts, and the dense mass of hulls along both shores almost hid the large square blocks of warehouses, and the huddled terraces of homes and businesses. On the River, the tall funnels of steamers belched columns of smoke and sparks.

One ship backed towards a wharf on the opposite shore, its paddle wheels whirling and twirling, forwards and backwards creating showers of spray and a smutty mist that spread on the wind across the River towards us.

Against our bank of the River was a squalid huddle of Dutch eel boats. Their cargo fed our foreign workforce and supplied the jellied eel stalls on every street corner in the poorer districts of the Metropolis.

Trading vessels of all sizes lay against the wharves on both sides of the River. Slab-sided and unpretentious, they carried tobacco, coffee, spices, and ton upon ton of essential and luxury commodities from our Imperial possessions and trading partners.

Further upstream, fast packet steamers strained at their moorings as they loaded mail, specie and passengers for the Continent.

Haughty steamers from the Peninsula and Oriental line, with their gilt sterns, mahogany deckhouses, and gleaming brass binnacles, showed white lamps on topmasts and red and green riding lamps as they steamed down the fairway bound for Aden, Colombo, Rangoon, or Sydney.

I had never beheld a better visual metaphor for the glory of Empire.

The door opened again and Wiggins led in an elderly woman in a grey bonnet with a dark shawl over her black dress. Churchill and I stood as he sat her opposite me. Wiggins struck a match and lit an oil lamp in a bracket above the door.

"Good evening, Madam," I said. "I am Doctor Watson and this is Master Spencer-Churchill. I believe you know Master Wiggins."

She nodded suspiciously. In the light, her face reminded me instantly of Mrs Punch in the street show. I avoided Churchill's eye.

Wiggins put a glass of hot, spiced gin on the table in front of her. "This is Mrs Plum, sole proprietor of the fine premises next door."

"I wonder, Madam —" I began.

"We are looking for a riverside property to rent," said Churchill, overriding me in a high-pitched patrician tone. "Mr Wiggins has suggested that you may have a suitable building."

Mrs Plum looked up at Wiggins, winked and reached for her drink. "I might have," she said, taking a slug of gin.

"You see," said Churchill. "We are looking for accommodation and for storage facilities close to the River."

"Storing what?"

"Bibles, Ma'am," said Churchill smoothly. "The Doctor represents a charity that aims to place a Bible in the hands of every seafarer visiting the Port."

"My old man were a seafarer," said Mrs Plum. "He were in the Whaling. When that fell off, we had hard shrift. Then he bleeding well fell off the ship hisself in a storm off California, the one in America. At least, that's what his captain said. A scheming, shifty-eyed villain as ever you'd see in a day's walk."

"Your old man, Mrs P?" asked Wiggins with a grin.

"The captain," she cried laughing, elbowing Wiggins in the ribs. "The sauce on him! Impudent rascal."

Wiggins grinned and slipped back into the pub.

"How long do you want the place for, then?" she asked, giving Churchill a narrow-eyed look.

"At least a year."

"Bit young, aren't you? Who's to sign the lease? The doctor is it?"

"No, Madam. That would be my father, Lord Randolph Spencer-Churchill, ex-Chancellor of the Exchequer. He is the patron of our society."

I spluttered in my beer and was instantly wracked with heaving spasms. Wiggins came back out with another hot gin. He thumped me heartily on the back.

"The doctor is not used to beer," Churchill explained. "He generally restricts himself to Champagne of the finest vintages."

"Oh," said Mrs Plum looking respectfully in my direction. "I see. You'll want to view the premises, My Lord?"

"We would like to have a look now," said Wiggins. "As we are pressed for time, like."

"We aim to lease a property immediately," added Churchill. "The Bibles are due at — at — Baker Street on the morrow."

Mrs Plum gulped the second gin in one long swallow and stood unsteadily.

"Come along, then." She led us to the adjoining building.

Mrs Plum opened a stout padlock with a heavy key.

I wondered how Wiggins had managed to enter the house so easily the night before. He guessed my thoughts because he gave me a wink and a nod at a ground-floor window. He mimed opening a clasp knife and fiddling the lock. I gave him a dark look.

Mrs Plum opened the front door and stood aside.

"I'll wait here. There's gas laid on. Mind you put it out when you're done."

Wiggins and I trooped through the door and along the corridor. Behind me, I heard Churchill addressing Mrs Plum.

"One of the fellows from the Christian Tract Association rented a space along here somewhere last month," he said. "The gentleman described a similar building."

"Did he, then?" said Mrs Plum.

"I believe so. I don't recall his name. He was a narrow, sharp-featured gent with a stoop and an inward twist to his leg. I am certain he was the fellow who rented from you last month. He spoke highly of the premises."

I followed Wiggins upstairs and we checked every room. The meagre furniture was cloth covered, and the floors were swept clean as he had reported. I opened a pair of French windows on the first floor and stepped out onto a wide balcony.

Churchill lit the gas lamps and examined the balustrade with Holmes's magnifying glass.

I looked down at the rowing boat moored below.

"Why is that here?" I asked. "The house is empty."

I looked up. "Wiggins, did you check the roof yesterday?"

"Roof? What's on the roof?"

"There must be some access."

We ran back inside and relit the gas in the top-floor rooms. We opened every door and cupboard. In the front room, what looked like a cupboard door opened to reveal a steep wooden staircase. We rushed up the stairs and out onto a wide, empty roof space with high walls on the street front and sides. I looked over the curving balustrade on the River side.

A thick rope tied to a pillar hung down to the water. Its end trailed with the tide. The rowing boat was gone.

"There, Doctor!" Wiggins pointed downstream. A boat was just visible in the pale moonlight. A single man rowed furiously. He wore a dark coat and had a top hat pulled over his face. It could have been Maxwell Taylor. I took out my revolver and sighted on the boat.

I shook my head and lowered my gun.

"Doctor, he's getting away!"

"I will not shoot at a man because he is rowing on the River Thames, Wiggins."

He pointed to a deep scratch in the wood of the balustrade and some stains, black in the moonlight. Churchill held up a lantern and examined the stains; through his glass, they were rusty red.

Wiggins looked expectantly at me.

I shook my head.

"I cannot, sir, be judge and jury. And now he is much too far away for a fair shot."

We dropped off Wiggins, in a foul mood, at a 'bus stop near Waterloo Bridge, and we continued west towards home.

"You were right not to fire," said Churchill.

"I know, but I may have let the murderer of that poor fellow escape."

Churchill was silent for a while.

"But we have a great deal more information for Mr Purchase."

"Well, I'm not sure that I can give a useful description. He wore a top hat, and I caught the white of his shirt. He was probably in evening clothes covered by an opera cloak. Not much use."

"Oh," said Churchill. "We can do better than that. The man is over six feet, in his sixties, swarthy-complexioned, and with a full salt-and-pepper moustache and grey hair, balding at the top. He is left-handed and he favours his right arm as if he has hurt it. He habitually wears evening dress. A surprising number of gentlemen in evening dress frequent the area, especially the Chinese opium dens and the houses of ill repute, so that is not singular. He carries a leaded cane."

"Churchill, how on Earth —"

"I described Inspector Lestrade to Mrs Plum as the man who leased her property for a month and supposedly left last week. She vehemently denied my description and gave hers. We traded detail for detail. Her lessee may be our man. He did not offer references, but he left a substantial deposit; he said that he had just arrived from America. He could easily have copied the key."

I was dumbfounded; I was also a little disconcerted. I had a great deal more experience in methods of detection than the aristocratic young whippersnapper seated so complacently in the cab opposite me. "How do we know that this lessee is connected to the case?"

Churchill leant back and steepled his fingers in an annoyingly Holmesian gesture.

"He signed the lease in the name of Richard Wilmer. And he spoke with a pronounced accent that Mrs Plum describes as 'Dutch or German'."

"Wilmer." I said. "Well, Mr Taylor and Mr Wilmer have too many similarities to be unconnected. Could he have been Taylor in disguise?"

Churchill nodded. "Perhaps."

I pursed my lips. "How did you know that the murder took place in Mrs Plum's house?"

"I didn't. But, if there was no boat, the body must have fallen from one of the riverside buildings. The violent blow to the head surely poured with blood. We had to make a more thorough search for stains. Mrs Plum's building, right next to the pub, was the most likely location for the murder. When you have eliminated the impossible, what is left, however unlikely, must be — oh, here we are."

The cab wheels screeched against the kerb as we stopped outside 221B; Churchill made to get out.

"I think, young man, that you had better make your number at home for tonight. Mrs Everest was worried about you. I am sure that your mother and father are too. I wrote a letter to Lady Randolph that said — ah — that you are a fine young fellow. I am certain that she misses you, and you her."

Churchill looked up at me, his eyes glistening in the gaslight. "I may come back tomorrow, mayn't I, Doctor?"

"Of course you may, Churchill. You have done well today. Holmes will be pleased with our progress."

He beamed, and I felt like a cad.

I handed him the cab fare and waved him off.

Lestrade on the Scent

I was exhausted.

I gathered my resolve and wrote a short note to Scotland Yard. Peterson across the road was still up, so I sent it by messenger. I then spent an hour or more leafing through Holmes's notebooks and scrapbooks looking for his patent method of detecting blood. When we had first met, at St Bartholomew's Hospital six or more years previously, Holmes had said, boasted rather, that he had discovered a method for detecting even minute quantities of blood. I wanted to test the reddish brown flakes I had scraped from the balustrade of the house in Narrow Street with his technique. It would pay Holmes back, I thought, for his presumption over the arsenical curtains.

I could make nothing of the cataloguing system, and by the time Billy came up with supper — a tureen of beef soup and some crusty bread — I had given up and placed the flakes in an envelope on the laboratory bench. Really, I thought, I should encourage Holmes to index his papers in a less eccentric manner.

I felt a sense of guilt; I had been hard on young Churchill. He had furnished several important facts in the case, in particular the description of the lessee of the murder house.

I had thought to acknowledge his acuity in the note I wrote to Lestrade at Scotland Yard. However, it seemed obvious that the inspector might be less, rather than more, inclined to act on the facts if I had explained their source. I had therefore not mentioned the boy's contribution to the interview with Mrs Plum. I had no doubt that I should have won the information from her by some means of my own, given time.

I poured myself a glass of Madeira and reviewed my notes on the case thus far, in preparation for briefing Holmes the following day.

Facts: the killing and the disappearance of Bobby and his friend were connected by the photograph found on the body, and by the resemblance between Aaron and the victim. They might be relatives, brothers perhaps. Aaron had been brought from America by Taylor as a servant. Why would his relative follow him, and how would he have obtained the money for the transatlantic steamer fare?

Mr Wilmer was the possible murderer. It stretched credulity to think that Mr Maxwell Taylor, Bobby Taylor, and Mr Richard Wilmer were unconnected. Mr Wilmer said that he had recently arrived from America, where Taylor and the boy had lived. He might have used his real name, or a fake one to rent the murder house. Why was he there a week after his lease had run out? Why was the dead man at the house? The case was less clear, not less clouded. I feared more and more for the safety of young Bobby and his friend. I could hardly wait to lay the facts before Holmes. I yawned and stubbed out my final cigar of the evening.

I heard a ring at the doorbell, followed by footsteps on the stairs and a knock at the sitting-room door.

"Come."

Inspector Lestrade came in looking annoyed.

"I got your remarkable letter at the Yard, Doctor."

"You work late, Inspector."

"And I catch my worm, given half a chance. I could have wished that you had wired this information to my office direct from Limehouse. We would have saved an hour."

"I did not expect you to be at your post at night," I said shortly. "Does Scotland Yard work twenty-four hour shifts like a Lancashire cotton mill?"

Lestrade sniffed in his uncouth manner.

"We have had an officer on duty at all hours since the Irish bombings. He has orders to fetch me if there is urgent need. We could have scoured the shoreline for a gentleman in evening dress rowing a boat; an uncommon sight on the River, as I think you will agree. I am certain that Mr Holmes would have —"

"I cannot swear that he was dressed so, or that he had anything to do with the murder. Would you care for a glass of wine?"

The doorbell rang again as Lestrade took his usual seat on the sofa and accepted a glass of Madeira.

"We are late on the scent," he said. "However, with your very complete description, we will have our man before the night is out. We have warned all hotels frequented by foreigners. I have men watching the premises in Limehouse, and our water station at Wapping has detectives rowing on the River looking for suspicious characters."

"You have been most active, Inspector."

There was a soft knock on the door, and Churchill entered. He wore a dark cutaway jacket over knee breeches and long socks. I guessed that this was his uniform at his preparatory school.

"Churchill," I said with a stern look. "What are you doing here? I sent you home. It is very late."

"Everyone has gone to Blenheim Palace, Doctor. The Duke of Marlborough is holding a Jubilee Ball. There are just servants in the house. I did not care to stay there alone. Billy said that Inspector Lestrade was here, so I came up."

He looked at his toes.

"Quite right," I said with a smile. "There's soup. Ask Bessie to warm some for you."

"Thank you, Doctor." He too sat in his usual seat.

"What I don't understand, Doctor," continued Lestrade ignoring Churchill, "is why this man Wilmer returned to the murder house the day after the killing. And what was he doing there a week after his lease expired? Did this landlady, this Mrs Plum, not have any opinion on the matter? You winkled out a great deal of information from her —"

I stood. "She said nothing more about Mr Wilmer. You will want to put that to her yourself before tomorrow morning is out."

Lestrade stood and shook my hand. He smiled.

"I hope you'll forgive my peevishness earlier, Doctor. We are most grateful to you for the information we received. The flakes of material you included in your note have been sent for analysis. I have no doubt that they are bloodstains."

He left.

I coloured and turned to the fireplace. I made a show of slowly filling my pipe.

"Churchill —"

"It's quite all right, Doctor. You could not involve me. The inspector would have laughed the matter away. I do understand."

He beamed shyly at me.

"Well," I said, "have some soup and get to bed. Today was a jungle of a day. We have a great deal to tell Holmes tomorrow. And we can have a lie-in: Holmes won't be here until lunchtime at the earliest."

"Goodnight, Doctor."

"Goodnight, young man. I shall smoke a last pipe and meditate on the facts of the case of the missing American boy. I feel it in my soul that he is in the gravest danger."

Churchill opened the sitting-room door.

"I say, old fellow," I asked softly. "Were you not invited to the Blenheim ball?"

He shook his head.

"I believe that I was forgotten, Doctor," he said, "in the excitement."

8. The Sprightly Correspondence

A Monstrous Imputation

"Watson!"

I woke to the familiar sound of my friend's voice and a hammering on my bedroom door.

I unhooked my pocket watch from its stand on the night table and checked the time in the weak light filtering through the curtains. It was not yet six.

"Good morning, Holmes," I croaked.

"Coffee in the sitting room in twelve minutes," he called.

I heaved myself out of bed. I wondered what emergency had brought Holmes back so much before his expected time, and indeed how the deuce he had managed to get from the North to London so early.

"This coffee is excellent," said Holmes as I opened the sitting-room door. "Spencer-Churchill is coming along. If he learns one new fact daily, and a new skill every fortnight, he will do well. He seems set on the Army; he has a large collection of toy soldiers. I shall write to Gamages Store to encourage them to add a set of miniature consulting detectives to their collections."

"You are early, Holmes," I said as I joined him at the breakfast table.

"I caught the milk train. I could not stand a moment more of Stockton, that miserable town. I am astonished that the good people of Darlington should have been so eager to establish a railway link with the place. Let me pour you a cup of this excellent brew and you can acquaint me with your adventures in the Caspar case. Spencer-Churchill assures me that the witnesses were entertaining."

I described the visit to Madame Audet and my lack of success in getting a clear statement from her. Churchill came in carrying a stack of morning newspapers, followed by Billy with a tray of bacon and eggs. Holmes grabbed the *Pall Mall Gazette* and scanned the pages.

"More abuse thrown on the police by that monstrous regiment of political women, ha! They have nothing new. Ha, ha! They do not have it; they do not have the answer."

"Do you?"

Holmes looked up from the paper with a vainglorious grin. "Naturally, my dear Watson. I have all my birds lined up but one, and that will flutter into my net within the day."

"How is the coffee, Mr Holmes?" asked Churchill.

"First rate, young man. I could be on the banks of the Orinoco. I see from the newspapers that Venezuela is in its usual state of unrest. I hope that does not mean a rise in the already abominably inflated price of coffee beans."

He applied himself to his breakfast with the air of a pilgrim who fasted with reason and deep conviction for a week and who was let loose at last.

"Stockton, Holmes," I said. "What did you discover?"

"Oh, I learned everything the police did not. Lestrade's men were still at the local police station poring through their rancid records when I arrived. I went directly to Miss Caspar's home, a pleasant corner property where her mother caters to travellers in the commercial line. She was in a deplorable state, had taken to her bed in fact, and her maid had even less understanding of the culinary arts than our dear Bessie. When I disclosed that I acted in the case, Madam Caspar was kind enough to offer me a room. After a long day of coaxing and bed-side-mannering, she produced the evidence I had hoped for and that was that. The Scotland Yard detectives did not deign to visit her. Ha! Ha, ha!"

He waved his fork in triumph.

I looked across to Churchill. He seemed as confused as I was. What possible evidence could the lady's mother in Stockton offer?

"I say, Holmes —"

"Tell me about the Major," said Holmes, looking up with a sly smile.

"He lives in Oriental splendour a stone's throw from the Fulham Road." I described the house, the lounge and its furnishings.

"Attendants?"

"He mentioned an Ahmed, perhaps a cook. We saw only one, a young Indian or Malay girl. He mentioned Ceylon, so she may — what?"

Churchill and Holmes convulsed with laughter.

"I'm sorry, Watson," said Holmes, recovering his breath. "We have played upon you. You had better tell the Doctor, young Churchill, although I do not envy you that heavy task."

There was a loud ring at the doorbell.

"Ah," said Holmes. "We are saved by the doorbell. This will be the first of my bird dogs."

The door of our sitting room opened and Wiggins strode in. He wore a clean and respectable tweed suit and a soft wide-awake hat. He saw my surprised look.

"Investment, Doctor: tools of the trade. I'm on the Dead Faint game, though it's not a big earner without Bobby."

"Wiggins," said Holmes. "You are to confirm that the person named in this paper lives at that address. Do so discreetly, and have your men follow if necessary. Take care, your quarry will be wise to the street. Wire me when you coop your prey. Usual rates plus meals. Give Wiggins ten-bob, Watson."

He took the money, saluted and left.

Holmes and Churchill buried themselves in the morning papers.

"Ahem," I said. "We were in the middle of a conversation when the doorbell rang."

Holmes looked across the room to Churchill and raised his eyebrows. The boy responded with an impertinent shrug.

"The girl who served us tea, Doctor," said Churchill. "She was no girl."

"And Major Massingham is undoubtedly one of nature's gentlemen," added Holmes. "A confirmed bachelor."

They looked at me with a kind of pleasant speculation. I was utterly taken aback.

"I do not believe it," I said stiffly. "It is a monstrous imputation upon a retired official in the Indian Colonial Administration in Ceylon. They maintain the highest standards."

"My dear chap," said Holmes. "Spencer-Churchill has described the nude painting of bathing boys, the dainty furnishings. You would have been entirely convinced had you stayed to view the photograph albums."

I remained silent as I recalled the delicate features and compelling gaze of the young girl at Major Massingham's home. Her wide, almond eyes and soft skin were entirely un-boy-like; I could not imagine such a creature playing rugby football.

"I do not believe it."

"Do not feel gulled, Watson. The practices of the East, to which Major Massingham has evidently succumbed, are intractable to the wholesome, English mind."

I helped myself to a last half-cup of coffee as Holmes continued.

"I do not discount the Major's evidence despite its moral inadequacy. It is of the first importance; it is the final piece of the puzzle. As I have said before, the investigator must recognise, from the mass of data that constitute the facts of a case, the vital elements and the merely incidental. It was clear to me from the beginning of this affair that the key to the solution was the discrepancy between the witnesses as to the location of the arrest. PC Endaby and Madame Audet state positively that Miss Caspar was arrested in one place, while Major Massingham and Miss Caspar firmly assert that she was arrested in another. Neither

Police Constable Twyman nor Police Constable Dyer, on duty in the area, saw the arrest.

"It seems inexplicable," I said.

The doorbell rang downstairs.

Billy ushered Inspector Lestrade into our sitting rooms.

"Coffee, Inspector?" I offered. "We can make another brew."

"Thank you, no."

He sat at our breakfast table opposite Holmes and slid a large grey envelope across to him.

"Chapter and verse, sir," he said shaking his head.

"The Stockton papers," said Holmes. He handed the envelope to me. I opened it and slid a wad of official forms onto my knees.

"These are arrest records for Miss E. Caspar of thirty-eight, The Railway Embankments, Stockton. Mostly dated last year and the year before: loitering, various noise nuisances, ah —"

I looked up and across the room to Churchill. He sighed and stood. Holmes waved him back into his seat.

"Cautioned on suspicion of importuning for a certain purpose," I continued. "Cautioned for suspicion of soliciting for same, and again, and again; the list goes on Holmes. It is most damning."

"The date of the last arrest?" he asked.

"Eleven months or so ago. There are also envelopes here addressed to Miss Caspar in various hands that contain certain letters."

I stuffed the papers back into the envelope and flung it onto the table in disgust.

"I hope that you heeded my warning, Mr Holmes," said Lestrade in his nasal bray. "I trust that you made no rash statements as to Miss Caspar's innocence that might be awkward to repudiate. The letters are from various male acquaintances. The contents are sprightly, sir, very sprightly indeed. A Royal Navy commander with the Mediterranean Fleet offers to set the lady up in keeping, as his paramour."

Billy appeared at the door with a telegram on a tray.

Holmes stood, but waved for me to take it.

"Thank you Inspector," he said. "You have been most thorough. May I beg you to return at two of the afternoon? I may have some information vital to the case by then. Oh, I would caution you not to make any statements on the guilt or innocence of Miss Caspar, despite the Stockton materials, until you have returned to me here."

"Is there any news of Mr Wilmer?" I asked.

"None at all, Doctor. If we had been on the track earlier —"

"Show Inspector Lestrade out, Billy," said Holmes.

The door closed and Holmes turned to me.

"Cooped," I said as I read the telegram. "Garrick Street, Covent Garden. Meet at Lamb and Flag, Wiggins."

Churchill slapped his hands together and grinned. "Got you, My Lovely."

"Our leopard is treed," Holmes said. "Our case is complete. I must to the Lamb and Flag pub at Covent Garden; Spencer-Churchill, kindly ask Billy to fetch me a four-wheeler."

I watched from the window as Holmes hurried out to the growler. Churchill jumped in beside him.

I was rather surprised that Holmes had not asked me to accompany him as he usually would when the game was afoot. Of course, my friend liked to keep his cards close to his chest during an investigation. He would lay them out with a flourish when he was sure of his conclusions. However, in this case, young Churchill had insinuated himself into Holmes's confidence, and he appeared to know much more than I did.

I had to confess to myself that I felt only confusion when I examined the facts of the Caspar case; I could not imagine why the location of the arrest should be of such significance. My feeling was that Constable Endaby had panicked when he heard Miss Caspar's explanations while he was conducting her to the police station. He felt that he had to bolster his case, so he made up the frequent visits earlier in the year. It was to me utterly inconceivable that the young lady who had graced our waiting room was capable of the indelicacies described in the materials from Stockton.

I put the problem aside and went downstairs to visit Mrs Hudson. She was making a most remarkable recovery for a lady of her age.

I was with Mrs Hudson in her room reading her a comic story from *Punch*, when I heard a four-wheeler cab draw up outside our door. I went out into the hall just as the front door opened and Holmes led a lady by the arm into the house. Young Churchill followed them. I was astonished to see that it was Miss Caspar, dressed in the same blue skirt and white jacket that she wore on her first visit to us, and with the straw hat and mauve band that Major Massingham had described. She looked pale and nervous. I bowed and murmured a greeting as she was swept past me by Holmes and hurried upstairs.

"Tea, Bessie," Holmes called over his shoulder.

I caught Churchill by the arm. "Miss Caspar does not look well."

"She's had a shock, Doctor," Churchill replied with an impudent grin. "And another's coming."

The doorbell rang again. Billy admitted Inspector Lestrade and Constable Endaby. They looked understandably pleased with themselves. Lestrade had no doubt passed on to Endaby details of the vile Stockton papers. I felt a surge of anger against them, and a counter-surge of pity for the young lady upstairs.

I followed them up the stairs, with Churchill at my heels.

Miss Caspar was not present in the sitting room as Lestrade and Endaby took their places on the sofa. Holmes saw my puzzled look; he nodded his head towards the curtained alcove where Billy had recovered from his faint. No doubt, I thought, poor Miss Caspar was preparing herself there before she met her fate at the hands of her accusers. I was disappointed to note that Churchill could not restrain a wide and unseemly grin from distorting his features. I gave him a stern look of rebuke and reproach that brought him to his senses.

"We have just enough chairs for the expected company," said Holmes. "Make a fresh pot of tea, Bessie, and bring more cups."

I could not think why would need them; who else might have an interest in the revelations of Miss Caspar's guilt? I wished that she had brought support in the shape of the formidable Mrs Barker.

The doorbell rang, and a moment later, to my utter confusion and chagrin, Billy showed in Major Massingham. He spotted me immediately and crossed the room to shake my hand in an unpleasantly intimate manner. I was obliged to introduce him to Holmes and to Inspector Lestrade. Massingham took a seat at the table with Churchill. They began an animated conversation about the boy's impending attendance at Harrow School. Massingham, it seemed, was an alumnus of that institution. Churchill was much more self-possessed than I should have been in his situation.

The bell rang yet again. This, I thought, was beginning to resemble the last act of a French farce, with all the characters gathered in the drawing room waiting for the various misunderstandings to be unravelled.

The door opened and I was pleased to see that Mrs Barker was at the door. Then I was struck completely out of countenance when I saw that following her was Miss Caspar! I could not for a moment imagine how or why she had been spirited outside and brought back in again. I looked to where Holmes stood at the alcove curtain.

"Ladies and gentlemen," he cried in his most theatrical style. "I present to you —"

He pulled the curtain along its runners to reveal the alcove and the small sofa on which Billy had lain. A lady stood and turned to face the company.

"Miss E Caspar," said Holmes.

"Twins," I said as the last of our guests left.

I helped myself to a Scotch and soda.

"Not quite," said Holmes. "Elizabeth, our client, is one year older than her flighty sister Eliza."

"Eliza was dancing along Regent Street waving her parasol," I said.

"Yes, she had just received a wire intimating that her protector, the commander in the Royal Navy of whom Lestrade made mention, was returning to Town on leave. She was in the West End buying new gloves and a smart hat for the occasion of their reunion. She has, as you saw, an open, pretty nature, and she had enough experience from her time in Stockton and London to deal with the remarks made to her by male pests as she walked along. She rebuffed their advances, but she enjoyed their attention. I do not find it in my heart to condemn her."

"So said *Pest* in the newspaper, Holmes." I said stiffly. "I can hardly believe it. She must have been thoroughly debauched in Stockton to have behaved in such an untrammelled way in the streets of London."

"That is what PC Endaby thought; he glossed her excitement at the return of her lover as an advertisement of sexual availability. He arrested her and brought her back to Oxford Circus. There, the crowd jostled them, and he lost her. Eliza skipped across the road and caught a 'bus home to Covent Garden."

"And Endaby hurried through the strolling pedestrians along Oxford Street and caught sight of what he thought was his quarry outside the Chrystal Palace Bazaar."

"Exactly. That was the older sister, Elizabeth, who is perfectly innocent. The Stockton allegations referred to Eliza: Miss E Caspar, junior."

"Why didn't Endaby mention that he'd lost hold of the girl?" I asked.

"Professional embarrassment, perhaps. He would not and did not think it had any bearing on the case. You saw his astonishment at the revelation of the two Miss Caspars."

"I think it vile that Eliza did not come forward to relieve her sister," said I. "She must have known; it was all over the newspapers."

"The only periodical that the younger Miss Caspar subscribes to is *The Girl's Own Paper*. She was reading an article on pearl buttons when I visited," said Holmes. "She had no idea of her sister's plight."

"Surely Miss Elizabeth Caspar must have realised —"

"Perhaps; we shall never know. She and her sister were estranged. The younger Miss Caspar left her family home last year. Her nautical admirer has set her up in a comfortable position near Covent Garden. The two sisters have not communicated since that time. I gambled a trip to darkest Stockton to see if the mother had received any letters from her errant daughter. After much persuasion, she admitted that she had. A simple matter, then, to set Wiggins and his men to stake out my quarry."

"The clothes, Holmes. They wore almost identical costumes."

"Sisters, Watson. And all the clothes were made by Miss Caspar senior. Two of each; it is a common trope."

"And what of the policemen who saw nothing?"

"Untrained observers. I have written to the Police Commissioners to acquaint them with the inadequacy of their training system for constables, let alone for detectives. They reply that they suffer a twenty-two per cent turnover in police officers yearly and that it is impossible to institute the ten-week course on basic principles of detection that I advocate."

"Well, Holmes, I saw, but evidently I did not observe. When did you first guess — I'm sorry, when did you realise that there were two ladies involved?"

Holmes waved his pipe stem at young Churchill. "Would you like to answer that, Spencer-Churchill?"

"Me, sir?" said Churchill. "Oh, my suspicions were immediately aroused when we met Miss Caspar and Mrs Barker outside in the street below us. After Major Massingham's testimony, it was clear that there were two ladies involved."

I looked across at Holmes. He blinked back at me.

"How so?" I asked.

"PC Endaby insisted that Miss Caspar waved her parasol in a suggestive way. Miss Caspar did not bring a parasol with her when she came here to Baker Street, despite the bright sunshine. She wore a wide-brimmed straw hat. And Major Massingham stated that the lady arrested before him in Oxford Street had no parasol; there had to be two ladies."

"Exactly," said Holmes after a long pause.

9. Left for Dead at the Diggings

A Simple Experiment

Holmes and I had a pleasant dinner, and shared a fine Claret, at a chophouse in the Strand.

"You advertised for Taylor in the agony columns," he said. "That was an excellent idea. And it bore fruit."

"A ploy that you have used on any number of occasions, Holmes."

He nodded.

"If Taylor killed the Negro boy," I asked, "why did he do it in Limehouse? Is that where the boy lived? And why did he return to the scene of the crime the following day? Was it Taylor in disguise who took the lodgings under the name of Richard Wilmer? Or is there another Cape Colonial hunting for Bobby and Aaron?"

"The boy is thirteen," said Holmes. "Taylor took him to America when he was six. Taylor must have been in Southern Africa at the time of the Zulu Wars in '79; that is interesting."

"I do not see a connection, Holmes."

"Nor do I," he answered with a smile.

We left the restaurant, and Holmes led me down the nearby steps to the River. "Hire us a steam launch, would you, Watson?"

"Where to?"

"The Grapes, Limehouse."

I sat with Holmes in the prow of a small steam launch.

The engineer kept to a steady pace, manoeuvring smoothly around other traffic and calling out imaginative curses at the fat, sluggish Thames barges bumping along with the tide.

"Why are we returning to the Grapes?"

Holmes smiled again. "A simple experiment."

We landed at the steps of the Grapes, climbed past where the body of the young man had been recovered, and stepped again onto the small wooden balcony that jutted over the River.

"We are just on our time," said Holmes sitting and consulting his pocket watch. A boy pushed open the door to the pub and edged out holding a tray of drinks.

"Ahoy, gents," he said. "Grog's up."

"Wiggins!" I exclaimed.

"Good to see you again, Doctor. Mr Holmes was worried about us out here in the wilds of Limehouse. He doesn't know the half of it, does he?"

Wiggins distributed half-pints of ale.

"Now, to business, gentlemen," said Holmes. "Our quarry is due in two hours, but were I he, I might arrive an hour or so before my time to reconnoitre the ken, don't you agree? Let us drink up and take our positions."

"Who are we waiting for?" I asked.

"Well, let us see who turns up," said Holmes with an annoying grin. "Wiggins, I want to show you something." They went inside the bar.

Holmes emerged a few minutes later.

"Come, Watson." He led me through the pub, ignoring Wiggins leaning against the bar, and out the front door. We walked along the busy road for a few yards and turned in to the front yard of Mrs Plum's empty building, next along the riverfront from the Grapes.

He knocked softly on the door. It opened and we filed inside and up the stairs to the large front room on the floor above. The gas lamps glowed weakly. A half-dozen chairs were grouped around a large table on the terrace outside. Holmes lit a tall oil lamp that illuminated a tray of drinks and glasses.

"Well done, young man," said Holmes. "Everything is as it should be."

"Thank you, sir," said Churchill emerging from the shadows. "I'll keep watch."

"Holmes," I said, taking a seat at the table. "What is going on?"

He passed me a note. "I sent that telegram today from the central post office to Mr Taylor's suite at the Langham Hotel."

For information whereabouts Bobby meet 75 Narrow Road, Limehouse, eleven pm. W.

"I don't understand, Holmes."

Churchill appeared in the doorway. "He's here."

We followed Churchill into a dark front bedroom, and to a window from which we could see the busy street below us.

"In the opera hat," said Holmes pointing to a tall, heavyset man who had just alighted from a cab.

"It is Taylor," I said. "He is looking at the building next door."

Churchill giggled. "We took off the number plates."

"Vandals," I murmured.

"He is lost," said Holmes. "He does not know this building."

"He is going to the pub to ask directions," said Churchill, beaming at Holmes. "Just as Mr Holmes predicted."

Holmes rubbed his hands together.

"It was an unlikely hypothesis and now it is scotched. He is not the murderer of the young Negro. He does not know this building. It was worth our effort just for that. I hope that we may be able to glean more information from Mr Taylor before the night is out. Here he comes, with the helpful Master Wiggins showing him the way."

I heard a loud knock on the front door downstairs.

"It's open," Churchill whispered.

The sound of a door opening and slamming shut came from the hall downstairs.

"White?" Taylor shouted in his coarse Colonial accent. "Where the hell are you?"

Holmes met my gaze and put his finger to his lips.

"White? Come out, you cur."

Doors slammed open and closed on the ground floor. A silence, and then I heard a heavy tread on the stairs.

"White! If you have harmed the boy, I will do for you if I swing for it!"

The door crashed open. Taylor stood in the doorway flushed, sweating and breathing heavily. He wore evening dress and a top hat that scraped the ceiling. His red mutton chop-whiskers were unbrushed, and his clothes were dishevelled. He held his heavy stick in one hand and a large pistol in the other.

"Mr Maxwell P Taylor, I presume," said Holmes. "I am Sherlock Holmes. It is a fine evening. Let us take a seat on the terrace."

"A tray of beers from the pub, Wiggins," said Holmes. "Unless you prefer something stronger, Mr Taylor?"

"Scotch," he growled.

Holmes waved Wiggins off and led the way out onto the terrace. Wiggins tapped me on the shoulder.

"Dosh, Doctor?"

I handed him a half-sovereign. "I expect change, Wiggins."

He laughed a most impertinent laugh and thundered downstairs. We sat at the table outside.

"Now, Mr Taylor," said Holmes. "I must apologise for summoning you here on false pretences, but it was in your interests. The police are investigating the case of the dead Negro man and interviewing all likely foreign persons. They suspect the murderer has a Cape accent. They will get to you eventually, and you will find yourself in an awkward position."

"I did not kill that man," said Taylor.

"Doctor Watson was convinced of your innocence. I arranged this little charade to prove it. You had trouble finding the house — we had removed the house numbers — and you decided to ask for directions at the pub. Mr Wiggins, one of our confederates, guided you here."

Holmes smiled. "You do not know this house."

"Never been here before in my life," said Taylor in his thick accent, made thicker, I suspected, by drink. He looked around the terrace. "Never in my life."

"The young Negro man was murdered on the roof above us, and thrown into the Thames. I think you know, or at least suspect, who did it. And you think that the same person is searching for Bobby and his companion."

Taylor shook his head and said nothing.

"Spencer-Churchill?"

"The suspect is over six feet," said Churchill. "He's in his sixties, swarthy, with a salt-and-pepper moustache and grey hair, balding at the top. He is left-handed, and he favours his right arm. He habitually wears evening dress. He carries a leaded cane and speaks with a thick Cape Colony accent."

"My God," said Taylor softly. "You know everything."

"His name is White," said Holmes, "Richard, or more probably Robert White. You and he are, or were, close associates, probably at the Cape in diamond or gold mining. He is Bobby's natural father."

"All right, Mr Holmes," said Taylor after a long pause. "You have most of it."

Wiggins passed around drinks and we settled ourselves around the table.

"Rob White and me were in the diamond business together in Griqualand," Mr Taylor began. "That's on the Transvaal side of the Vaal River at Klipdrift. We went through our little capital in a short while. Coal to heat our sorting basins came from Kimberley at thirteen pounds per ton. It shipped to the diggings at three times that cost. Life was hard, but we struck lucky in our second year. The dig gave up garnets, agates, and diamonds of value, of considerable value."

"White was married?" asked Holmes.

"He had a woman. She was a Boer lass that he'd picked up in Natal when he lived there in the mid-seventies. Bobby was their son. It was not a marriage; it was a convenience."

Taylor drained his whisky. Churchill refilled his glass.

"The long and the short of it is that we quarrelled," said Taylor. "Not over the money, as was the usual way with partnerships; it was over the woman. She cleaved to me, sir, more than to her husband. White slit the woman's throat for infidelity. I found the corpse in their hut at the diggings when I came a-visiting. He laid in wait. We fought, and we cut each other. I had the better of the match and left him bleeding his heart out. Yes, I got the best of it and left him for dead. So I thought.

"I loaded up the wagon, and I contemplated on the boy. He was six, and as cute as a button. He had her character: soft and sweet and loving. I could not let him come home to that blood and death. It was not in me to permit it, Mr Holmes; you understand that. I rode to the kraal of his nanny, a Bantu woman, and picked him up. I discharged her with a payment, and made some excuse about trekking north with Rob: Rob White, the dead man."

He took the whisky bottle from Wiggins and filled his glass.

"The nanny, as I found out later, had her suspicions. She went to the hut, found the girl dead and White clinging on to life. I tell you straight, sir, it would have been better for all if he had expired. She sent for a wise man and he nursed White back to health with evil charms, the devil.

"I outrode a warrant for my arrest, and sold enough gems at the Cape to secure a passage on a Yankee ship to Baltimore, and thence on to Milwaukee, where I made an attempt at going for a gentleman and making a life for Bobby. I kept his name, Robert White Taylor, as I thought it fitting, despite my partner's cruelty and the murder of the girl.

"The rest I have told Doctor Watson. I brought the boy to England to give him a start as a gentleman. I discovered that it was not possible in America."

"And?" said Holmes.

"I heard from friends at the Cape that I was inquired for; someone was on my tail. I thought it might be detectives chasing me for White's killing and maybe for his woman's. Then I received a letter in New York from a man that I had thought was long dead. It was postmarked from the Cape. He required me to return the boy that for half his young lifetime had been my son. I could not do that, and I defy you gentlemen to tell me to my face that I was wrong. It would have broken my heart, and put the boy in the power of evil. I took flight with Bobby to Wisconsin, thinking to outrun the fiend. I received another threat, this time mailed in New York. He was on my trail."

"He is the boy's father," I said.

"And he killed his mother. He will murder me, and the boy, if does not get his way. He has already killed the Negro lad."

"How do you know that?" asked Holmes.

"You told me. You have his description pat, plus seven or so years of ageing from when I knew him. Who the murdered man was, and what their relationship was, I do not know, but Rob White is your murderer, sure."

"Has he made any attempt on you?" asked Holmes.

"No," said Taylor. "He will wait until he has the boy in his power. Then my life will not be worth a bent nickel."

"Why did the boy run?"

"He caught sight of a letter from White. He is a bright boy, sir. He realised that White must be his natural father. I was forced to tell what happened at the diggings."

"Did he believe you?"

Taylor shrugged. "I don't know. The servant, Long, poisoned him against me, so I gave him his notice. Bobby left with him a few days after."

"Thank you, Mr Taylor," said Holmes, standing. "We need take up no more of your time."

He turned away as Taylor stood unsteadily and held out his hand.

I shook hands and guided him to the top of the stairs.

"Oh, Taylor," said Holmes quietly. "Where were you wounded?"

Taylor stopped and touched his cheek with his hand.

"Natal."

"The Zulu War?"

"No, just a bar fight. I am no soldier. Good night to all."

He clattered down the steps and outside into Narrow Street.

"Well," said Holmes. "Do we believe our Mr Taylor?"

He turned to Churchill.

"He is still not telling us everything, sir," Churchill said. "What was that about the wound?"

"The whiskers almost hide the scar. A bullet wound in the neck and cheek. I would say that Taylor was shot from behind."

"Perhaps by White," said Churchill.

"Perhaps," Holmes agreed.

"This White is a vile fellow," I said. "How did you know that he is the boy's natural father?"

"It is a matter of elementary genetics," said Holmes. "Once you had met Taylor and confirmed his fox-red hair and green eyes, I made a calculation using the formula of Brother Mendel, the Augustinian monk, to determine the likelihood of a parental relationship with a blond, blue-eyed boy as described by Wiggins. I then determined the character differences between Taylor and his supposed son, and weighed Taylor's frantic fear that White had the boy in his power. The middle initial was conclusive: Bobby is White's son, not Taylor's. White had the power to deprive Taylor of the boy by legal as well as illegal means. When you have eliminated the impossible —"

"I wonder that White has not been apprehended by the police," I said. "The description is exact."

Churchill and Wiggins indulged in a cheap form of wit at the expense of the London constabulary.

"Why then, you may laugh," I countered stiffly. "But the Baker Street Irregulars have not covered themselves in glory."

"You're a sporting gent, Doctor." Wiggins said quietly. "A fiver at evens will see what the Irregulars can achieve."

"Done," I said.

Churchill shook his head. "Oh, Doctor."

"Money down, sir." Wiggins pulled a thick wallet out of a breast pocket and laid a crisp, white five-pound note on the table.

"Watson —" Holmes began.

"No, no, Holmes. Let us see what your vaunted gang of young miscreants may do. I will venture a fiver that they will not find White before the authorities catch him. Inspector Lestrade may be trusted to get his man; he is dogged in pursuit."

I slipped a five-pound note from my slim pocketbook. It was the last one left from that month's pension after Wiggins's earlier depredations. I laid it on the table.

"Mr White is in Room 34, St Pancras Hotel," said Wiggins. "Checked in under the name of Wolff, Wilhelm Gunter. Thank you very much." He scooped up the money and stood. "I gave the Doctor evens, as being your mate, Mr Holmes. With any other gent, I would have made it a tenner at three to one. I had the honour of the Irregulars to uphold."

I sat back in my seat as the four-wheeler rattled through the empty streets.

"Did you replace the house numbers?" I asked.

"We did, Doctor," said Churchill instantly. "And all in the right places too, with no larking about."

"What now, Holmes?" I asked as we alighted at Baker Street.

"Sleep, Watson," said Holmes. "We will see what tomorrow brings. Do not over-tip the driver. He has not brushed the benches in the cab this age."

The Servant Cooped

"Good morning, Watson," said Holmes the next morning. "I am glad to see that Mrs Hudson is on her feet again."

I joined Holmes at our breakfast table.

"She is indeed," I replied. "How did you guess?"

"No guesswork is involved, my dear sir. It was a matter of simple deduction: here is a perfect six-minute boiled egg, and these are faultless toast soldiers. Our breakfast is undoubtedly the work of our dear landlady. She is up and about."

"She can hobble to the kitchen. Indeed, she insists on doing so."

I leafed through the *Daily Telegraph* as I sipped my coffee. I will not say that I was in the best of humours, but Mrs Hudson's excellent notion of breakfast: streaky bacon, sage-stuffed sausages, black pudding, eggs, and fresh roasted coffee, had returned me to a state in which I might be cajoled into a reasonable humour, given a quiet day with no surprises.

"I see that the Caspar case has disappeared from the front pages," I said. "I expect both sides in the dispute were happy to let it fade from view. It will be a salutary lesson to that flighty class of females who think that they may venture forth unescorted to any part of London at any hour. It has scotched their plans, I fancy."

"I would say, Watson that the effect of this case will be absolutely to the contrary. It will open the West End to women. It will fox every policeman in the metropolis to determine the women 'on the game' and those who are merely exercising their right to assemble freely at Piccadilly Circus and to chat merrily with passing strangers."

"Monstrous," I exclaimed.

"There is already a scheme to erect a public convenience for women in Oxford Street."

I blinked in astonishment. "Good Lord. I trust that no municipal funds are involved."

"From now on," said Holmes, "any police officer who makes a mistaken arrest can expect to be pilloried as Endaby was pilloried. And the Southern Railway will have to run excursion steamers from Boulogne-Sur-Mer and special trains from the coast to accommodate the influx of French *boulevardiers* who will throng our streets looking for likely lasses."

"Nonsense, Holmes, you mistake the virtuosity of our English maidens."

I heard a faint knock at the door, and Churchill entered.

"Ah, our stormy petrel," said Holmes. "Coffee?"

"Thank you, I have already breakfasted."

Holmes raised his eyebrows.

"Twice, sir: once with Billy and once with Mrs Hudson. She is much improved."

"How are your parents?" Holmes asked.

"Quite well; still taken up with affairs. They are at Blenheim Palace. The Jubilee Ball is scheduled for tomorrow."

I coughed and shook my head slightly, willing Holmes to catch my meaning.

"You did not join them," said Holmes. "That was selfish and unpatriotic of you. I am surprised; you were coming along so well."

Churchill blinked at him; I saw tears welling up and I drew in a breath to remonstrate with Holmes.

"Watson acquainted me with your exemplary extraction of Mrs Plum's evidence," Holmes said. "But just because you are showing such promise in the science of deduction, does not mean that you can neglect your familial duties. Blood, in your case in particular, is blood. You must send a telegram expressing a wish that the dance is a success. Do not forget Her Majesty's good health."

Churchill beamed, and I sighed in relief.

"I have a job for you this morning, Spencer-Churchill," Holmes continued. "I intend to make certain enquiries at the British Museum. I must assist the prosecution in the appalling Netherlands-Sumatra Company case in Brussels. I will ask you to stand by at the Reading Room, as I may have to send urgent and confidential messages."

Churchill snapped a crisp salute.

"What are your plans for this morning, Watson? Should you care to join me in a visit to the Diogenes Club? My brother Mycroft requires my presence at eleven precisely for a conference on the Brussels case. I should warn you that the luncheon menu at the Diogenes consists entirely of dishes that once graced the tables of the members' public schools: the leathery toad is in its hole, the comforting roly-poly pudding is smothered in sulphurous yellow custard."

"Thank you," I said uncertainly. "I have several neglected tasks, duties rather, that I should attend to. And we must surely inform the police of the whereabouts of White. He is the chief suspect in a brutal murder. And Bobby and the servant are still in danger."

"I have Herr Wolff close watched. Hotel employees have been bribed, the cab rank nearest to the hotel is ours to a man, and the Irregulars are camped opposite the door. He may yet lead us to Bobby. It is no part of my charter as a consulting detective to do the work of the regular police. Lestrade has an excellent description of the man, although White has gone to some trouble to disguise himself. That was how he was discovered."

He went back to his newspaper and there was a long pause.

I sighed. "How?"

Holmes flipped down a corner of his *Times*.

"He hired a couple of brutes to aid him in his search for the boy. One of them enquired at a pub in Southwark where top-quality slum paper might be had."

"Slum what?"

"False documents. The enquiry passed through several intermediaries and a deal was struck for White to become Herr Wolff. The papers were excellent. They were produced by a master screever."

"Wiggins's uncle!" I said.

"Exactly."

"Ha, so much for the honour of the Irregulars. White came to them!"

Holmes shrugged. "A good regiment is invariably a lucky one. Is there any coffee left? I must away too, Watson. That devil, Baron Maupertuis wove a most intricate web in eight countries and three empires. Let us meet at the British Museum at five."

Billy entered with a brown-paper wrapped package for Holmes.

"What do you make of it, Watson?" He passed the package to me.

"It is about quarto-sized. It could be a book: a thin, light book." I examined the address and stamp. "Posted in Holborn yesterday. Addressed in a female hand in violet ink, wrapped with best-quality brown paper and twine; the paper is very well-folded."

"Notice that all the knots are the same, exactly spaced," said Holmes. "There are no unsightly wisps of twine to spoil the effect."

"Yes, and the corners are as tight as could be."

"Well?"

"I confess that I have nothing more to add, Holmes."

"Ha! I wrote to Gamages Store in Holborn some days ago to suggest an addition to their range of lead toy soldiers. I proposed that they commission a set of detectives. I enclosed a portrait photograph of myself in a suitable pose, pistol at the ready. As a courtesy, I recommended Alphonse Bertillon and François le Villard in France and Von Waldbaum in Germany as other candidates.

"I was hesitant at first. Bertillon, although technically brilliant, has little practical knowledge, and he is quite possibly insane. Le Villard merely plods along in the profession, limited by his intellectual capacity. He also has a considerable paunch. I wrote to Barker, my rival across the River, and he has agreed to the scheme. Mr Leverton of the Pinkerton Agency is still considering —"

"What of Lestrade?" I asked. "Or Inspector Gregson?"

We mopped our eyes with our handkerchiefs and stifled our laughter as Bessie came in and cleared the breakfast table.

"My brother Mycroft has naturally refused to become involved. I have no doubt that this package, so professionally wrapped with the special paper used by the parcels department at Gamages, contains the proofs for the lead figure of me brandishing my pistol."

"I see, Holmes," I said, taken aback. "You told me of the models; I had no idea that your proposition was serious."

He snipped the twine with a pair of scissors and unwrapped the package.

"I hope that they have not portrayed me in some eccentric position, or wearing a ridiculous hat, or smoking a peculiar — oh, it is a book."

I looked over his shoulder. "It is an illustrated edition of the poems of Edward Lear. Who is it from?"

Holmes opened the cover. "There is an inscription: ah, just so." He put the book down on the table, open to the inscription. "I must away. Come, Churchill."

He left; I read the inscription.

To my knights in shining armour, Mr Holmes, Doctor Watson and Master Churchill, with my enduring gratitude.

It was signed, Elizabeth Caspar, Miss. A pale-blue envelope peeked out from halfway through the book. I opened it to the page and found that the letter was addressed to Churchill, Holmes, and to me.

At lunchtime, I determined that the alphabetical order of the names of the addressees suggested an equality that allowed me to open the envelope and read the contents.

It was an invitation to tea at five that day.

I put down the letter and looked at the strange little drawing of a chick that accompanied the poem on the page in which the envelope had been inserted. I read the poem aloud, beating the rhythm in the air.

"WHO, or why, or which, or what,
Is the Akond of Swat?
Is he tall or short, or dark or fair?
Does he sit on a stool or a sofa or chair,
OR SQUAT?
The Akond of Swat?

Is he wise or foolish, young or old?
Does he drink his soup or his coffee cold,
OR HOT,
The Akond of Swat?

Does he sing or whistle, jabber or talk,
And when riding abroad does he gallop or walk,
OR TROT,
The Akond of Swat?"

The doorbell rang downstairs.

"Does he wear a turban, a fez or a hat?
Does he sleep on a mattress, a bed, or a mat,
OR A COT,
The Akond of Swat?

When he writes a copy in round-hand size,
Does he cross his T's and finish his I's

WITH A DOT,
The Akond of Swat?"

A voice joined me from the stairs.

"Can he write a letter concisely clear
Without a speck or a smudge or a smear
OR BLOT,
The Akond of Swat?"

"Ah, Churchill," I said as he appeared at the door.

"I was at the British Museum, Doctor. Guess what I found."

"I need to send two telegrams," I said. "And then I have a mind to teach you percentages. A subaltern friend in Afghanistan said that they always came up at the entrance examination for Harrow."

"Oh dear," said Churchill. "Surely not in the modern age?"

"It is almost three o'clock. We started our studies at one. What percentage of an eight-hour day have we spent on our mathematical endeavours?"

"A considerable one, Doctor," said Churchill yawning. "A large proportion; much, in fact."

I sighed. "Are you not ashamed, young man, that our pageboy knows more of percentages than you, the son of a Chancellor of the Exchequer?"

"Not at all, sir," Churchill said sharply. "Billy gets a cut of all tips to deliverymen and telegraph boys. If my income were thus dependent, I would be a mathematical genius."

We arrived at the pavement outside the British Museum and found Holmes waiting with a uniformed attendant.

We dismissed our hansom, and the museum attendant hailed us a four-wheeler. I batted away a street urchin trying to get my attention; another boy accosted Holmes. I checked my pocketbook — thinner after the latest depredation by Wiggins — and found that it was untouched. As we drove off, I was astonished when Churchill waved goodbye to the attendant in a most familiar manner. He called out that we would see him at nine at the World Turned Upside Down, south of the River.

"You received my wire, Holmes?" I asked as I checked my watch. "We are expected at 19, Southampton Row for tea with Miss Caspar and Mrs Barker. I sent them a polite note of acceptance. We will just make it on time."

Holmes called to the driver.

"Spitalfields, the Ten Bells."

He turned to me.

"Spencer-Churchill has been busy. However, I have other, more urgent, news. Wiggins just sent me word. They have cooped the servant, Aaron!"

10. Leather Apron

The Ten Bells

We alighted at a busy corner of Commercial Street at the entrance to a dilapidated pub.

On one side of the pub door was a clutch of street vendors selling broken crockery, a few wizened apples, some sad fish, and a nest of cracked and leaking meat pies. On the other, a man rested against the wall, sweating profusely and smoking a pipe. He was sandwiched between two enormous advertising boards showing the Spiritualist harridan Mrs Weldon commending Pear's Soap.

The road was hot, malodorous and noisy. A deafening crush of wagons and buses crowded the highway and pedestrians ducked and weaved between them. The only patch of colour in the grey and brown mass of humanity and horseflesh that teemed in the roadway behind us was a muscular, magnificently-whiskered, scarlet-uniformed, sergeant of Foot Guards. He was in undress uniform, with his forage cap at a rakish angle on his head. He adorned the passenger seat of a parked wagon that carried a hoarding advertising life insurance.

"No, no," said Holmes glancing at the sergeant as he swept past the advertising boards and entered the Ten Bells public house. "Wrong shade of scarlet, buttons awry, and sabre instead of sword. The Duke of Cambridge would be livid."

"His sabre is rusty," said Churchill following him. "And his boots are cracked."

"His moustache is surely non-regulation," I added as I closed the door behind us.

I reflected on the gullibility of the lower classes. Would they flock to buy insurance for the spurious reason that a fake guardsman endorsed the company? Would they buy a particular brand of soap because Mrs Weldon, the celebrity agitator who had brought several doctors and madhouse keepers to court, suggested that it protected her complexion? The sad truth of course was that —

"Doctor," said Churchill breaking into my reverie, "four pints of ale."

I mopped my brow with my handkerchief, and handed him a coin.

"A half for you. Why four?"

"Wiggins is with Mr Holmes, Doctor. They are beckoning us to that table in the corner."

I followed Churchill. He pushed through the throng of pub patrons, men and women, all loud and smelly, and bought the drinks with a worryingly practised ease.

"Evening, Doctor," said Wiggins as we sat. "The Irregulars strike again, eh?"

I ignored the gibe.

"Wiggins, the facts," said Holmes.

The boy bent forward and spoke in a low tone.

"First off, we'll need our wits about us here, gents. I'm not known, and this ain't a polite neighbourhood."

I snorted.

"You may laugh, Doctor, but you haven't seen the half of it."

"So I am constantly being told."

"I had a couple of the lads on the canary paint shop, like I told you gents," Wiggins continued. "We was stretched, what with the so-called Mr Wolff laired in his hotel, his two heavy geezers searching for Bobby's track down Blackfriars way, and then keeping a watch on Mutton-chops. I had to take on extra help, Mr Holmes, all accounted for down to the farthing."

Churchill laid a tray of pints of ale on the table. I took my drink and sipped; it was surprisingly good, cool and nutty.

"What of Aaron?" Holmes asked.

"Yesterday, as the second shift at the canary paint shop was going in, one of the lads spots a Negro man slipping in with them. The man goes up to the office and stays ten minutes. Then he's off along Brick Lane until he turns in to a court. It was a regular rookery, gents, and my lad was unknown and not young enough to pass unnoticed. He reported, and I talked to a mate or two, and found a bloke that knows the courts back there. He's the bald cove in the leather apron up at the bar."

Holmes looked over my shoulder. I held Churchill's gaze and resisted the temptation to turn around.

Holmes turned back to Wiggins and raised his eyebrows.

"I know he's a rum-looking bugger, sir, but you work with what you've got, as my old dad used to say. Leather Apron says he knows where the Negro kid lives, and he can lead us there. I bunged him five-bob up front with a half-sovereign more promised on delivery. And I don't trust the bugger an inch."

Holmes touched my arm.

"Do you have your pistol with you?" he murmured.

"I do not, Holmes. I did not think that there would be much call for a revolver while taking tea with Miss Caspar. It is heavy, and it makes my jacket pocket droop. Do you have yours?"

Holmes frowned and shook his head. He turned back to Wiggins.

"Can your Leather Apron persuade the boy to join us here for a drink?"

Wiggins slipped out of his seat. I followed Churchill's gaze and found that I could see the bar reflected in a mirror above us. I saw Wiggins approach the counter and buy a cigar. He stood next to a short, fat, bald man in a black shirt and waistcoat wearing a filthy leather apron. I watched as Wiggins accepted a light for his cigar and sauntered back.

"No go, sir. He says Aaron is main flighty, all of a quiver, like. He won't talk on it, but he knows he's being sought."

"Does he not go out?" asked Holmes.

Wiggins shrugged. "He goes out with the dippers. He does the fakery that gets folks staring and not minding their pockets, the Faint, maybe, or a Bedlam dance. People stare at him anyway for his colour. On the street he's mob-handed, so he feels safe."

"Nothing on the boy, Bobby?"

Wiggins shook his head.

"What do you think, Watson?" Holmes asked softly.

"I have my cane," I said. "I'm game."

Wiggins slid the end of a thick leather cosh out of his sleeve and grinned.

"We must send Churchill home in a cab," I said firmly.

I was surprised when he did not object. He merely smiled.

"I'm sorry," I said. "But you must think of these courts as primitive jungles teeming with wild beasts that would think nothing of killing you for your socks."

He laughed. "Whatever would wild beasts do with my socks? Anyway, they wouldn't get them. Not while I have this."

He laid a two-barrel Derringer pistol on the table. Wiggins instantly swept it off and into his lap. He blinked and looked nonchalantly around the pub.

"I say," cried Churchill. "You beast —"

"Shut it," said Wiggins fiercely. "You'll have us all in lavender."

"Give it here," I said.

I surreptitiously examined the gun under the table. It was the same type that I had seen Taylor carry. I looked a question at Churchill.

"Mr Taylor gave it to me," he said with a sulky look. "He didn't have much ammunition and it's not readily available here. I told him about a shop in Bond Street where he could buy a bigger gun that takes our regular loads."

I looked at Holmes. He shrugged.

"If the police go in to this rookery," said Wiggins. "If they go in, mind, if they venture in at all, they go in threes with barkers drawn. We ain't in Lambeth now, gents."

"We are four," said Churchill with a wide grin.

I passed the pistol to Churchill under the table. He nodded and slipped it into his waistband. I pocketed the two cartridges I had removed from the chambers.

"Gentlemen," said Holmes standing.

Leather Apron left the pub without looking at our party. We followed at a slow saunter.

The Rookery

Outside on the street, the heat was even more oppressive.

The insurance wagon was gone, and in its place was a reeking butcher's cart. A line of men wearing sandwich boards trooped past. They advertised a bare-knuckle fight between Joe Heenan, the Mayo Mauler, and Bethnal Green's own, Bruiser Bonner. The contest would take place that evening in the yard of the Horn of Plenty pub just up the road in Dorset Street.

"Might we look?" asked Churchill.

"The fight starts at seven-thirty," Holmes answered with a grin. "We might have a peek."

I shook my head. Bare-knuckle fighting was a dying art, strangled by public opinion. Several bouts had ended in death or permanent injury.

"I expect the police will intervene and forbid the fight," I said.

Churchill muttered something under his breath, that, had I caught it, might have earned him a cuffed ear.

We followed Leather Apron along Fournier Street and into the teeming heart of Brick Lane. I saw Holmes tuck away his gold watch chain, and I did the same. I regretted putting on my pearl tiepin that morning. Churchill followed along whistling a tune from *The Mikado*.

Tawdry shops lined both sides of the street, some of them already lit up to lure customers to their wares. Here the fruit on display glowed freshly, and from a dozen steaming cook-shops an enticing smell of roasting meat and baking pies wafted along the pavement until it was overpowered by the stench of crowds, smoke, and horse dung.

We passed a line of glaring gin-palaces, a dark church and mission hall, and a rickety house that advertised waxwork facsimiles of several gruesome murders. Horrible pictorial representations with all the dreadful details were posted up outside. Boys, men, and women, some with children in their arms, crowded through the doorway, pennies in their hands.

A street preacher stood on a box in front of a shop overflowing with rags and made-up clothes. A dozen loafers gathered around him as he discoursed on the wages of sin. We edged past the crowd. I had one hand on my pocketbook and my cane at the ready. The owner of the rag shop, evidently a foreigner from his accent, called to the preacher to move on; he used a coarser term. The crowd's sympathy was with him; a pair of laughing oafs knocked the preacher off his box and pushed him away. If not for our mission, I should have intervened.

Suddenly Leather Apron was gone, and Holmes with him.

"This way, Doctor," said Churchill, plucking me by the sleeve.

We went through a narrow archway into a festering alley that was as almost as dark as in full night. The cobblestones at my feet were uneven and slimy and the walls were streaked with filth. The alley opened out after twenty feet or so into a dim, high-walled court with several gloomy openings. Leather Apron leaned against the far wall, next to an arch. Holmes stood to one side, lighting a cigar. A dozen or so men lounged at the doorway openings, or against the walls, and smoked evil-smelling pipes. Bare-headed women with thick arms clustered in twos and threes, or sat gossiping on steps leading to upper passages dark as Erebus. A shallow gutter or conduit ran down one side of the yard; a black liquid oozed along it and overflowed where masses of stinking, decaying filth blocked it. The yard, gutter and passageways teemed with half-ragged children, fighting, chasing one another or kicking a broken bottle back and forth. The older boys lounged in doorways smoking and spitting like their elders.

A pack of little children swarmed around me, begging and plucking at my clothes. As Churchill shooed them away, I saw the loafers exchanging glances and looking in our direction. I took a firm hold of my stick.

Leather Apron slipped into another alleyway; I followed close behind Wiggins and Holmes, with Churchill at my heels.

People moved aside to let us by. Some cowered fearfully in doorways staring wide-eyed as we slipped past, others spat in our path and only moved to let us through with evident distrust and disdain. I had an uncomfortable feeling that a hostile group was assembling behind us. I pushed Churchill ahead of me. The smell of foetid, unwashed bodies and fresh and festering excrement was overpowering. I rejected the impulse to cover my nose with a handkerchief. I ignored the sleek brown rats that pattered unconcernedly before us.

We entered another tiny square, again with a dozen black doorways off it and an open sewer running through it. No children played here, and no loungers stood in the doorways. Two ragged bundles that might have been bodies lay against the wall to the right. Leather Apron stopped in a doorway on the other side. He lit a pipe. I looked away and fumbled for my cigar case.

Not a glimmer of light came from the dark windows that looked out onto the court from the four floors above us. I turned back and thought I caught a signal from Leather Apron to Holmes: a gesture with his pipe stem and four fingers extended. Then Leather Apron was gone.

Holmes nodded.

I followed Churchill and Holmes into the dark doorway that Leather Apron had indicated. A brick staircase with no handrail stood before us.

"Stay in the hall, Wiggins, and guard our backs."

Wiggins nodded, his eyes wide and fearful.

"Fourth floor, right," whispered Holmes.

He led the way. More rats squeaked and gibbered at us as we ascended. I heard no other noise except our heavy breathing. The stench was worse: the staircase had been used as a communal lavatory. I staggered and thought I might swoon and topple off the unguarded edge. I pulled out my handkerchief and breathed through it. Holmes and Churchill quickly followed my example.

From the third floor, the stairs were steeper and made of tarred wood, sticky to the touch. We stopped at the fourth floor landing. Again, there was no rail, only a black yawning empty cavern down to the ground level. We had not seen a single soul on the stairs or in a doorway.

Holmes lit a match. In its flare, I saw a door of peeling wood blocked the doorway on the right. It hung on one hinge.

Holmes knocked with his stick. "Aaron?"

There was no answer. I thought I heard a scuffle within; it might have been rats, or my imagination.

Holmes called again.

He looked back at me and gestured a warning, then he took hold of the edge of the door and inched it open. It ground across the uneven wood of the landing, the single hinge creaking.

"Aaron?" Holmes called again. "We are friends —"

The door burst open, Holmes fell back, and I was knocked off my feet onto the landing. I heard a screech and a thump, then silence.

Holmes and I heaved ourselves up. He lit a match.

The slim body of a young man in a dark suit lay face down, hanging off the edge of the stairs. Churchill clasped his trouser legs and held him.

"He's slipping," he said.

Holmes and I grabbed at the body and hauled it onto the landing. Holmes lit another match and I examined him. It was a young Negro, in his early twenties perhaps. He looked like the corpse at the mortuary, except he was younger and very thin. He was unconscious, but he was breathing.

"He fell over me," said Churchill. "He banged his head on the wall and bounced to the edge."

"Well caught, Churchill," said Holmes.

He turned to me. "Will he live?"

"It's a serious contusion, but yes. He needs be cleaned up, and by the look of him, given some proper nourishment."

"Let us withdraw. Take a shoulder, Watson. For God's sake watch yourself on the way down."

He handed Churchill his box of matches.

"Light our way."

We staggered down to the ground floor. No one was in sight, but I had a strong feeling that we were watched. The light was slightly better in the archway, and I examined the young man again.

"We should get him into the air, Holmes," I said.

Holmes put his hand on my shoulder. I looked up and saw that, where before the yard had been empty, a throng of ragged, silent men now stood at the entrances to the alley and the rooms. They stared across the court at us. Each carried a club or a blade.

"Back inside the entrance, Watson. We must make a stand. Our backs will be to the wall."

Holmes and Wiggins guarded the entrance, as Churchill and I dragged the body back inside the dank corridor and laid the man on the paving stones.

I joined Holmes, my stick at the ready.

The men stared; they made no move to molest us. I stepped forward.

"I am a doctor," I said. "I must take this young — oh."

A lump of masonry crashed into the yard from above. It missed me by inches. It spattered us all with dust and fragments. A woman screeched from a window above us.

"Resurrection men! Body snatchers!"

The crowd growled menacingly and moved forward, brandishing their weapons.

"Oh, dearie me," said Wiggins.

"Wrong place, wrong profession, old man," said Holmes, smiling at me. "They are not fond of doctors."

The mob circled, shuffling and shoving, elbowing one another. Their eyes gleamed with bloodlust.

A high-pitched scream and Churchill burst past us and into the centre of the yard. He wore no jacket or shirt, and he had blackened his torso and face with dirt. His hair stood up wildly. He whooped like a Red Indian. He pointed one arm up into the air.

Crack!

The sound of a revolver shot reverberated around and across the court.

The crowd fell back; some ran. A man in a battered bowler crossed himself and cried, "It's Spring-Heeled Jack!"

Churchill ran, whooping and twirling, up the alley towards Brick Lane.

"Quick," said Holmes. "Now's our chance."

I leapt back into the hall and slung the body over my shoulder. Churchill's shirt and jacket lay on the floor and I threw them to Holmes. Wiggins led the way at the trot, slapping his cosh in his hand. I followed with the body. Holmes covered my back.

"It's not Spring-Heeled Jack," I heard Holmes cry. "It's his ghost come up from hell!

Angels and ministers of grace defend us!
Be thou a spirit of health or goblin damn'd,
Bring with thee airs from heaven or blasts from hell,
Be thy intents wicked or charitable,
Thou comest in such a questionable shape
That I will speak to thee: I'll call thee Winston Spencer-Churchill,
Spring-heeled Jack!"

We trotted along the alley towards the first court. I glimpsed Churchill ahead of Wiggins. He screeched, whooped, and capered wildly.

Crack!

Two shots, I thought. He has fired both barrels of his Derringer. I reached the first yard, empty now, and paused to catch my breath.

"We must get on," murmured Holmes. "They are recovering their wits."

In front of us, a group of armed men emerged from a doorway and blocked off our escape route to Brick Lane. I heard cries and the rustle of running feet, and a mob surged from the alley behind us.

"*Incidit in Scyllam qui vult vitare Charybdum*," muttered Holmes.

Wiggins gave him an odd look.

"He falls in Scylla's jaws who would escape Charybdis, or out of the frying pan and into the fire," I said. "I translate loosely."

"In here," said Holmes. We backed into a dark doorway. I laid the body down again and checked the corridor behind us. It was clear.

I joined Holmes and Wiggins outside. The mob of men advanced slowly towards us. They grinned, laughed and brandished their knives, clubs and blackjacks. Behind them, a crowd of woman egged them on with a horrible blackguardism that made me shudder to think that humankind could descend to such a level.

I had a nauseating sense, in this festering, black, warren, of the depths of depravity to which humanity could sink. I saw how brutish that most noble piece of work, man, might become when his life were lived apart from the intellectual stimulus of art, music, books, travel, and the soft, health-giving influences of verdant fields and fragrant flowers. The brutish denizens of the rookeries were inured to filth and indecency. They lived in the absence of the gentle amenities: stimulating companionship, friendly intercourse with educated and cultured friends, and interesting enterprise; they had no experience of the pure and moral atmosphere of team sports —

"Wake up, old chap," said Holmes clasping my shoulder. He stepped forward and stood in the centre of the yard, his feet set wide and his top hat at a rakish angle, and stared at the mob with contempt. He grasped his walking stick in both hands and held it out before him. Our attackers watched wide-eyed as he slowly twisted the silver knob at the end of the stick and unhurriedly slid out a thin sword blade that gleamed in the weak light. He swished the sword into the salute.

"Come, then," he said.

"Come: you but dally;
I pray you, pass with your best violence;
I am afeard you make a wanton of me."

I stood beside him on one side, Wiggins on the other. I held my stick high and cried my war cry.

"Do his people like him extremely well?
Or do they, whenever they can, rebel,
OR PLOT,
At the Akond of Swat?"

Wiggins gave me another odd look.

The crowd parted, and a short bald man stepped forward: Leather Apron. He hefted a long-handled single-bladed axe. He grinned at us.

Holmes nodded to him and took up the *en garde* position.

I heard a wild whoop and the sound of running feet came from the alley in the direction of Brick Lane. Churchill bounded out of the archway and skidded to a halt next to Holmes. Behind him, a group of tough-looking, heavy-built men stalked into the court. They carried weighty clubs and long, wicked-looking knives. They ranged behind one man who had his hands bandaged and strapped with strips of leather.

"Evening, Mr Holmes," he said.

"Good evening, Bruiser," said Holmes, sheathing his sword stick.

Bruiser Bonner turned to the mob across the yard.

"Nice evening," he called to Leather Apron. "You out for a stroll or what?"

Leather Apron walked into an open doorway without a word. The mob dispersed as suddenly as it had gathered.

"I hear that you are against the Mayo Mauler," said Holmes, offering Bruiser a cigar. "Should I have a guinea or two on you?"

"The Fancy's betting two to one on the Mauler, sir. Was I you, I'd go a few guineas at that price."

"I shall do so."

Blackmail

We carried the young Negro man along Commercial Street and into the Horn of Plenty public house.

The pub was packed, but Bruiser cleared a place for us. I examined and cleaned the young man's bruises and brought him around with smelling salts.

"That's Aaron," said Wiggins. "Certain sure."

He was a handsome young man with the same light-brown complexion as the dead man. In the light, the resemblance between him and the corpse from the River was evident. I gave him a glass of brandy, and he began to come around. Churchill returned from a wash and brush up in the kitchen of the pub.

"The hero of the hour," I said, raising my glass.

"Well done, Churchill," said Holmes.

"I just heard that Leather Apron's a bleeding pork butcher," said Wiggins. "You saved our bacon."

"What was that theatrical nonsense with your swordstick, Holmes?" I asked with a discreet wink at Wiggins and Churchill.

"In war, moral power is to the physical, as three parts out of four," he replied. "Who said that young man?"

"Napoleon," said Churchill. "I ran here to the Horn of Plenty. Mr Bonner recognised me immediately. He and his mates were eager to help."

The pub emptied as the bare-knuckle fight was announced. The Fancy was directed to a secret location farther up the street and assured that refreshments would be available at a special rate for the duration of the bout.

Churchill and Wiggins went to see the fun. Aaron sat between Holmes and me, looking dazed and nervous.

"You are Aaron Long," said Holmes. "You are a friend of Bobby White Taylor. You were valet to Mr Maxwell P Taylor of the Cape Colony and Milwaukee, and you ran off with his son and his silver."

"I didn't run off," he said sullenly. "I was dismissed."

"You took the valuables."

"I helped Bobby take them. Anyway, I was owed back wages."

He spoke in a marked American accent.

"Mr Taylor," I said, "accuses you of persuading his son to run away."

"Bobby needed no persuasion to run."

"Tell us about it," said Holmes. "We know that both Taylor and White are looking for you and for Bobby. We tracked you. So eventually will one of the men searching for you. We have most of the pieces in our hands. We want to find Bobby and help him."

"He needs no help from you."

Holmes stood.

"It seems we have wasted our time and risked our lives for nothing, Watson. This young man scorns our help."

"The man in the apron," I said. "He sold you out once and will again."

Aaron looked down at the table and shook his head.

"Very well," I said. "But you must visit the coroner, Doctor Purchase at 9, St Laurence, Pountney Hill, EC, to identify the body held there."

Aaron looked up startled.

"The body of your brother," said Holmes. "We believe that he was killed by Mr White."

I ordered another brandy for Aaron. Holmes sat again, and we waited.

"Yep, it must be my brother, Joe. He went to see someone two days ago, on business."

The drink arrived and he gulped it.

"What kind of business?" I asked.

"Blackmail," said Holmes quietly.

Aaron looked up. "Looks like you know it all."

"Tell us from the beginning," said Holmes.

Aaron explained that about seven years previously in Baltimore his mother had found a job as cook for a rich foreigner, Mr Taylor. She had moved into his house, and taken Aaron, then fifteen, with her.

"What about your brother?" asked Holmes. "Did he live with you?"

"No, my ma threw him out before that. She said he was a bad 'un. He ran with a wharf gang. He got picked up and jailed for robbing a warehouse and blackjacking the guard."

Aaron said that Mr Taylor had given him a job as valet, but his real job was looking after Bobby. Mr Taylor wanted his son to grow up like a gentleman. He hired private tutors, and he wouldn't let the boy out of the house except to ride with his riding master. Aaron was fifteen and Bobby six, but Aaron had been Bobby's only friend. Aaron would smuggle him out to a theatre show, or a baseball game, or just to play softball on the street.

"Mr Taylor would get mad if he found out and he would beat us; mostly he didn't catch us. Bobby is like a kid brother to me."

I nodded. "Go on."

He shrugged. "Everything was all right until about two years ago. Then Mr Taylor went crazy. He put new locks on the house. He hid guns in every room and drank more than he had before. He was half-drunk most of the time, cussing us out and laying into me. His craziness was connected to letters that arrived from Southern Africa. When I brought him one in the post he would go wild."

"You moved to Wisconsin," said Holmes.

"Yeah, to Milwaukee, all of a sudden, and in winter. The furniture had to follow by train. We set up in a grand house, and things went on as before. Then, another letter arrived, this time from New York, and Mr Taylor went *loco* again. One evening, as I sat in a whisky joint on the lakeshore, my brother Joe sat next to me. He said he'd just got out of prison and he had tracked us from

Baltimore. He'd been to see Ma, but she wouldn't talk to him. She wouldn't open the kitchen door.

"He said that if he could talk to her face to face he would make things right. Joe was my older brother. When I was a kid he was my hero, like Bobby and me, so I said I'd help."

Aaron explained that they got back to Mr Taylor's house too late to see their mother. They were drunk. He found a place for Joe to stay in the attic and he went to bed.

The next day the house was in an uproar. Several valuable items, including Mr Taylor's watch and over a hundred dollars in cash had been stolen from his bedroom. The thief had also rifled his papers.

"My mother and me knew for certain sure that it was Joe. What could we do? I hoped he would go away and not bother us again."

He shook his head.

Aaron explained that he had been in the same bar as before a few days later when Joe had walked in again. He didn't deny that he was the thief. On the night of the theft, Mr Taylor had been out drinking until late so Joe had plenty of time to examine the documents in his desk. He had read threatening letters from Mr White in Cape Town and New York that told the story of the fight at the gold diggings and that that Bobby was not Mr Taylor's son. Joe planned to blackmail Mr Taylor; he would threaten to tell the story to Bobby and the police. He wanted Aaron to come in with him.

"I said I wouldn't. Joe said he'd tell Mr Taylor that he and I did the theft together if I didn't go along."

"So, your brother blackmailed you and Taylor," I said.

Aaron shook his head.

"When I got home, the house was again in a racket. We were to sail to England on a liner in three days. I was glad. I thought that we would be rid of Joe. Ma thought so too."

Aaron described their arrival in Liverpool and the setting up of their house in London.

"We were all homesick after a couple of months, except for Mr Taylor. Bobby was wild to go back to America. He didn't understand all these moves and why he was kept like a prisoner. He went crazy when Mr Taylor told him he was putting him to an English school."

Aaron laughed.

"He poked the old geezer at one school in the nose and kicked another in the bawbles."

He grew serious again.

"Then the letter from Joe arrived, postmarked in Liverpool the day before. I had been in London since we arrived, but Mr Taylor figured me as the blackmailer. He compared my writing to the handwriting of the letter and naturally, it was similar. He didn't know anything about Joe, so he blamed me. He threw me out. He said if he saw me again, or heard that I had contacted Bobby, he would hunt me down like a dog. I knew that he would too."

"Bobby went with you?"

"He did not."

Aaron explained that Taylor had locked Bobby in his room for a week, then kept him indoors. They could communicate through a kitchen window left open by Aaron's mother. Aaron told Bobby about White, and the next day the boy had run. He had taken clothes and valuables. They had wandered across the River in search of lodgings and fallen into the hands of Wiggins and his pals.

"They were main good to us, sirs," he said. "We ran because we heard that a man was on our trail, asking for us in Lambeth and offering a reward. We hopped it to Whitechapel."

"How did your brother find you?" asked Holmes.

"I went to see my ma. I would meet her at a pub near Mr Taylor's house. He bushwhacked me as I left."

"How did Joe know Taylor's address?" I asked. "He sent a letter there from Liverpool. And how —"

"He found correspondence between Taylor and the house agent in London in Taylor's bureau," Holmes said. "And he obtained money from White by telling him that he could contact Bobby and persuade him to run to him. He bought his steamer ticket with that money. Is that right, Aaron?"

"Exact, sir."

"Your brother visited White in Limehouse to squeeze him," said Holmes. "But White knew by that time of Bobby's disappearance. He killed Joe out of hand."

Aaron put his head in his arms and rocked back and forth.

"He and Taylor both think that you know where Bobby is. Do you?" Holmes asked softly.

"Bobby ran when I brought Joe to our lodgings in Whitechapel. He guessed that he would turn him in to Taylor or White, whoever would pay the most. He said that he would never go with either of the cowards. I have no idea where he is."

"Cowards? Not murderers or attempted murderers," I said. "An odd choice of words."

"Do you know where Bobby is?" Holmes asked again.

Aaron shook his head. "I searched, but I couldn't find him. Maybe he has gone back to America. That's all he wants to do."

Holmes sat back, and I checked my watch.

"We are far, far too late for tea with Miss Caspar."

11. A Certain Spectacle

A Noble Scar

Wiggins and Churchill came through the door with a crowd of disgruntled punters.

"The Mayo Mauler by a knockout in twenty-two minutes, eight seconds," said Wiggins. "The Fancy is disappointed, Mr Holmes. They expected a fearful spectacle of pugilistic delight. There's talk of fight fixing and dark deeds. Time we was off."

"Watson, give me five sovereigns, will you?"

I took the coins from the meagre collection in my waistcoat pocket and counted them out.

"You know, Holmes, our finances —"

He scooped the money up and gave it to Wiggins.

"Bruiser," he said. "To ease his injured pride."

I could hardly complain. Wiggins disappeared outside.

"How are you for the ready?" Holmes asked Aaron.

He shrugged. "All right. We do the street fakements, and we've another dodge or two on."

"The canary dyer's pay roll," said Holmes.

Aaron looked at Holmes in astonishment.

"You worked there for a while recently to eye the ken and the security arrangements on payday," Holmes said. "I would bet that your brother took over your job on the day he died. Were you ill?"

"On a lead for Bobby," said Aaron "Turned out to be a false trail."

"You went back to the factory to collect your back-pay."

Aaron nodded.

Holmes stood. "I would advise you to hide yourself somewhere until Bobby is found. I would suggest the docks; you would not stand out there. Better still, work your return to America and turn your back on this foul affair. It has cost the life of your brother. Do not trust Leather Apron."

We shook hands and Aaron slipped away.

We four musketeers climbed into a four-wheeler and drove away from Whitechapel, not without, for me at least, a sense of considerable relief.

"A near-run thing, Holmes," I said.

He nodded.

I turned to Churchill. "You owe me an explanation, young man."

"Mr Taylor gave me six shells with the palm gun. I have two left, plus the two you tea-leafed, Doctor."

Again, I could hardly complain.

Holmes looked at his watch. "We shall be seven minutes late."

"I say, Doctor," whispered Churchill pulling at my sleeve. "In the pub, Mr Holmes called me Churchill, not Spencer-Churchill."

His bright-eyed grin lit up the carriage.

"This is more like it," said Wiggins.

We stepped from the cab at the World Turned Upside Down in the Old Kent Road. He gazed about him, put his thumbs in his waistcoat pockets and took a deep breath. "Give me south of the River any day."

It was dusk, and the bright-coloured windows and fanlight of the pub were most welcoming after our ordeal in the black, foetid courts of Whitechapel. I eyed our young companion.

"Churchill," I said, "I am concerned that you are getting too familiar with these sorts of premises. I suggest that you wait in the coffee public house across the road with Wiggins. I do not expect that we will be —"

I followed my friends into the pub.

The World Turned Upside Down was a far cleaner and less malodorous establishment than the Ten Bells. The clientele was mixed in gender, and composed of members of the more responsible echelons of the lower class: tradesmen, small shopkeepers and their wives, neat clerks and perhaps a smart artisan or two from one of the respectable trades, watch repairers possibly, or bookbinders.

Holmes enquired at the bar, and the barman directed us to an upstairs room. There, in a quiet corner booth, sat the attendant from the British Museum that I had seen earlier. He was still in uniform, nursing a pint of ale. Wiggins held out his hand and I paid for pints of beer and a sarsaparilla for Churchill.

He made the introductions.

The attendant was Mr Henry Hook from Churcham in Gloucestershire, fifteen miles or so from Ross. I smiled as I heard his West Country burr. He had been married when he joined the Army at the relatively old age of twenty-six. He had been mustered into the twenty-fourth regiment of Foot and thereafter served in Africa.

He had a long oval face with a high brow and brushed back, slightly greying hair. He wore a moustache similar to my own; his was straggly and unbrushed.

The drinks came, and I sipped my beer. I saw that Wiggins had given Churchill a pint of beer, despite my clear instructions. I was about to remonstrate with him when I checked myself and looked instead at the pair of medals pinned to the attendant's chest.

I coughed and spluttered in my pint glass as I recognised the first medal. It was the Victoria Cross, Britain's highest award for gallantry in the field of battle.

Churchill kindly slapped me on the back until I recovered.

"You are Private Henry Hook," I said rising from my seat, "hero of the defence of Rorke's Drift against the Zulus in '79. The Queen awarded you the Victoria Cross. May I have the great privilege of shaking you by the hand? Why did you not tell me, Churchill?"

I shook hands with Hook, and a thrill of emotion caught me off guard. I stiffened my upper lip.

"Pleased to make your acquaintance, Doctor," said Hook. "In fact, I received the medal from the hands of Sir Garnet Wolseley at the Drift about seven months after the engagement."

I sat in a daze.

"The young man told me that you were in action, Doctor, in Afghanistan."

"I was," I said, smoothing my moustache.

He nodded and smiled. "Then you know."

Churchill beamed at me, and I nodded shyly.

"I understand," said Holmes in a tart tone, "that this gentleman has information for us."

Churchill explained that he had noticed Hook's medals when he waited for Holmes at the British Museum. Hook was the Umbrella Attendant at the Reading Room. He had told Churchill something of his history. He had purchased his discharge from the Army a year or so after the battle and gone home. In Churcham, he found that he had been declared dead, his property had been sold and his wife had remarried.

He had moved to London and obtained a job as labourer, and then got the job as Inside Duster, then Umbrella Attendant at the British Museum.

"What has this to do with the missing boy?" asked Holmes testily.

"Nothing much at all to do with Bobby, Mr Holmes," Churchill said with a grin.

Holmes stood, glaring at the boy. "While I appreciate the great service Mr —"

"Tell us about White and Taylor," Churchill said to Hook.

Holmes flopped down in his seat.

"Them buggers," said Hook. "I don't like to think on them."

"Another pint, Mr Hook?" said Churchill.

"Very kind." He drained his glass.

"All round, then, Doctor?" said Wiggins with a grin.

Hook described the layout of the Rorke's Drift mission station on the late afternoon of 22 January 1879, drawing in beer on the polished wood of the table. I could see that he had done this many times before. He described a lazy day cooking for the patients in the hospital and helping Surgeon Reynolds with various small chores.

"Not a soul suspected that a dozen miles away the men that we had said 'Goodbye' and 'Good luck' to the previous day were either dead or standing back to back in a last fierce fight with the Zulus.

"Two gallopers appeared. They were white officers of the Natal Native Horse. They brought word that a British column had been massacred across the Tugela River at Isandlwana with more than five hundred soldiers and many more native levies killed. Four thousand Zulus were on their way towards us.

"My officer, Lieutenant Bromhead, ordered preparations for a fighting withdrawal, but Acting Assistant Commissary Dalton, an old campaigner, had a quiet word and persuaded him to stay and fortify our post. Mr Dalton is the reason I am alive and talking to you gentlemen, for if the Zulus had caught us on the march, we would have suffered the sad fate of our comrades at Isandlwana.

"Now, we had about a hundred men of B Company, 24th Foot, plus officers and details, making us a hundred thirty-nine in all. There was a much larger force of native levies, the Natal Mounted Police and the Natal Native Contingent.

"A strong troop of Natal Native Horse fleeing the battle at Isandlwana swept by our position; they would not join us. That was the signal for our levies to lose heart and scarper. The NNC jumped the barricades and ran off after the riders. I can't say the lads were much bothered; we never thought much of the native troops. Most of them hadn't guns, and those that had weren't properly trained. No, we wasn't much bothered when they buggered off. We gave them a cheer and a wave."

Hook took a long gulp of beer.

"What got our goat was seeing their white officer, Captain Stephens by name, galloping off with them. Then their white NCOs legged it too. That irritated the boys, and there was a splatter of musketry. Corporal Anderson fell dead; shot in the back. Colour-Sergeant Bourne brought us back to discipline. He was a fine man, though young for the position at twenty-five, and short for a CSM at five-foot nothing and a half. The two other corporals escaped; I could see that they were wounded."

He looked across at me.

"You know it, sir: it's being with your own lot that stiffens your backbone. We were Welsh and English, all hugger-mugger, with even a few Scotch to tell the truth, but we were all the Queen's twenty-fourth regiment of foot, and proud of it. We had a proper gentleman in our officer, Mr Bromhead; that makes a difference. Of course, he would have killed us all by marching us off into the hills if Mr Dalton had not been there. We would have followed Mr Bromhead to our certain deaths without a murmur. That's the difference a true gentleman makes, sir.

"Them NNC corporals were local, see? Half Boer by the sound of them. They weren't part of the regiment, so they had nobody to look out for, and nobody to look out for them. They were Corporal Robert White, and Corporal Max Taylor."

Holmes fidgeted while I insisted that Hook tell us of the battle and especially his part in the heroic defence of the hospital.

"How many men did you lose?" I asked.

"Seventeen, with eight seriously wounded."

I looked at Churchill.

"Just under a quarter of their force, Doctor."

"And the Zulus?" Holmes asked.

"Hundreds, sir," said Hook. "I read it was more than five hundred."

"One-eighth," said Churchill on a look from me.

"Rifle against spear," said Holmes pursing his lips.

"No, sir, Mr Holmes," said Hook. "If I may correct you there, sir. Most wounds I saw on the Zulus were from the bayonet. The Zulu had a lot of respect for the British bayonet."

"And the man behind it," I said.

He smiled and nodded.

"I was teetotal before the battle, and during too. When Colour Sergeant Bourne gave out a tot of rum to each man the next morning, I took mine gladly: 'Oy', says he, 'what's this?' as I held out my mug. 'Well', says I, 'I feel I want something after that'. That is how I went on the drink; it has been the ruin of me. Cheers."

Holmes stood.

"Thank you, Mr Hook; it has been a fascinating story. I congratulate you on your experience and your bravery. We must get along now." He rattled down the wooden staircase to the lower floor.

I stood and solemnly shook Private Hook's hand again. It was hard to believe that he was, like me, in his thirties; he looked much older than his years. I looked closely at the decoration he wore on his breast.

"Would you like to hold it, Doctor?" He slipped off his Victoria Cross and placed it on my palm.

"Be careful," he said. "I got a wound in the scalp during the battle, but my worst stab came from Sir Garnet Wolseley with this." He turned the cross over to reveal two long, sharp prongs.

"They were to make it easy for Her Majesty to award the Cross from horseback with one hand. Sir Garnet impaled me on my breast. I still have the scar."

I passed the medal reluctantly to a wide-eyed Churchill. We shook the gallant soldier's hand again, and with glistening eyes, I followed Holmes downstairs.

We said our goodbyes to Wiggins and took a four-wheeler. On the way home, Churchill and I talked over the engagement at

Rorke's Drift. Eleven Victoria Crosses were awarded to the garrison.

"I once had the privilege of meeting Surgeon James Henry Reynolds, VC," I said. "He saved many lives at Rorke's Drift and played a gallant a part in its defence. I have therefore shaken the hand of two members of that distinguished company of heroes, one in Lambeth and one in Eastbourne. Remind me to send a letter of apology to Miss Caspar for missing tea."

We returned to our home in Baker Street with some satisfaction at our progress.

and Mrs Hudson served tea; she handed me a telegram

"This is from the amiable Doctor Purchase at the mortuary," I said opening the envelope and scanning the contents. "He says that he has been in communication with his colleague for Whitechapel and — good Lord, Holmes, it is Aaron. It must be Aaron."

"Dead?"

"A young Negro man bearing a remarkable resemblance to the body in his keeping found dead in Commercial Street, Whitechapel two hours ago."

"An axe wound?"

I nodded. "Leather Apron."

I indicated my intention to visit Doctor Purchase to acquaint him with our identification of Joe, Aaron's brother, and our suspicions regarding the killer.

Churchill looked glum.

"The body will wait," said Holmes. "This young man wishes to invite us to a certain spectacle. His mother's friend, Prince Kinski, offered to get tickets to *Ruddigore*, the latest Gilbert and Sullivan offering; he was able to get some harder-to-obtain tickets. Am I right, young sir?"

"Exactly, Mr Holmes," Churchill said shyly. "But I don't know whether it's quite fitting now, after Aaron —"

"Aaron made his decision, and it was an unwise one. He was warned. Our duty now is to Bobby. Show the doctor your tickets."

Churchill took out an envelope from his jacket pocket and slipped three long tickets onto the table. "It's Buffalo Bill's Wild West Show, Doctor. It is a gala event, with a grand reception afterwards."

I examined the luridly-illustrated tickets. "From the posters that I have seen plastered all over the city, I see that the Wild West Show is entirely unrestrained; it is rowdy, undisciplined, and uncultured. It says on the ticket that they exhibit herds of wild beasts, and gun-toting cow girls — whatever they are. The illustration shows shabbily-dressed riders being chased by a band of feral Indians. *Ruddigore*, on the other hand, is, by all accounts, pleasingly droll, melodic and —"

"How did you know about the tickets, Mr Holmes?" asked Churchill.

"Ha, your vandalism gave you away. As a subtle hint to Prince Kinski that you would prefer Wild West tickets to those of a comic opera, you cut the advertisement for the Buffalo Bill show out of my *Times* two days ago. I noticed an envelope addressed to His Highness with our outgoing correspondence. I am sure that the cutting was attended by a heart-rending begging letter. Your face when you opened your correspondence this morning told me that you had been successful."

Churchill nodded, beaming. "I asked for four tickets, three for us and one for Billy, as he's dying to go. Prince Kinski has decided views on my mixing with members of the servant class and he refused my request." He looked at me.

"What? My dear boy, you must realise that Wild West tickets are very expensive, particularly compared with tickets for the Savoy Opera." I turned to Holmes. "Our finances have been seriously depleted recently."

"Take it out of Churchill's salary. Do you agree, young man?"

"Oh, yes, Mr Holmes, with pleasure."

"We will see what we can do," Holmes said. "Thomas Cooke's have the agency for the tickets, I believe. Send Peterson from the commissionaire's stand. Money, Watson."

Churchill bounded out the door.

"Salary, Holmes?" I asked. "What salary?"

The Boy on the Palomino

Our cab joined the throng of carriages moving slowly towards the new grounds at Olympia.

Billy was one of our party. We had battered our poor pageboy with so many injunctions to behave himself before his betters that he had visibly shrunk an inch or two, and he started like a nervous colt at every noise.

We could tell that we were nearing the grounds by a strange animal smell that pervaded the air.

"Buffalo," said Holmes.

"Or Red Indians," I suggested in a jocular vein. My remark went unappreciated by my fellow passengers.

Prince Kinski's influence provided us with comfortable seats in a section close to the Royal Box. Application of five-shillings grease to an attendant afforded us an extra seat for Billy, much to the annoyance of an American couple with a fat child who shared the box.

I saw Holmes nod and wave his stick in his Bohemian fashion to several acquaintances.

"That is Mr Oscar Wilde," said Holmes. "I acted for him in an unconventional little matter."

I looked across into a neighbouring box where the aesthetical gentleman sat with a lady that, by his attentions to her, was clearly his wife. His hair was ridiculously long, of course, but his dress was far more sober than I would have expected. I had read some of his pieces in the *Pall Mall Gazette*, and thought them clever and well argued. I had recently seen a notice that he was to take over as editor of the *Lady's Journal*. His manners did seem foppish — he turned, smiled at me and waved. I was instantly abashed and furious with myself for staring at him. I hid behind my programme until he looked away. I confined my future attentions to the scene before me.

A vast, circular, open ground lay before the stands. On one side, we could see the tents of the Indian Village with people moving about and smoke rising in curls. On the other, various groups of performers assembled. Small herds of wild animals wandered here and there. I saw a buffalo for the first time, and I realised that Holmes had been right about the source of the stink. There were also deer, antlered elk, and wild horses. A huge backdrop of white-topped mountains and curious rock structures curved behind the ground giving a vivid impression of reality. A band played popular songs. I recognised 'Yankee Doodle' and another tune the name of which escaped me.

I consulted my programme. The ground was a third of a mile in circumference, it claimed, and could hold forty-thousand spectators. Ha, ha, I thought, we are in America now, where everything is bigger and, at least according to its inhabitants, better.

A sudden flourish of trumpets, and a rider cantered into the arena on a fine chestnut horse. I knew him instantly as Colonel William F Cody, the frontier scout and impresario popularly known as Buffalo Bill. His long, black hair spilled over his shoulders, and he wore the same tan jacket, black trousers, long leather boots, and wide sombrero hat that adorned the thousands of colourful lithograph posters that had blanketed London that season. His moustache and beard were even more luxuriant in real life than in the portraits plastered across the city. He received a loud cheer and a burst of applause.

He bowed to each section of the crowd. "Welcome to Buffalo Bill's Wild West Show!"

A rider entered the arena at full pelt carrying the largest American flag that I had ever seen. It looked big enough for the topmast of an ironclad. He drew up in a cloud of dust beside Buffalo Bill and waved the flag furiously. The band played the national anthem of the United States and the crowd stood. Men doffed their hats, Holmes and our party included, and officers saluted. The American couple in our box sang the anthem lustily.

At the conclusion of the song, they beamed at us, and we bowed. International relations were thus restored to amiability, and we cordially traded slices of Mrs Hudson's beef loaf for four oranges and a paper bag of butter-popped corn; the latter was tasty, but had to be eaten by hand, a ticklish business if one were loath to have butter dripping from ones chin, or one's fingers made gummy.

A blaze of naphtha light lit the Indian village. It was dawn. The Indians came out of their tents and performed their morning routines. A cry of welcome, and another tribe arrived and they danced an energetic war dance together. It was a strange, shuffling, rhythmic dance that relied on heavy drumbeats and ululation by a top tenor to provide the melody.

I had to cuff Churchill and Billy for improvising their own war dance in our box.

The scenes followed one another, all with highly elaborate costumes, settings and lighting effects.

Immigrants travelled west in their covered wagons, with Buffalo Bill scouting forward. He led a hunt in which cowboys chased the shaggy buffalo herd around the stadium to whoops of delight from the boys and yells of encouragement from me.

Night fell, and the settlers slumbered. A red glow appeared in the distance. It grew, and to cries of alarm, the Indians identified it as a wildfire. That scene, and the following that simulated a cyclone, were masterpieces of stage illusion.

In an interval between scenes, Buffalo Bill exhibited his prowess with the lasso, and in shooting, at full gallop, glass balls thrown into the air by another rider. Two young ladies, whose names I could not catch above the wild roars of the crowd, demonstrated an astonishing celerity in marksmanship using repeating rifles.

The high point of the performance was the series of mock attacks by Indians on a wagon train, and their gallant rescue by a company of scouts under the command of Buffalo Bill.

As a finale, he called for volunteers to act as passengers in the Deadwood Stage Coach on a journey fraught with danger of attack by wild Indians. I turned to make a remark to Churchill and found that he and Billy were gone.

"I say, Holmes," I said.

He pointed to where the boys were clambering aboard a closed carriage similar to the mail coaches we used before the railways took over. The coach was lightly built, but six horses pulled it.

The Deadwood Stage started with a jerk that almost had it over on its side; it sped away with driver and guard clinging to the box. A column of Indians gave chase, whooping, screaming, and firing guns at the coach. The coachman whipped the horses into a wild gallop. The coach bounced over ruts with sometimes all four wheels in the air. Heads appeared at the windows as the passengers fired back at the Indians with rifles and pistols. Churchill was to the fore, shouting imprecations that would have made his mother blush: they made me blush.

Buffalo Bill galloped out into the arena and surveyed the scene through a telescope. He formed his troop of scouts and chased the attackers. The Indians fled and the Deadwood Stage Coach pulled up at the grandstand to tumultuous applause. Young Churchill, as *de facto* leader of the coach passengers, shook the hands of Buffalo Bill, his scouts and the Indians.

He returned to our box with Billy, both sweating furiously and with bright feathers in their hats.

"Colonel Cody said that Billy and me would have plugged at least a dozen Indians, had it been real," cried Churchill, panting furiously. "Mr Red Shirt, the commander of the attacking column, said something cordial in his language that I could not quite catch."

"Billy and I," I corrected.

The boys took their seats to a smattering of applause from our neighbours.

The band struck up 'God Save the Queen', and we stood. I was pleased to see that the American family stood stiffly and put their hands over their hearts in an affecting gesture.

Churchill leaned towards me during the anthem, unfolding a sheet of paper.

"Do you see that short cowboy in the big white hat?" he murmured.

I looked at the line of riders at attention during the Anthem. Towards our end of the line, a shorter man or boy sat on a palomino pony holding a huge, white Mexican hat to his heart.

"On the Palomino?"

"That's Bobby White," Churchill said. "That's the missing boy."

Peace Pipe

We joined the stream of people leaving the stands and crossing the ground towards the gates and the Great American Exhibition souvenir shops.

The lights went out behind us as the gas and blazing naphtha lights were extinguished, and a sprinkling of stars and a bright Moon appeared overhead.

Holmes pulled us aside.

"This way." He tipped his top hat over his eyes in his droll way and marched off towards the Indian village with his cane over his shoulder, whistling 'Yankee Doodle'.

Churchill, Billy and I followed.

We passed through the village, where the natives were preparing their dinner. Haunches of meat roasted across open fires, and Indian ladies stirred aromatic soups or stews in pots. I doffed my hat and uttered a friendly 'How', the universal Indian greeting according to my programme, to the natives as we passed.

Holmes stopped a young Indian boy and asked for directions to the residence of Colonel Buffalo Bill. The boy pointed towards a large, brightly lit tent across the plain. I gave him a thruppenny-bit that he took with a practised air and a wink. We walked on, ignored, through a group of grazing buffalo, and pitched up outside the indicated tent. It was more like a marquee, and a party was in progress. The tent flaps were drawn back and a large group of people chatted and drank Champagne both inside and outside.

"Holmes," I said urgently taking him by the arm. "We cannot just —"

"Oh, hello, Mr Phelps," Churchill said to a tall, elderly gentleman with prominent grey side-whiskers. He wore a sash across his breast covered with glittering orders and medals.

"Winston, how are you, my boy?" the man said in a strong American accent. "How is Lady Randolph? And your father, of course."

"Quite well, sir. May I introduce my companions, Mr Sherlock Holmes, Doctor Watson and Master William? This is Mr Phelps, the United States Ambassador to Great Britain."

We shook hands. A waiter offered us Champagne and, despite a stern look from me, Churchill and Billy claimed glasses from the tray.

Holmes chatted with Mr Phelps — he could be sociable if the mood took him — while I looked about me at the heterogeneous collection of people conversing under Mr Cody's canvas. About half the guests were men in evening attire or dress uniforms, with their ladies beside them in glistening gowns and scintillating jewels. The others were men and women in cowboy or Indian dress; they had evidently come directly from the show. I did not see young Bobby.

I noticed that the two boys had found a buffet table in one corner of the tent and I walked over to keep an eye on them. At one end of the table, a tall Red Indian man stood with a boy of about Churchill's age. Churchill, a sandwich in one hand and a Champagne flute in the other, chatted with the boy. The contrast between young Churchill in his dusty, modern clothes and the Indian boy, resplendent in a waistcoat of white porcupine quills and grey leggings, was very striking. The Indian boy had a pair of red feathers stuck in his long, plaited hair.

"Oh, Doctor Watson." Churchill said indicating the tall Indian. "May I present Chief Red Shirt of the Oglala Lakota?"

The chief had a handsome bronzed face, high cheekbones, Asiatic eyes, and a straight Roman nose. He wore a high-necked white cotton blouse with red leggings. His most remarkable feature was his hair, which fell in a graceful tumble of curls to below his waist. A single white eagle feather was tucked behind his head. It brushed the canvas roof of the tent. In his hand, he held a long, highly decorated wooden pipe.

We shook hands. Red Shirt had a firm grip and looked straight into my eyes in a manly way.

"How?" I said.

"Good evening," he replied affably.

"This is Running Deer, Doctor," said Churchill introducing the Indian boy. "He speaks English."

Red Shirt smiled at me and said something to the Indian boy.

"Chief Red Shirt asks whether you are a doctor of healing or of another thing," said the boy.

"I am a medical practitioner."

He looked blankly at me.

"Doctor Watson is indeed a healer," said Churchill helping himself to another sandwich. "He was in the Army and was jolly brave. He was wounded in Afghanistan, twice."

The boy translated, and Red Shirt's eyes narrowed. He spoke again.

"Is that why you carry a pistol? The Chief says that most English do not carry guns."

I did not know what to say. I had tucked the revolver into my waistband as we left home without a thought. It said something about my state of mind, and the nature of our current case, that I should so unthinkingly carry my service piece. I wondered what effect the American show, with its glorification of rifle and pistol shooting and of killing out-of-hand one's own wounded and mutilating the defeated enemy, might have on the criminal classes of London. Our robbers, usually content with a cosh or a knife rather than a firearm, might take up the American custom of continuously carrying arms. That might mean the regular arming of the police, a grotesque idea that —

The Chief put his hand on my arm and smiled. It was as if he had read my wild and anxious thoughts.

"Come," he said. "We smoke."

I followed the two Indians onto the show ground. They walked across to the Indian Village. The Chief sat on a blanket spread outside one of the tepees and before a small fire; the boy sat beside him. Several Indian girls emerged from the tepees and spread more blankets and cushions. The chief invited me to sit with a sweeping gesture. I did so with some difficulty: the ground was hard, and my leg had been awkward since I had carried Aaron from the vile court in Whitechapel.

"Squaw of Red Shirt," the chief said indicating one woman. "Great White Chief Queen Victoria."

I struggled up again and shook her hand. She showed me a necklace and medallion of the Queen. I sat, again with an effort.

Red Shirt barked an order and, at his direction, a dozen or more men and women brought saddles and blankets and fashioned a rough armchair for me. It was exceedingly comfortable. I bowed thanks to the chief.

Churchill and Billy joined us carrying plates of sandwiches, sausage rolls, and fruit. A waiter followed them with a bucket of Champagne bottles and a handful of glasses.

"Courtesy of Mr Cody," Churchill said with an impish grin.

Several Indians joined our circle, and Red Shirt and I greeted them in turn. They did not appreciate the Champagne, but a whisky jug appeared from Red Shirt's tepee and it was passed around, together with tin plates piled with delicious roasted meat. I kept a careful eye on the alcohol and the boys.

"The Chief says sorry about the stink," said Running Deer.

"Oh," I replied. "It is strong. I expect that you get used to the smell of buffalo, in time."

The Indian boy dissolved in giggles, and it took some moments and a nip of whisky before he could be prevailed upon to translate my remark to Red Shirt. The Indians laughed uproariously, abandoning their previous stern and unflappable demeanour and slapping one another on the back. They beamed across at me in the firelight.

"Chief Red Shirt," said the boy wiping his eyes and grinning at me, "meant the stink of London."

Red Shirt bowed to me and gestured for silence.

He began to speak in soft tones. Running Deer took the Chief's long pipe and filled it with tobacco from a leather pouch. The Chief spoke slowly and the boy translated sentence by sentence. It was clearly a well-told tale.

"I will tell you the story of the death of Heova'ehe," said Red Shirt. "Pa-e-has-ka killed him in the time of the Great Wars. That day, two chiefs rode from the line of warriors to challenge the Great White Hunter to a duel. The first, Heova'ehe, called out in a strong voice, 'I know you. You are Pa-e-has-ka, Long Hair, and want to fight you.' The white man shouted back, 'Come on, you red devil, and have it out.' He was a rude man in those days; he has learned better manners."

Red Shirt passed me the long pipe. I drew in the surprisingly mild and aromatic blend and blew out a long stream of smoke. A murmur of approval came from the ring of Indians.

"Heova'ehe dashed at full speed toward the white man. He, with a wild yell, rode toward Heova'ehe. They fired, the Chief with his rifle and Pa-e-has-ka with his revolver; down dropped both horses. Heova'ehe was pinned under his horse.

"With a loud war cry, Pa-e-has-ka rushed upon him. The Chief succeeded in releasing his leg from beneath his horse and again fired, as did Pa-e-has-ka, both with revolvers. The Indian's bullet cut a gash in the white hunter's arm, while he struck Heova'ehe in the leg; in the next instant, the white man sprang on him with his knife. The hand-to-hand fight lasted a few seconds, and Pa-e-has-ka drove his knife into the breast of Heova'ehe. He tore from his head the Chief's scalp and war-bonnet, and waving it over his head, shouted 'See, the first scalp to avenge Custer!'"

"Good Lord," I said. "A white man took the Indian chief's scalp!"

"That I did," said Colonel Cody squatting beside me with practised ease. Holmes sat next to Cody in an Oriental meditation position with his legs tucked under him. He had his top hat on askew and I strongly suspected that he had taken too much Champagne.

"I took the scalp of Heova'ehe: Chief Yellow Hair," Cody continued. "Then I took that of Chief Red Knife. I am Pa-e-has-ka: Long Hair. They were not my first scalps, but I hope and pray that they will be my last. Yellow Hair's scalp is hanging in my quarters if you'd like a look."

He took a long puff on the peace pipe.

Churchill nudged me in the ribs. "Running Deer says it is your turn, Doctor."

"Eh?"

"You have to tell a story."

"Oh." I looked around me for inspiration. "Very well, I will tell the story of one hundred and thirty-nine valiant soldiers defying four-thousand brave and fierce warriors, of two cowards, of three murders, and of a boy in grave danger."

I pulled out my packet of Arcadia Mixture from my pocket.

"Pass that to the Chief, would you, Churchill? He might like to fill the pipe with a local blend."

I walked away from the campfire with Colonel Cody, Holmes and the boys.

"I'll take you to see Bobby," said Cody. "The Indians call him Little Big Hat. We are the circus and Wild West rolled into one, so we attract a lot of children. You would be surprised how many London boys want to join up. Bobby has been coming to the grounds since the day we set up, more often every week. He knows horses, he can rope, he gets on with the braves, he is a willing lad, and he speaks American, so we took him on. He made out that he was an orphan. I will not say that we believed him. A couple of weeks ago, he turned up with his traps and moved in with Running Deer. The boy is half-white and speaks both lingos as you saw."

He pointed to a tent set against the painted backdrop of the field.

"That's their tepee."

"You let the Indian boy run ahead," Holmes said.

"I did. If Bobby doesn't want to see you, it's his choice. I will not force him to go with you, or with the two men that he detests who call him son. This may not be US sovereign territory, Mr Holmes, but here every man is free to follow his conscience until we pack up in the Fall."

Holmes sniffed.

"You speak as if there were no freedom of thought in England, Colonel," I said.

Colonel Cody considered.

"I was impertinent. We are your guests. I hope that you will forgive an intemperate Yankee. I will leave you here."

"Buffoon," I muttered under my breath as Colonel Cody walked away. We continued past a group of stinking buffalo to Bobby's tent.

"No, no," said Holmes. "He is more enlightened than you might think. We had a long talk in the marquee. He introduced me to some American Army officers who brought up the affair at Little Big Horn in '76. Cody infuriated them by refusing to accept that the affair was a massacre. He said that the soldiers hunting the Indians were skilled fighters with orders to take no prisoners. The Indians defended their wives and little ones. He said that the commander who led the Americans thought more of his plumage than of the art of war. These are not the words of a buffoon. Colonel Cody values truth over the regard of his compatriots."

Holmes took me by the arm with uncharacteristic intimacy.

"The Indians hold him in high esteem. It is the simple judgement, that of a ship's crew or a company of soldiers, that shows whether a man rings true or false, Watson. You know that."

We arrived at the opening of the tent. The flap was pinned back and we could see people silhouetted inside by the light of a lamp.

"Hello?" I said tentatively.

A head popped out.

"Doctor, come on in."

I crawled carefully inside with Holmes and the boys close behind me.

"Hello, Harry," said Churchill.

I looked up. "Wiggins! Damn your eyes, Wiggins. You knew that Bobby was here!"

"No, Doctor, I did not; at least, not for sure. I guessed it. I came here to tell him about what happened. I mean it's the obvious place for him to hide out, isn't it?"

"A hit, Watson, a palpable hit," Holmes said, as he gracefully folded himself onto a blanket next to me. Facing us was the Indian boy, Running Deer. Sitting next to him was a round-faced, handsome white boy in a tan frilled jacket with a mop of blond hair that almost covered his blue eyes. He looked back at me without expression.

"You must be Bobby White," I said. "You have caused us all a great deal of bother."

Bobby shrugged. "No bugger asked you to chase me."

He spoke with a slight American accent, and with the vocabulary of Lambeth.

"There, young man, you are wrong. Mr Holmes was engaged to find you by your worried friends."

The boy glanced across at Wiggins.

"Well," he said. "I didn't know of that. It was main good of you to look out for me, Harry."

"Our current client is Mr Maxwell Taylor, of Milwaukee," said Holmes.

Bobby stiffened. "I want nothing to do with him."

"He claims a father's rights," said Holmes.

"He is not my father. I do not have a father."

"Young man," said Holmes, "I have had nothing to eat since luncheon but an orange and the disgusting puffed corn dripped in butter that caused the dreadful stains on Churchill's jacket. May I invite you all to join me in a late supper? Doctor Watson is in visible distress, my joints are creaking, and Churchill and Billy will need to be carpet beaten to rid them of prairie dust. We have much to tell you, Bobby. Let us adjourn to Baker Street." He waved his programme. "We can have a 'pow-wow'."

Holmes ducked out of the tent, and I stumbled after him. My leg ached abominably. The boys followed us out.

Wiggins immediately took Holmes aside. Bobby came up to me.

"I'll go with you, Doctor Watson," said Bobby. "I'll go out of respect for Harry and because I know from his face that he has some bad news for me and I'd better hear it. But no power on Earth will make me return to that coward Taylor, or to the murdering coward, White."

"I'll get horses," said Running Deer.

"Billy, a cab," said Holmes.

A light drizzle began to fall.

Four-wheelers were impossible to find at the gates of the Olympia Ground. We caught a hansom dropping off a passenger. The driver agreed to take Billy squatting outside the doors at our feet. The other boys rode, with Wiggins looking terrified two-up behind Churchill on a huge bay. Bobby was on his palomino. He wore a giant sombrero that almost extinguished his head. The Indian boy rode bareback on a chestnut pony.

As we set off, Bobby rode alongside our hansom and leaned across to Holmes. "Churchill and me will scout ahead for bushwhackers." He slapped the leather rifle case attached to saddle and rode off.

"Do they know the way?" I asked Holmes.

He shrugged. "Cabby," he called up through the hatch. "Follow that cowboy!"

Holmes turned to me.

"Grave news from Wiggins, Watson. Herr Wolff, or Mr White as we know him, has slipped our net. The murderer of Bobby's mother, of Joe, and perhaps of his brother Aaron, is loose in the city."

12. The Deadwood Stage

Nay to Derring-do

We arrived at Baker Street in good order, although all of us were more or less damp.

Billy recruited a couple of street Arabs to help him lead the horses around the corner to the mews. Bobby hung his oversized hat on the hat stand in the hallway, and stood his repeating rifle in the umbrella bin below it.

Churchill led him, the Indian boy, and Wiggins out to the back kitchen to wash, while I tackled Mrs Hudson regarding supper.

We assembled upstairs in the sitting room. Billy served coffee and Holmes offered cigars. Wiggins took one with an insouciant air. I guarded the whisky Tantalus.

"Do you begin, Wiggins," said Holmes. "How in the name of reason did you lose White?"

"Reason weren't in it, sir. He paid more. We was outbid by the Herr. The reception clerks got five pounds each to look the other way when he scarpered, all in solid yellow gold. He paid his room bill too. It ain't natural, Mr Holmes. A fiver would have tempted a cardinal of Rome to wear blinkers. It's bad for business when foreigners are paying over the rate; it harms the local trade."

"All right, tell your tale," said Holmes.

Wiggins explained to Bobby that he had come to Holmes for help after Bobby and Aaron had suddenly disappeared. Churchill showed the portrait done by the forger, and described his first mission to Lambeth and his interviews with boys who had been approached by Mutton-chops.

"Taylor," said Bobby. "I knew it must be him on our trail, so we took off. I am sorry about that, Harry. We should have told you everything straight up, so we should."

Wiggins told Bobby about the arrested pocket-picker who had identified the corpse of a Negro man pulled from the River as Aaron. I described our visit to Doctor Purchase at the mortuary and Wiggins's inability to identify the corpse.

"White did for Joe, I guess," said Bobby. "He was a bad 'un, mind. When I heard that Joe and Aaron were in cahoots putting the squeeze on White and my dad — I mean Taylor — I ran for it. The only place I could think to go was the Show. They have been good to me."

He and Running Deer exchanged shy smiles.

Holmes described the trap that we had set for Taylor at the murder location in Limehouse. He emphasised Taylor's fierceness when he thought that White held Bobby in the house.

Bobby listened impassively.

Wiggins detailed White's transformation to Herr Wolff, and I gave a description of our journey into the courts of Whitechapel in search of Aaron. We laughed as we recalled Churchill's impersonation of Spring-Heeled Jack.

"And Aaron?" asked Bobby.

"Dead," said Wiggins.

The sitting-room door opened and Mrs Hudson and Bessie carried in trays of food.

"I have telegraphed to Mr Taylor," Holmes said. "I have a duty to my client to say that we have found you and that you are well. I have asked him to visit at ten tomorrow morning. If you should choose to call at the same time, you would be most welcome."

"I don't see why I should," said Bobby.

"I suggest that you give Taylor the opportunity to tell his side of the story before you rush once again to judgement."

"I know the story," said Bobby.

"There is also White," I said. "We found you out. So may he. Taylor has promised to return with you to America. You will have a far better chance of disappearing there."

"All right," said Bobby. "I'll come and talk. I won't go anywhere with him."

"Good," said Holmes rising. "It is getting late. Should you boys like to stay here or return to the show ground?"

"We'll go home," Bobby said. "Thanks for supper."

We shook hands.

"A word of advice, Bobby," said Holmes. "If you do not want Mr Taylor to know where you are staying, you might want to come dressed more soberly, and in a less voluminous hat."

The boys clattered downstairs.

"Well, Holmes," I said, "a most satisfactory conclusion."

I sat back in my chair and filled my briar pipe.

"Indeed," said Holmes. "Whether the boy goes with Taylor, or continues with the Wild West Show is his affair. I have written to Lestrade with all the information we have about White's alias, and with details of his confederates. They are ex-Detective Force, kicked out of the police in that betting and corruption scandal a few years back."

"Monstrous," I said. "Let us hope that Lestrade can bring them all to book without further involvement from us. I have had enough adventure for this month, more than enough. Let us say nay to derring-do until at least the autumn, if not until 1888."

I lit my pipe.

"One question must be resolved, Holmes. We must let Churchill return to his home, loving or no. I am sure that Lord and Lady Randolph —"

A thunder of hooves and a deafening rumble of wheels came from the street. We sprang to the window. A closed carriage skidded to a halt in a shriek and a shower of sparks as the wheels creased the pavement edge below us. It ground to a stop under the gas lamp outside our door. The two horses attached to the carriage capered, prancing and rearing, striking sparks from the flagstones and spray from puddles. A dark figure in a top hat, swathed in a cloak, sat on the driver's bench wrenching on the reins.

Our horses had bolted in terror, except the huge bay; it plunged and kicked with Billy hanging on to its bridle.

As we watched in horror, two men leapt from the carriage and charged into the group of boys below. They grabbed the boy wearing a sombrero and hustled him towards the coach.

"They've got Bobby," I cried. I turned and darted for my pistol. Holmes made for the door.

I heard wild screams and shouts, then bright flashes lit the window and a burst of gunfire echoed from the street below. I got back to the window just as the coachman whipped his horses and the black carriage surged away, the horses slipping on the wet road and bucking in the traces. I sighted the revolver, but could not get a clear shot.

A boy with a rifle leapt into the centre of Baker Street and fired a blazing fusillade of shots at the rear of the carriage, to no effect that I could see. The carriage roared along the street, turned on two wheels at the station, and was gone.

The attack had taken seconds. I looked down and saw Holmes standing with two boys. As I watched, a yellow tendril wrapped itself around the lamppost: fog.

I made my way downstairs and out onto the pavement. Lights were lit in the street, neighbours called across to one another from windows, and I heard the watchman at Portman Mansions furiously springing his police rattle. Billy clung to the bridle of Churchill's bay horse as it plunged and jumped; horse and boy both wide-eyed with fear.

The Red Indian boy stood on the pavement in the light from our doorway holding a large knife.

"I cut one," he said. He put his fingers to his mouth and whistled a loud, undulating sound like a birdsong.

There was an answering whinny and a clop of hooves as the chestnut horse appeared through the wisps of fog and stopped in front of the boy. He stroked its nose, said some soft words and leapt onto the pony's bare back. He galloped away, not in the direction that the coach had taken, but in the other, towards Paddington Street. I moved up beside Holmes and the two boys.

"Muster the Irregulars, Wiggins," said Holmes. "Damn this fog. Go when you've calmed the horse. Get an apple from Mrs Hudson. Ah, Watson."

"They took Bobby," I said. "I couldn't get a proper shot."

Holmes raised an eyebrow and pointed.

"I could have done for the lot of them," said Bobby waving his Winchester rifle at me. "But this danged thing is full of blanks. I shot to scare them off, but they grabbed him."

I blinked in astonishment.

"Churchill wore Bobby's cowboy hat," said Holmes.

"He wanted to try it on," said Bobby. "They got him instead of me. I don't understand what's happened to *Ciqala*."

He whistled.

I clutched at the lamppost for support. "Dear God, we've lost a Marlborough."

The palomino pony appeared out of the fog dragging a street Arab along the ground by its bridle.

"Get the hell away from my pony," said Bobby. He cuffed away the child, leapt into the saddle, holstered his rifle and took off after the black carriage.

"I shall have to inform the Churchills."

"It can wait," said Holmes. "Nobody is getting far in this pea soup. The Irregulars will be on the trail soon."

We stood at the window with restorative brandies and sodas and looked out at the yellow muck that obscured the other side of Baker Street.

"Running Deer lived up to his name," I said. "And Bobby is chasing the devils with an empty rifle. Good Lord, Holmes, an hour ago I congratulated us on a job well done."

"Billy says that he saw a group of men arrive at the mews when he went to check our horses after supper," Holmes said. "They had hired the coach, and they wanted top-quality horses for it. They must have had a watcher who saw Bobby with us. They lay in wait at the top of the street for him to emerge from our door."

"What will they do when they discover that they have the wrong boy?" I asked.

"They might not. White — we must suppose he is the devil behind this business — last saw his son when he was six. Churchill is the right age. He is quick thinking enough to fake the accent; his mother is American."

"I don't agree, Holmes. Churchill will plant his legs wide; his arms akimbo, declare that he is Winston Spencer-Churchill, son of Lord Randolph Churchill, and demand that White take him immediately to Blenheim Palace. What is that noise?"

A tremendous clatter of hoof beats, a loud rumble of wheels and jingle of harness came from the street below.

We looked down into Baker Street as a huge glare of light illuminated the street. A crowd of riders reined up below us, followed by a six-in-hand coach.

"Is it White come back for Bobby?" I asked.

Holmes smiled. "It is the Deadwood Stage."

I pocketed my loaded revolver and joined Holmes and Colonel Cody on the pavement outside our door. Billy served nips of Scotch from a tray to us and a dozen or so riders dressed in cowboy clothes that sat on their horses in the road. It was ridiculously like a stirrup cup being served to a pack of foxhunters.

The flimsy-looking stagecoach with its six feisty horses was parked on the other side of the road. Our neighbours again hung out of their windows and clustered in doorways looking annoyed.

"It took a while to harness up," said Cody. "Then we had to reload our guns with fighting ball and fix some naphtha lights to the Deadwood. And the Indians had to put on their war paint."

"Where are they?" I asked.

He pointed up the road. "They're picking up the trail."

I chuckled. "You expect to follow a carriage trail through London in a fog with a pack of Red Indians? Are you serious, Colonel?"

"Speaking as one tracked by Lakota Sioux for three days over rocky ground and very, very, nearly scalped, I would say that I am, Doctor," he replied warmly.

The Indian youth, Running Deer, rode up and said something to Colonel Cody.

"All right, boys," he called to his men. "Let's get after them."

"Is this legal?" I asked.

"I am holder of the Congressional Medal of Honour, Doctor," said Colonel Cody stiffly. "And as Colonel of Scouts in the United States Army, I have the authority to lead these men — with Annie as female sharpshooter — on the trail of those no-good kidnapping varmints, and no power on this Earth will stop me. Excuse my French there, sir."

"I say, Colonel —"

"We have formed a posse, Doctor. What did you expect me to do, summon a beefeater?"

He rode away shouting, "Yo!" to his men.

"What infernal cheek, Holmes."

"Come," he replied. "Let us hasten aboard."

We clambered up into the stagecoach and grabbed straps as it lurched forward and the driver whipped the horses into a spanking trot.

"Posse, Holmes?" I asked.

"*Posse Comitatis*," he said. "To have the right to an armed retinue. I translate loosely. The sheriff may appoint deputies to help catch a felon. The hue and cry."

"An ancient practice."

We hung on to the straps as the coach swung past Baker Street Station and around the corner.

"There is a legal precedent," said Holmes.

I inwardly doubted that Colonel Cody's medal or his American rank gave him sheriff's rights in the Cities of London and Westminster, or in the Metropolis generally. It was, I thought, typical of Americans of the Cody type that he would attempt to transfer their injudicious blend of mob and six-gun rule to the streets of London.

I looked out of a side window as we clattered along York Terrace. The fog was lifting. I saw that the Indians ranged ahead, hooting and calling "Yip, yip". Colonel Cody and his riders had formed a column in front of the stagecoach. It was, I had to admit, a stirring spectacle.

Cody held up his arm. "Column, yo-oh!" The coach shuddered to a halt.

Two fiercely war-painted Indians rode up dangling a white-faced police constable between them.

"Good evening, Constable," Holmes said gently. "Did you see a closed black carriage go past an hour ago, driving furiously?"

The policeman nodded and his helmet flopped over his eyes.

"Direction?"

"Portland Place, sir."

Holmes pointed south. The Indians dropped their policeman and raced off yelping.

"Thank you, Constable," I said, patting him on the helmet and giving him sixpence.

We started again with a jerk and a body slid off the roof and slipped down beside the door. Holmes and I grappled it and dragged it into the coach. We sat him on the opposite seat.

"Billy," I said with a sigh.

It was a very effective method of tracking.

The Indians scooped up several more police constables and private citizens and presented them to us for examination. We directed our column towards the River.

"Do you remember, Holmes," I said as we passed along Oxford Street, "how we raced home this way in the fog, with the street Arabs lighting the way and the policemen trotting with us? When Mrs Hudson was in danger from the arsenic poison."

"You have read my mind, old friend," he said. "I was thinking exactly that thought."

He leaned out of the coach window and called over a splendid Indian who had ridden alongside us from Baker Street. The Indian ran his horse closer and peered through our window. His cheeks and brow were striped in red, black and white; his eyes were outlined in yellow. He wore a magnificent eagle feather headdress and carried a huge silver medallion on a chequered ribbon around his neck and a necklace formed of dozens of tufts of hair tied into beads.

"Good evening, Doctor," he said with a huge grin.

"Red Shirt," I said.

"Could you kindly fetch Colonel Cody, Mr Shirt?" asked Holmes.

A few moments later Cody stopped the coach and appeared at the window.

"I believe I know where we are going, Colonel. Mr White is heading for the River. He may have a steam launch already engaged. He will land at number 75, Narrow Street, Limehouse. He knows by now that he has the wrong boy; he will want to negotiate. We could hire a launch, but I fear that he will get there well before us and have time to make his preparations."

"How far is this Narrow Street, Mr Holmes?" Colonel Cody asked.

"We are close to Charing Cross. I would say about four miles to Limehouse, as the crow flies, with half that much again along our winding streets. At least there is not much traffic at this hour."

"We will ride then, sir. We will need a scout: my boys don't know London."

Holmes opened the door of the coach. "I am at your service, Colonel. I have an intimate knowledge of London."

"I'll get you a horse." Cody galloped off

"I say, Holmes, is this wise?" I asked.

Holmes grinned. "The Western saddle looks quite rational. It will be an interesting experience."

Holmes stepped out of the carriage, and a huge man dressed as a cowboy got in and folded himself onto the seat opposite me.

"Hiya, Doctor. I'm Dick Johnson, the Giant Cowboy."

He held out a leather pouch. "Would you gents care for a chaw of tobacco?"

The coach lunged forward tipping Billy onto the floor. I grabbed at a strap. The horses' hooves drummed on the road, the wheels hummed and roared and the leather and metal harness groaned and jingled. We built up to a spanking pace as we tore along the Strand and into Fleet Street, the driver cracking his whip and urging the horses on. We swerved and skidded around the newspaper vans that lined up for the early editions, scattering the loaders. I glimpsed Holmes at the head of our column on a gigantic black horse, whooping and waving his top hat as he jumped his mount over a stack of newspapers. Newsboys cheered and hallooed us. Billy and the Giant Cowboy hung out of the windows and cheered back. I waved a friendly handkerchief.

We pounded through the empty streets of the City past St Paul's on our left and the Tower on our right and galloped along Cable Street to the end of the notorious Ratcliff Highway. Holmes slowed the column as we entered the network of streets and alleys that led to Narrow Street.

I called Holmes to the coach.

"There's a stable in Shoulder of Mutton Alley. We can leave the stagecoach and the horses there."

I directed the coachman down a narrow lane. I smelled again the rich mixture of coffee, oil, tobacco, and the aroma and stench of a dozen other commodities. It was early morning, well before dawn, and the lights were lit in the warehouses and packing houses that lined the street.

The stable boys seemed strangely unmoved at the appearance of a dozen or more cowboys and Indians at their establishment. We left them to unharness the coach, and settle and water our mounts.

We left a guard and continued on foot. Narrow Street was much quieter than when I had last visited. The few pedestrians on the street scurried away in alarm when they saw armed men. The Indians melted into the night, treating Limehouse as if it were their native prairie. I indicated the house next to the Grapes, and it was soon surrounded. Billy led three cowboys and, astonishingly, a young cowgirl, into the pub to cover the River from the terrace.

Holmes, Colonel Cody, Red Shirt and I took up positions in a doorway opposite the gates of number 75. We held a council of war.

"Colonel Cody," said Holmes. "What are your views?"

"I'm not thinking to storm in guns blazing, Mr Holmes, if that's what you are expecting." He grinned. "I propose that Red Shirt and his braves get inside, stealthy like, and cut Mr White's throat neat as you please."

Running Deer translated and Red Shirt sliced his palm across his neck, grinning broadly. He looked immensely fearsome in his full-feathered headdress, lurid paint, and glittering medallion. I saw not the showman of the Olympia ground, but a highly trained warrior from a strong, warlike race. He reminded me of the valiant Sikhs I was privileged to soldier with in India.

"That would certainly be a solution," said Holmes with a smile. "But ideally, I would like to talk with Mr White before he is killed. He came here to be talked to. He will want to swop Churchill for his son."

"And I must warn you, Colonel," I said. "You would do well to realise that the stealthy assassination you describe would be a capital offence in this country. And that the discharge of firearms in the street is a public nuisance for which a policeman can take you in charge without a warrant."

"Thank you, Doctor," said Holmes. "Now, I suggest —"

A low whistling hoot came from the top of the house opposite. A boy in a feather bonnet loped along the edge of the roof terrace. He waved his tomahawk, pointed down, and disappeared behind the balustrade.

A light appeared in the room below as the gas was lit. A window opened. Red Shirt sighted his rifle at the silhouette framed in the window.

"Mr Holmes," called a slightly tremulous voice. "Would you like to come up?"

I laid my hand on Red Shirt's arm. "That is Winston Churchill," I said. "Let us go across, Holmes."

Holmes looked at me, saw my determination, and made no objection. We walked together across the road, through the open gates and into the house in which Aaron's brother had been cruelly murdered.

A tall, heavily built man in a dingy suit and dusty bowler stood at the bottom of the staircase.

"Barkers, gents," he said. "On the table, if you please."

Holmes placed his revolver on a dustsheet-covered table, and I put my service piece beside it. The man nodded us upstairs.

I poked him on the chest with my cane. "Understand this, I carried that revolver at Maiwand. If it is missing when I come down, I will look to you."

He blinked down at me.

Holmes took the lead and I followed him up the stairs to the next floor. The large dining room was empty, its furniture covered, as it had been on my previous visit. The French windows to the terrace stood open. Another heavyset man in shirt and braces with a pistol in his hand and a bandage around his upper arm waved us through and onto the terrace.

The oil lamp on the table and the two wall-mounted gas burners brightly illuminated the terrace. A tall man in evening dress and an opera hat stood on the far side of the table, up against the balustrade. He was in his sixties, dark-complexioned and with a full, salt-and-pepper moustache. The man held Churchill by the collar. In his left hand, he held a large calibre revolver.

"Good evening," he said in a strong Cape accent. "Take a seat, eh."

"Robert White," said Holmes, sitting at the table. "You purchased two tickets to New York on the SS Murray Castle under the name of Wilhelm Gunter Wolff and son. She sails on the tenth of this month. I must say that you had more faith in my ability to find Bobby than was justified by events. We stumbled across him by chance. You might have wasted your ticket money if we'd not found him for you by sailing day."

I sat next to Holmes.

"It is a simple matter," said White. "I bought several steamer tickets. Give me my son and I will return this arrogant brat. If not —"

He pointed his pistol at Churchill's head.

I made to jump up; Holmes hand on my arm restrained me. The boy stared at us wide-eyed and pale. I saw that he had his right hand in his jacket pocket. I was terrified that he might try to use his Derringer.

"You killed Joe Long, Aaron's brother," said Holmes.

The man shrugged.

"He strung me along. He said that he could persuade Bobby to come to me. I sent him money. He told me that Taylor had brought the boy to England. I followed and I paid Joe to pass messages to Bobby. He cheated me."

"He blackmailed you and Taylor about Rorke's Drift."

"You know about that, eh, Mr Detective? What a canny bugger you are."

"You lured him to this house."

"I took lodgings here when I arrived in London and I tried to contact Bobby. When he ran, I moved to a hotel. I copied the key."

"You also killed — or had your minions kill — his brother, Aaron."

White shrugged again. "He knew where Bobby was; he wouldn't talk."

"And you murdered Bobby's mother, your wife."

"A Jezebel, and no wife to me: no church wife anyway. She bedded Taylor so I paid her back for it."

"And your plans for Taylor and Bobby?"

White lifted his eyebrows and smiled grimly. "Kill Taylor and take my son back. I have money. We can make a new life in California. Give me my son. You can have this brat and I'll pay you well."

"It's not as simple as that, White," Holmes said. "We do not have your son."

White shook his head and pressed his pistol into Churchill's temple.

"If you cooperate, we can find Bobby and arrange a meeting between you. You can make your case," Holmes continued.

"He is a child, Mr Holmes. I am his father; I decide what is best for him. He will come with me to America, and we will start a new life. I'll marry again to give him a mother. There's a good life to be made in the West."

"We last saw Bobby in Baker Street," Holmes said. "He galloped off after you."

White blinked and his gun hand wavered.

"I shot at a rider that followed us on a palomino," he said. "I shot at glimpses of him that I saw through the fog. I hit him, I think."

Holmes said nothing.

"I hit him. Was that my son? Then, it's all over, Mr Holmes," said White. He shook his head as if to try to clear it. "I shot him down. Now there's nothing left. Why should my son die and this brat live?"

He cocked his pistol.

"Father!" A cry came from below.

White turned and peered over the parapet.

"Down, Churchill," Holmes yelled, jumping from his seat.

A gunshot split the air. White's revolver flew off in a spinning arc as Holmes barrelled into him and tipped him over the parapet. White fell into the River with a loud splash.

I saw a movement above Holmes and watched in astonishment as a slim-shouldered Indian boy swung down onto the parapet from the roof terrace above. I recognised Running Deer. He held something in his hand.

"What the devil?" a yell came from behind me. I turned. The bodyguard at the door raised his pistol.

A whirling object swished past me and a tomahawk embedded itself in the man's neck, handle down. The bodyguard dropped the gun and slumped to his knees.

Running Deer leapt onto the floor, and trotted past us, silent in his soft leather shoes. He kicked the body over, retrieved his tomahawk, and tucked the man's gun in his belt. He put his fingers to his lips and slipped inside the house through the French windows.

Holmes helped Churchill up. I took his Derringer and checked it. He had somehow contrived to load the pistol while held captive in the carriage, but thank goodness, he had not tried to use it against White and his men.

I looked over the parapet. Two steam launches were moored below, chugging quietly. One was empty. Bobby sat in the other with Wiggins beside him. He waved. Directly below me a group of men dragged White from the River.

I glimpsed a movement on my left, on the tiny terrace of the Grapes. A girl in Western dress waved her rifle.

"I told White who I was," said Churchill. He was pale, but he was already regaining his self-possession. "I demanded that he drop me at the nearest police station, take me home to Connaught Place, or deliver me to my uncle's house."

"Blenheim Palace," said Holmes with a grin.

"I could have plugged him with my Derringer when his back was turned, but it wouldn't have been sporting. And there were his associates to think of."

"You did well," I said.

Running Deer came back onto the terrace looking disappointed. "Red Shirt got the other one." He handed Holmes and I our pistols. As I watched aghast, he casually slit the throat of the man he had tomahawked and sliced off a large piece of his scalp.

Churchill joined him for a closer look.

"Great Scott, Holmes," I cried.

He shrugged. "When in Rome, et cetera."

"My dear fellow, we are in Middlesex."

It was the hour before dawn.

Colonel Cody, Churchill, Holmes, Wiggins, and I sat tight-squeezed on the outside terrace of the Grapes sipping coffee and smoking cigars.

Inside, the pub was packed with revellers from the Wild West Show, including Bobby, 'whooping it up' as they put it.

"I was wrong about Running Deer," I said. "He behaved admirably, apart from the scalping. Do you have an outline of the action in your mind, Colonel Cody?"

"I do not. Red Shirt and I crashed inside when we heard the gunshot. Red Shirt dealt with the guard in his customary civil fashion. There will be one more feather in his war bonnet by this evening."

"And one more scalp," I said stiffly.

"No, he will keep that in his tepee to bring out on special occasions," said Cody. "The Prince of Wales complimented me on my collection. Red Shirt will put a wisp of hair on a bead and hang it from his necklace."

"What?" I cried. "But he's got dozens and dozens of tufts — oh." Colonel Cody had opened his jacket to reveal a bead-studded waistcoat. Each had strands of hair attached.

There was a strained silence.

"I know you," Colonel Cody said to Churchill. "You were the boy on the Deadwood tonight. You're the Duke of Marlborough's son we chased after?"

Churchill smiled shyly. "He is my uncle."

"Maybe he'd like a ride on the stage coach. I'll send you some tickets."

"I hardly think that would be possible," I said coldly. "He is a duke of the realm."

"Last week," said Cody with a smile, "the Prince of Wales packed four majesties with him in the Deadwood. Let me see: Denmark, Saxony, Greece, and Austria. A couple of them hid under the seats when the Indians got a mite carried away. A good poker hand: four kings and a Royal Joker."

I was stunned into silence.

"Wiggins, you must have had a good view of things from the water," said Holmes.

"I saw Mr White's fall, sir," he replied, looking down at the table.

"What were you doing in a steam launch?" I asked.

"I was on my way to stir the Irregulars when I thought that Mr White might hole up in his old haunt. I thought he'd want to swop Churchill for Bobby. The Narrow Street house was the obvious place for a meet. If he'd got Bobby, he'd have used another hideout, maybe upstream and handy for a steamer to America."

"The SS Murray Castle," said Holmes. "I had Lestrade check the passenger lists of transatlantic steamers. Go on, Wiggins."

"Westminster Bridge Steps was a likely place for him to moor his launch," said Wiggins. "I came up to a kerfuffle in the road just before the bridge. A dead horse lay in the road, a palomino. A copper was there already, and a crowd. I rode on to the steps and found Mr White's carriage abandoned. I watched White and his men drag Churchill into a launch and take off towards the Tower at full speed. Then I saw Bobby holding up a steam launch engineer with his rifle, and demanding that he follow White's vessel. I smoothed things over — another receipt, Doctor — and we set off after Churchill."

The door opened and a head peeked out.

"All right here gents?" said Billy. "There's bacon and egg all round coming up. Any more orders?"

"What are you doing, Billy?" I asked.

"I've been conscripted by the Grapes, Doctor. They need help with the Show folk. They're short-handed so they offered me half a crown and all I can drink."

"Go away," said Holmes. He nodded for Wiggins to continue.

"We saw the house all lit up, and the launch tied to the rail, so we coasted up beside it. I saw the Showgirl sharpshooter take up a position here on this terrace. We heard you and White talking, and him demanding Bobby. We saw him back up to the rail with his gun on Master Churchill. Bobby shouted 'Father!' to distract him. White turned and looked down, the girl fired and White's pistol flew out of his hand and he fell into the River."

"She hit the pistol in White's hand from here," I said with some disbelief. "Remarkable."

"Annie Oakley can hit a playing card, repeatedly mind, at ninety feet with a .22 rifle," said Colonel Cody stiffly. "The card is edge on."

"White fell," Wiggins said. "Hit or not, I don't know. I looked up again and I saw that young Indian boy drop to the terrace from the roof. He threw an axe inside and swung himself after it. That was that."

"And White?" I asked.

"Bobby and me dragged him to the dock. The Colonel and Red Shirt helped pull him out and inside the house. He was dead."

"Was he shot?" I asked.

Wiggins shook his head. He would not meet my eye. "Drowned, I expect, Doctor. Or hit his head on something."

Colonel Cody smiled. "A rifle butt maybe. White killed Bobby's mama. And maybe worse, he shot the boy's horse. I'm surprised the boy didn't take his scalp."

An hour later, it was full dawn.

Churchill slept with his head on the table. Billy was inside helping clear up after the departure of the Colonel Cody and his Show people. I shared a coffee pot with Holmes.

"What of White's body?" I asked. "And those of his followers?"

"Wiggins and the steam launch engineer reached an agreement to drop the dead louts downriver in the marshes,"

Holmes answered. "That is the proper place, according to custom. White's corpse is in his hired steam launch awaiting the coroner; it is unscalped."

"My God, Holmes, have we become inured to murder? Has slaughter become a commonplace? Can we sit idly by while men are scalped in the central city of the Empire? What example are we giving to boys of Churchill's class? He and his fellows will take on the mantle of responsibility for more than 300 million subjects of the Crown across the World. We won the Empire by the sword, and by the bravery of men like Henry Hook, but India cannot be ruled by the bayonet. Even Ireland cannot be ruled so, with honour."

"There is no such thing as a gentle bullet or a tender knife, Watson. Spare no sympathy for White and his thugs."

"Did Bobby kill his father?"

Holmes shrugged. "I do not know. White may have hit his head and drowned before they could get to him."

"Pass me your tobacco pouch, Holmes. I have run out."

I filled my pipe and passed the pouch back.

"Look at the city, old friend," said Holmes. "The cranes and ships' masts, the church spires and rooftops stand out against the clear sky with a sharpness that is only seen in London before its factories, hearths and cooking fires cover the town with their smoke. Almost four million Londoners cast off the season of all natures, sleep, and start a new day full of promise and peril. Ours is a stirring era, Watson."

He gestured to the sleeping boy. "I almost envy young Churchill. What advances will the new century bring? What opportunities for a young man with brains, daring, and ambition?"

He grinned at me. "He might even make a passable consulting detective, given the right tutor."

"It is easy to wax lyrical about promise and peril and the charm of London if you are not poor, Holmes," I said, more sharply than I had intended.

Holmes gazed at me mildly over his coffee cup.

I sighed. "I'm sorry, my dear fellow, it's just that I had supposed, and vehemently argued, that we are bringing enlightenment and civilization to savages in Africa, India and through our surrogates, America. Red Shirt said something to me this evening that has shaken me. He quotes a great medicine man of his people who claims that the Red Indians and even the animals know better how to live than the white man. He said that nobody can be in good health if he does not have fresh air, sunshine, and good water."

I helped myself to another cup of coffee.

"What have we in London to make up for our fogs, our dark, festering courts, and our foul water supply?"

"Lump sugar?" said Holmes, offering me the bowl.

"I wonder," I said stirring my coffee, "if Miss Caspar has replied to my note."

####

I hope that you enjoyed reading this book. If so, you might like to read two more books in the series:

Sherlock Holmes and Young Winston: The Jubilee Plot

In the sequel, set during the summer holiday in 1887, Winston Churchill is at 221B investigating a dastardly plot to assassinate Queen Victoria during her Golden Jubilee celebrations. All is not exactly as it seems.

Sherlock Holmes and Young Winston: The Giant Moles

The third book in the series, at Christmas in 1887, sees Holmes, Watson and Winston facing Moriarty's henchmen in the matter of the Giant Moles of Hereford.

For sample chapters of the books please visit my website at:

http:// mikehoganbooks.co.uk

Contact me online at:

https://www.facebook.com/sherlockholmesandyoungwinston

About the Author

I am British, living in Thailand, and writing for a living. My interests include classic films, good books and classical music. My favourite author, after the Bard, is Patrick O'Brian.

My obsessions include the British Empire and the Royal Navy, the Roman Empire and navy, all things nautical in fact, and, of course, Sherlock Holmes and his young friend, Winston.

Also from Mike Hogan

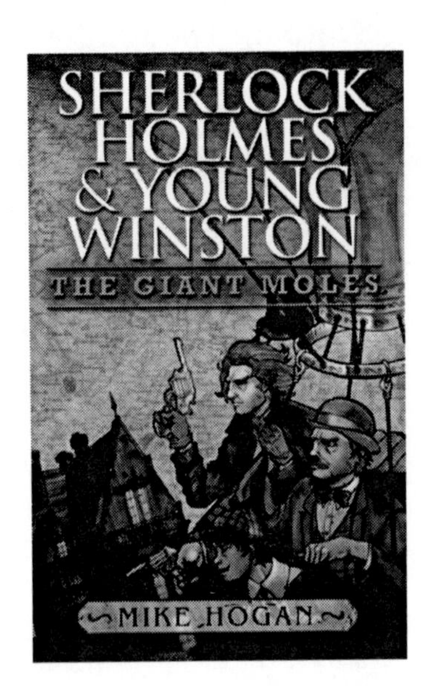

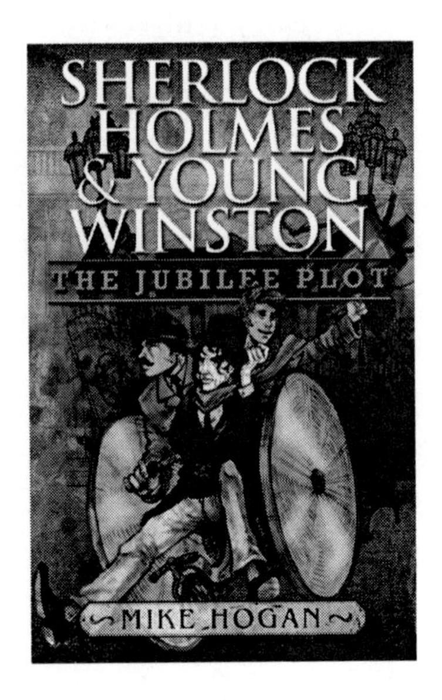

Part 2 and Part 3 of the Sherlock Holmes and Young Winston Trilogy.

Also from MX Publishing

MX Publishing is proud to support the campaign to save and restore Sir Arthur Conan Doyle's former home. Undershaw is where he brought Sherlock Holmes back to life, and should be preserved for future generations of Holmes fans.

Save Undershaw www.saveundershaw.com

Facebook www.facebook.com/saveundershaw

You can read more about Sir Arthur Conan Doyle and Undershaw in Alistair Duncan's book (share of royalties to the Undershaw Preservation Trust) – An Entirely New Country and in the amazing compilation Sherlock's Home – The Empty House (all royalties to the Trust).

Also from MX Publishing

Sherlock Holmes Travel Guides

In ebook an interactive guide to London

400 locations linked to Google Street View.

Also from MX Publishing

Cross over fiction featuring great villains from history

Fantasy Sherlock Holmes

www.mxpublishing.com

Also from MX Publishing

Carrying the seal of the Conan Doyle Estate.....

On the most secret and dangerous assignment of their lives, Sherlock Holmes and Dr. Watson are sent into the newborn Soviet Union to rescue The Romanovs: Nicholas and Alexandra and their innocent children. Will Holmes and Watson be able to change history? Will they even be able to survive?

CPSIA information can be obtained at www.ICGtesting.com
Printed in the USA
BVOW011906241212

309048BV00004B/21/P